CHENA

THE MAKING
OF
AN ORPHAN

Chena: The Making Of An Orphan
Copyright © 2013 by Lydia Callins.

ISBN: 978-615-87560-6

About the Author

An actress, model, writer, and personal trainer, Lydia Callins grew up as an orphan who lived life vicariously through every novel she could get her hands on. When she's not reading scripts, she's in the boxing ring slugging it out. She lives in Los Angeles with her significant other, a toy Maltese. Check out her website at www.lydiacallins.com or find her on Twitter, Facebook, and Instagram.

Chena

The Making Of An Orphan...............

Lydia Callins

Sex! Loss of Innocence! Death!
and
Secrets!

Two parallel worlds are connected,
revealing the ingredients that make up
an orphan named Chena

Contents

Acknowledgments

First and foremost, I'd like to thank the only father I've ever known and that is God, who has stood by my side since the day I was born and has blessed me with the opportunity to write this book. Thank you to the woman I admire and owe my life to, Latonya Randolph: I love you!

Special thanks to Jen Grisanti, my story developer, who told me, "This project will be realized, and touch lives"; Jennifer Brown, my amazing copy editor; Timmie Lee Thomas, an outstanding illustrator who took my vision with precise direction and brought it to life; and Frank Bongjio, a prodigious graphic designer and web designer who had the patience to deal with all my insatiable requests.

The above people could not have been hired and this book would not exist had it not been for the donations provided by Alexander Simpson, John De Voe, Ibrahima Sonko, Georges Asfar, and Protasio Rodriguez. Thank you so much for believing in me, and for proving that "the future of books belong to the readers that care."

My deepest gratitude goes to all my friends and loved ones who prayed for me, supported me, and encouraged me on what seemed like a never-ending journey to complete this novel. And most of all, thank you to the reader who picked up this novel and purchased it!

Introduction

Dear Diary,

Since the beginning of my earliest memory at two, realization that I was a being empowered me to survive. I often wondered what it would be like to be normal; to sit at a dinner table with a family that doesn't dissipate, abandon me, or fade away. Always seeking normality, but it never seemed quite in my grasp. That's not the life of an orphan. The dream of normality plays through my mind like a melody on a violin, the thoughts are music to my ears, oh how beautiful the sound of retaining lost innocence, and experiencing love, but the reality is the music always comes to a stop.

Now at the ripping age of seventeen I sit on the edge of uncertainty, willing and ready to jump into my destiny: saying good-bye to my childhood, daydreaming of what the future brings. Searching for clarity, and still very much in deep search of my identity, which I now know I will never find until I acknowledge my past...

CHAPTER 1
LIL CHENA

Dear Diary,

I looked out the bus
window
Hoped she'd see my face
and be reminded
she's all I got.
But it's a bittersweet
good-bye
She doesn't see me
anymore!
She doesn't hear me
anymore!
She can't remember me
anymore!
She doesn't love me
anymore!

CHENA, THE MAKING OF AN ORPHAN

It's Friday the thirteenth, so I carefully jumped to avoid stepping on any cracks, skillfully hopping from one leg to the other. "Step on a crack and break your mother's back," I sang, skipping the rest of the way home from school. Turning to walk up my street, I saw three police cars zip right past me with their lights and sirens on. Walking up to the forty-unit apartment complex, I immediately noticed that something was wrong. Our neighbors were standing on the lawn in front of my house with their arms folded, shaking their heads and talking to each other. Two teenage boys with red ginger hair, who lived above us, jumped out of the swimming pool and leaned on the iron gates surrounding the pool area, pointing towards my house.

As I got closer I could see Ford Crown Victoria cars parked in the parking lot and on the streets, red and blue lights flashing from the inside of their windshields. Three black and white police cars with red and blue lights on their hoods were parked directly on the lawn. Turning left off the sidewalk to enter the cobblestone path leading to my front door, I saw some men walking around in suits, but most of the men were wearing black pants, boots, and blue jackets marked with mustard-yellow letters: FBI. Entering my house, I saw men going through Mommy's things while writing on notepads. Some of the men were taking pictures, some were carrying things out of Mommy and Charlie's room, and some were just standing around talking to each other. No one noticed my little six-year-old frame walking into the living room. I took three more steps forward, and saw Mr. Bear on the couch. I ran to go grab Mr. Bear, but before I could reach him a tall black man with a small afro wearing a brown suit stepped in front of me.

"Hey, little girl, are you lost?" the man said in a kind voice as he leaned down.

"I want my mommy!" I demanded.

"You live here?"

"Hey! Dat's my bear," I whined as I flicked my gaze towards the couch, watching as a young Asian man wearing one of the blue FBI jackets reached down and picked up Mr. Bear. He turned him over, then threw him into a white box.

"Frank, hold up for a second, let me see that bear," the man wearing the brown suit ordered.

"Here you go, boss." The Asian man dutifully reached in the box and handed Mr. Bear over before he continued towards the front door. The black man picked Mr. Bear up and started squeezing him really tight. Then he turned him upside down and started shaking him. He pulled a knife from his pocket, unfolded it, and put it to Mr. Bear's back.

"Noooo, don't hurt Mr. Bear!" I yelled, as my eyes filled with tears. The black man froze and looked at Mr. Bear, then back at me, before closing his knife and putting it back in his pocket. He leaned down on one knee and handed me Mr. Bear. I quickly snatched Mr. Bear out of his hand and hugged him tight.

"Go ahead and have a seat right here. We're just asking your mother some questions, and then she'll be right out to get you. Everything is going to be okay." The man pointed to our blue and lavender floral love seat. I nodded my head, wiped my eyes, and climbed up on the seat, holding Mr. Bear tightly as I watched our house be destroyed. Despite my fear, I tried to hold back my tears and be brave. Some of the men started turning over the furniture in the house and cutting it open, while others continued carrying some of Mommy and Charlie's things out in white boxes.

After the men left the house, Mommy screamed, "Fucking pigs!" over and over as she vacuumed, dusted, swept, picked up glass and mopped. All of the books, vinyl records, cassette tapes, and beta tapes had been thrown in a pile that flooded the living room and dining room floor. The mattresses were turned over and ripped apart. My toys and Mommy's clothes were scattered all over the bedrooms. The men broke most of Mommy's china dishes and they cut up Mommy's sofa. It took Mommy all week to clean it up. Finally the house almost looked back to its normal self.

A week passed, and nothing new happened. Except for Mommy's things being broken and Charlie being gone, things seemed like they were back to normal. "Come on in here, breakfast is ready!" Mommy yelled from the kitchen.

"Coming!" I screamed as I put my Malibu Barbie down on the bottom bed of my cherry-stained oak bunk bed, and ran to the kitchen table.

Mommy walked over to the table carrying two plates, a sad look on her face.

"Mommy, are you otay?" I mumbled in a timid voice.

"No, baby," Mommy replied as she sat down and began poking at her eggs with her fork.

"When's Charlie gonna be home?" I asked, taking a bite out of my strawberry-jam-covered toast.

"He had to go back to the big house," Mommy said, looking at me with a small smile, her elbows on the table as she rests her chin gently on her hands.

"Are we gonna visit him?" I asked curiously.

"No sweetie, not for a while."

"Why not?" I replied, a confused look on my face.

Mommy took a deep breath and exhaled before answering. "Because he asked us not to. Now eat up, so you can go wash up. Shelly will be here for a visit this afternoon." Mommy scooted her chair back, walked into the kitchen, and dumped the contents of her full plate into the trashcan. Then she headed to her room. Seconds later I heard her door shut. I sat at the table, nervously swinging my dangling legs, while I finished the remainder of my eggs, toast, and sausage.

Mommy vacuumed and placed two sky-blue bed sheets over the sofa and love seat, covering the rips and tears made by the FBI men. She placed a plate of oatmeal cookies on the coffee table, and sat down on the sofa, reaching for her Marlboro Light cigarettes. I remained still on the floor with my back against the love seat, playing with my Barbies. Mommy was about to light another cigarette when the door bell rang. She smashed the cigarette down in the crystal ashtray on her lap, and placed it on the end table.

"Miss Shelly is here!" I said, excited, as Mommy got up to open the door.

"Who is it?" Mommy asked in her sweetest voice, smoothing her grey blouse down and rubbing her hands down the front of her blue jeans.

"Shelly Canaven," Shelly screamed into the door. Mommy removed the top chain, then unlocked the top lock and the bottom lock, and swung the door open.

"Hi, Shelly, come on in." Mommy ushered Miss Shelly in, closed the door, and led her into the living room.

"Hi, Miss Shelly!" I screamed as I jumped up to hug Miss Shelly's waist. Miss Shelly saved me and took me from my real mommy when I was three.

"Hi, Chena. Look at you, you are growing as fast as a beanstalk."

"I'm a first grader now," I said with a big bright smile, proudly showing my missing bottom tooth.

"Yes, and the prettiest one in your class I bet," Miss Shelly replied, patting me on the head.

"How was the drive?" Mommy asked, staying on her feet while Miss Shelly sat down.

"It was a long drive. I'm glad I left when you told me to. I saw all the traffic building just as I was leaving Oaktown—I can't believe you made that two-hour commute every day," Miss Shelly said with a smile.

"Well, a two-hour commute was a small price to pay for safety, peace, and quiet...but with this tendonitis, looks like I'll be going on disability. I won't be making that long drive anymore." Mommy pointed to her shoulder, shrugged, then headed toward the kitchen.

"Shelly, can I get you something to drink? Coffee, tea, soda?" Mommy asked, sticking her head out of the kitchen doorway.

"Coffee, black, would be great," Miss Shelly replied, as she reached for one of Mommy's homemade oatmeal cookies. Mommy returned with a wooden tray holding two white porcelain cups with tiny red roses bordering the edges on matching saucers, two silver spoons, and a small white porcelain bowl of sugar. Mommy set the tray down, then sat opposite from Miss Shelly and carefully passed her a cup of coffee.

"Thank you," Miss Shelly said, then took a couple of sips from her cup. Mommy just gave a slight smile in return, watching Miss Shelly place her cup down and scoot back into a comfortable position on the love seat. An awkward silence grew between Miss Shelly and Mommy, then Miss Shelly sat up and placed her hands on her thighs.

"Lucy, I'm going to be honest with you. I tried everything I could, but it's completely out of my hands," Miss Shelly announced.

"So what does this mean?" Mommy replied in a solicitous tone.

"As long as you're married to a convicted felon, you are not eligible to be a foster parent." Miss Shelly states, her tone suddenly stern.

"Why is who I decide to be with any of y'all's damn business?" Mommy yells. I knew something was wrong. I put my Barbies down and climbed onto the couch with Mommy, putting my head on her arm. Mommy grabbed my hand and squeezed it.

"Social Services has to do what is best for the child, and it is deemed that it would be in the best interest of the child to live in a home free of felons," Miss Shelly calmly replied. She looked at me, then looked down at her feet. "But the other option is that you could get a divorce, and apply to adopt Chena. I'd be more than happy to provide you with a letter of recommendation. I'm sure you would be approved." Miss Shelly's face brightened.

"How would I be able to afford to take care of her if ain't no more checks coming in? Money don't grow on trees! I'm on disability, and my husband is gone!" Mommy snapped.

Miss Shelly's smile faded, and she took in a deep breath, pressing her top lip. "Well, if money's the issue, then, unfortunately there is no other way. You have forty-eight hours to return her into our custody," Miss Shelly said in a shaky voice. A tear emerged from the corner of her right eye, and she placed her hand over her mouth as she looked up at the ceiling.

"Mommy what's wrong?" I asked, confused as to why Miss Shelly was getting upset. Mommy turned to me.

"Shelly said you can't..." Mommy stopped and cleared her throat. Rising to her feet, she glared at Miss Shelly and yelled, "You tell the child, I don't have the heart to." Then she walked out of the living room. I stared at Miss Shelly, waiting for an answer, but she didn't respond. She just looked at me with a smile of pity, and wiped her eyes. Then she began to nervously twist her two diamond rings around on her left hand. Only the slamming of Mommy's bedroom door broke the silence.

"Chena, I have some very bad news to tell you," Miss Shelly said in a soft voice. My heart dropped in anticipation. "You can no longer stay with Lucy, because she is married to a bad man. But we've found your cousin Tina, and she would love to take care of you." Miss Shelly smiled. Tears filled my eyes immediately.

"Please, please don't take me away from Mommy. I promise to be good!" I sobbed as I scrambled to the floor, falling to my knees in a praying position.

"I'm sorry, sweetheart, but there's no other way," Miss Shelly pleaded as she joined me on the floor, trying to hug me.

"No...no...I don't wanna go! I don't wanna go!" I screamed, shaking my head sideways, tears blinding my eyes. I pulled away from Miss Shelly's embrace and jumped to my feet. "You can't make me go... you fucking white bitch honkey. I hate you! I hate you! Mommy and me are happy, you're ruining everything! Charlie isn't a bad man.. you're a story teller!.. I hate you!" I yelled to the top of my lungs. Hyperventilating, choking on snot and tears, I ran to the door of Mommy's room. "Mommy, let me in! Let me in!" I yelled, trying to turn Mommy's doorknob with no success. I started kicking her door and banging on it with my hands as hard as I could.

"Moooomy....Mooooommmmmy! Mommmy!" I whined and screamed. But Mommy didn't answer me. I gave the door an extra-hard kick, denting it. The door opened slowly, Mommy fell to her knees crying and hugged me. My face soiled her shoulder immediately as she picked me up, placed me over her shoulder, and started rubbing my back.

"Shh...don't cry, it's only going to be for a little while. You'll like your cousin Tina, she's very nice," Mommy said as she patted my back like she was burping a baby. "Shh. Shh...I'll come and get you every weekend, and we'll go fishing." Mommy sat on the bed and cradled me.

"I don't want to go live with Tina, she's mean," I whined.

"How is she mean? You haven't even given her a chance to be nice." Mommy wiped the tears off my eyes and cheeks with her scarf.

"When she come to Grannie's house, she...she...hit me and Dominick with a shoe, and make...make...make us sit in the corner, I hate her! I...I...I hope a tiger eats her!" I sobbed and stuttered around my hyperventilation. Mommy just held me real tight like a bear and let me cry myself into exhaustion, until finally the hiccups stopped.

During the entire drive to the bus station two days later, I looked out the window, refusing to talk when Mommy talked to me. The whole ride I was hoping that she would change her mind and turn around, but she didn't, and before long we pulled into the bus yard.

"Okay, we're here," Mommy announced in a happy voice. I crossed my arms and poked out my lower lip as I looked straight ahead. Mommy opened her car door, then lightly closed as she watched me giving her dirty looks. She walked to the trunk of the car, opened it, and pulled out my duffel bag. One end had a stuffed animal panda face and the other a panda bottom and tail, with the blue mesh material in the middle part connecting them. She threw the black strap over her shoulder and reached in to grab a cardboard box that she had filled with my Connect Four game, Monopoly, checkers, Uno cards, Mr. Bear, Barbies, and my twelve-piece Disney book collection with audio cassette player. She had taped it up with grey duct tape and written "TOYS" across the front with a red smelly marker.

Mommy headed for my door, placed the box on the hood of the car, and opened the door. "Okay, Chena, come on now. The sooner you go, the sooner you'll be back," Mommy said as she held the door open for me to climb out. Tears started to well out of my eyes as we entered the Greyhound bus station. A smelly stench of musk and alcohol immediately hit my nose as we walked through the doors. I saw three homeless people laying and sitting on the wooden benches in the waiting area as we walked past. One had covered his face in newspapers and lay stretched out and still, taking up an entire bench. The other two just sat up with their plastic bags full of cans and bottles underneath them.

"Mommy, please don't make me go, I promise to be good," I pleaded. Mommy ignored me and continued walking past the smelly men, towards the ticket counter.

"Hello, one one-way child's ticket to Oaktown...the 5:15 p.m. bus, please," Mommy announced into the tin circle cut into the center of the glass window.

"Ten dollars," an old white man with glasses and a head full of silver hair replied. Mommy reached into the right pocket of her blue Jordache jeans, pulled out some money, and slid it under the glass window. The man wrote something on a clipboard, opened his cash drawer, then slid a long white rectangular card and some dollar bills under the glass window. "Bus leaves in 15 minutes." The man looked down at me.

Mommy picked up her change and the ticket and tucked it into the pocker of her purple windbreaker. She picked the box up off the counter, slid it under her left arm, secured my duffel bag over her shoulder, then grabbed my hand with her right hand, and led me outside towards a big silver bus. In the middle of the bus red and white rectangular stripes framed a painting of a greyhound.

"Now remember what I told you. Don't talk to strangers, you sit up front next to the bus driver so he can see you, and don't use that bathroom, you hold it till you get to your stop...Oaktown." Mommy said as we stood in line to get on the bus.

"You said you would be my Mommy...why are you giving me back?...I praaawmise to be good," I whined and looked up at Mommy.

"I packed you a lunch and I put your favorite fruit roll-up in there for you to eat," Mommy said in a soothing tone, ignoring my question.

Mommy handed my box to a stocky Mexican man wearing a grey captain's hat, a grey jacket with the same greyhound picture on his sleeve as on the bus, grey pants, and black boots. He took the box and checked the sticker on it, then carefully placed it in the compartment under the bus. Mommy handed me my duffel bag and handed the man my ticket. While he punched a hole in it, Mommy leaned down to hug me tight, then reached in her purple jacket, pulls out five one-dollar bills, and stuffed them into the right pocket of my pink-and-silver coat. Then she stood to retrieve the ticket stub from the bus driver and passed it to me. I placed the small square paper in the front pocket of my blue jeans.

Slowly boarding the bus, I stopped on each step long enough to look back at Mommy, who waved and smiled at me. Tears poured down from my eyes like a waterfall, as I walked up the last two steps. I turned left and took the first seat on the right-hand side of the bus. I slid over to the window and put my duffel bag on the floor, in between my legs. I sat and looked out the window at Mommy, hoping she would tell me to come off the bus and take me home, but she didn't, she just looked at me with pursed lips, and smiled with her arms folded.

The last three people in line boarded the bus. The bus driver followed the last person up the stairs and sat in the driver seat, started the engine, and closed the door. I put the palm of my right hand up to the window and looked at Mommy. The bus started to move and Mommy turned around to walk away. I kept staring at her until the bus pulled too far away and she was out of my sight. I leaned back in my seat and pulled my purple turtleneck up to my nose, trying with no avail not to cry. The bus driver glanced at me and gave me a small reassuring smile, before quickly turning back to face the road.

Staring back out the window, I desperately tried to memorize my location, so I could find my way back, but all of the buildings, street signs, people, and parked cars started to blur and vanish as the bus driver accelerated and steered onto the highway. I slumped in my seat with defeat, finally accepting my fate. I would never see Mommy again. This was my second mommy and fourth foster home that I had to say good-bye to forever. Tina's plump evil face ran through my thoughts; I was headed to beatings and I knew it. "Why doesn't no-one love me, why do they leave me?" I mumbled as I sat back up to look out the window onto the road, hoping to see Mommy's car. I started to wonder. What it's like to live in heaven? Is Nanna there? If I die would I go there?

Sitting in my seat staring out the window, feeling scared, cold and alone, I saw a moving light in the sky. The tiny star grew bigger as it got closer to the bus. Suddenly my body fills with a warm tingly feeling, and I feel safe and loved all at the same time. It's the same familiar feeling as when Star Lady saved me and my brother from the fire.

I started rapidly rubbing my eyes with the cuffs of my purple sleeved turtle neck. "I have to be a big girl, I have to take care of myself, I don't have a mommy, nobody loves me. I have to be a big girl, I have to take care of myself, I don't have a mommy, nobody loves me," I mumbled to myself under my breath until the tears dried up.

Sitting up in my seat, I zipped my jacket up to my neck, and put my hands in my warm jacket pockets. I turned to look back out the window, watching the sun fall into the violet-sherbet colored clouds as it disappears into the abyss. As the sky becomes dark the moving star seems billions of miles away, but I continued to focus on the light until it moves out of sight. A feeling of relief flooded my body. "I'll survive," I whispered as I closed my eyes, allowing the vibration of the bus to rock me to sleep, like a baby in her mother's arms.

CHAPTER 2
CHENA

Dear Diary,
One morning
I woke to realize
I don't like him...like
I want to be with him
I want him to be my man
I want to marry him...Shhh
I don't even know him
I don't even know his last name
I don't even know if I like him
Or...if I like the way he makes
my body feel.
Or...do I like this strange,
strong, smooth, tall man.
Or...do I like him
Cuz he makes the heat rise in my body
Butterflies rushing to my head
Juices flowing out
and around the sweatiest spot
on my cookie box!
The thought of him disappears,
Every time I call for him,
He's not there
But I love him...

CHENA, THE MAKING OF AN ORPHAN

He just grabs me, turns me around, and starts to kiss my virgin lips like there is no tomorrow. His kiss is deep and hard, and unconsciously I open my mouth, desiring the feel of his tongue against mine. I can't see who this man is. I should scream but I don't want him to stop. The light is too dim to see clearly, but the silhouette of his body is giving me immense gratification. He's about 6'4' with broad, muscular shoulders. His large hands are unbelievably soft to the touch. He looks like a ball player. I can't make out who this man is, but somehow I feel so safe and loved in his arms.

As I relax from my tense stance, I slowly bring my hands from a defensive pushing position against his chest and place my right hand around the base of his neck and the left on his side near his hips. Instinctively I started to explore his body with my hands, and immediately, I can feel his abs through his cotton wife beater. Slowly moving my hand towards his back, I run my hands over his strong back and firm behind. His large soft hands explore my body and I quiver with each and every touch, yearning for more with every kiss. I inhale the manly scent coming from his neck, he smells good...Pleasures for Men by Estee Lauder...my favorite.

His skin is smooth, yet I can still feel the after-five hairs prickling my neck and jawline. He's no boy, he's clearly a man. His massive height is overwhelming to my arms, causing me to fall back and land against a wall. He instinctively grabs my left leg with his muscular right arm and pulls me upward with a smooth upward thrust, causing my nightgown to rise above my hips and exposing my left butt cheek, which is only covered by my sheer pink panties.

His forearms wrap underneath my butt; lifting me into the air, he continues kissing my neck, making me feel like a super-hero is sweeping me away from all my pain. As his tongue makes its way up my neck towards my jawline, I move my lips towards his left ear, asking in the sexiest whisper I could muster, "Who are you?"

Suddenly he stops licking my neck, looks in my eyes, and gently lowers me to the ground. Putting his left hand on my cheek, he replies in a smooth deep voice, "I am love."

"But what's your name? I have to know," I reply with urgency. He begins to speak, but the sound coming from his mouth is too faint to hear. He repeats his words, "I am..."

Ring...Ring...

"Nooo!" Fuck, why did my alarm have to go off now, right when I was getting the best sleep I had had in weeks? I quickly slapped the top of my clock, jumped back under the covers of my twin bed, squeezed my thighs together, and closed my eyes. After an eternity of unsuccessfully trying to jump back into dreamland to learn the name of my dream man, I opened my eyes in defeat. It wasn't working, I wasn't sleepy. Pushing the covers off in disgust, I grabbed the remote on my nightstand, punching in the numbers 6-8 for my BET music videos.

"How ironic!" I blurted out as I wiped the sleepiness out of my eyes, focusing in on the image of a heavenly man gyrat-ing. "If you want it come get it...Ride it....My pony!" I tried to give my full and undivided attention to Ginuwine, my other dream man, whose posters cover my bedroom walls and my locker at school, but I couldn't stop thinking about the man in my dream. He seemed so perfect; it was as if he was my soulmate. I glanced at the clock. "Oh shit, it's six a.m. Gotta get my ass up!"

"Turn that noise down I said!" My foster mom Dena hollered. What was she talking about? The volume on my thirteen-inch TV was already just two notches from being off, and this was her first time saying anything! Dang, I can't even hear the damn videos now. I can't wait till I go to college and get my own place. Shit, what am I going to wear, let's see. Oh yeah, I got class with Brandon today, so I got to look good! I know he ain't seen my new black spandex boot-cut ski pants 'cause I just bought 'em last week.

A blustering windy sound came from my window, reminding me how cold it was outside. "Shit, I hope I didn't sleep with that open all night. I'm going to catch a cold." Reaching to close the window, I noticed it was raining hard. I don't care, I'm still looking cute. Just like Dena said, sometime a lady has to choose fashion or comfort. It was Wednesday, the only day I had class with Brandon, so I chose a little of both. I wore my ski pants, a midriff-showing blue sweater, black lug hiking boots, and my yellow Ralph Lauren puff coat. Couldn't forget to grab my black gloves and matching scarf, which would enable me to walk down the halls with my jacket unzipped so everybody could see my body's best asset—my abs!

Speedily walking the normal path to school I had walked for the past two years, I tried with no avail to stay dry and keep warm. Since it was my senior year, this would be my last year walking this path. Thank God Dena became my new foster mom. Not only did I escape that horrible group home from two years ago that felt like a prison, but I also got to transfer out of the public schools in Oaktown. Kids there were tying up teachers and setting them on fire. Welcoming calm peaceful suburbia's Sal Valley High took me in with open arms, and I gleefully accepted. Most kids my age are too old for foster homes, because most foster parents want to have kids who can't fight them back, so we usually end up in group homes or juvenile halls. But Miss Shelly went to bat for me and convinced Dena that a teenage daughter who was a straight "A" student was just as good as the little girl that she would never be able to birth.

Standing on the corner of Bancroft Avenue waiting to cross the street, I see Sheila in her white 1995 Geo Metro, honking and waving at me. I smiled and used every muscle in my body to raise my hand so I could wave too, as she rode by bumping her music hella loud, reminding me that I wasn't just walking, but I was walking in the damn rain. Bitch! That's okay. I was going to get my license as soon as those three points I racked up from stealing Dena's car fell off my driving record. I ain't tripping anyway 'cause no matter what Sheila's driving she's still ugly inside and out and ain't never gonna find a man! Shit, I seriously doubted that this broad would even graduate this year with us.

Honk! Honk! "Hey girl, you want a ride?" Bee yelled out of the passenger side window of her car as she pulled up.

"What's up, girl? You know I do, wish y'all woulda saw me five blocks ago before my coat got soaked." Bee and Tanisha both lived in town and carpooled every morning. They were my girls—we were tight. But these girls were always running late to school—I couldn't figure out why when you were riding in a brand-new 1999 purple Camaro on twenty-inch rims. Bee's mom is well-off, from what I can't tell. Oddly, she ain't got no job. Bee's dad died right before she was born and Bee is her only child. Well whatever or whoever was paying was properly breaking her off. Me and Tanisha were peas in the same pod, although she's being raised by her mom and I'm in foster homes. We were both hustlers, fighters, and smart, and you couldn't tell we grew up hella poor.

"Chena, you can't speak," Becky said rudely from the backseat.

"What?...Girl, I didn't see you back there. What's up? I see you decided to come to school today, huh?"

"Shut up, I go to school when my modeling allows it." Becky, short for Rebecca lived on another planet, called "cool." Half of the time she was off traveling the world, or being dismissed from class early to go pursue her modeling career, while we were just some regular high school kids in class everyday. We were only seventeen and she had already been to Europe, New York, Vegas, and had lived in L.A. half of our junior year to model.

Becky was the most experienced out of our clique, and I mean that all the way around. She only dated men, not boys! She'd already had three abortions, starting at the age of thirteen, and had been engaged twice. She almost got married, but her grandmother caught fiancé number two out to lunch with another girl. Becky was very beautiful, but she was a little vain and self-centered, and we all blamed her evil youth-sucking mother for that. Deep down she was just a down-to-earth girl with insecurities who wanted to be loved, and we all loved her.

"Move your backpack, Becky, so I can get in! Bee, you better smash. We got fifteen minutes and I still got to get my breakfast!"

Bee looked back at us in the rear view mirror and replied, "Okay," arching her eyebrow as if to say, "Yeah, right." While they ate breakfast at home I was used to my free breakfast in the mornings. It had been a morning ritual since preschool: go to school, get fed. That's what I'd call a "win-win" situation.

Bee rolled up hella slow in the parking lot, trying to weave in front of the damn football team leaving their six a.m. practice. As a front-seat passenger, Tanisha was scouting for a parking spot that would give onlookers a full view of Bee's Camaro but making sure she wasn't too close to the secondhand junk-mobiles. She signaled Bee to park near the front entrance. Bee didn't turn the car off until she ensured that the other cars near her wouldn't scratch up her custom candy-purple paint job.

"Turn that music down now!" yelled a familiar but annoying voice. It was Romonia, school security. This he-she of a woman was a city cop–reject on a power trip. Shit, she looked like a dog, husky and hairy. Make-up couldn't help her mean ass. To warn our peers we would yell out "Captain Nark!" whenever she was around. She had built up a reputation for catching kids trying to get off-campus during school hours. Once she hid under a car and in a tree to catch kids cutting school, and she was known for pulling kids right out of their cars if they tried to drive out of the student lot without a pass. I knew this could easily become a ten-minute lecture, so I had to think fast or I'd be stuck in this two door car.

"Tanisha, get out quick!"

"Why?"

"'Cause I got to use the bathroom! I'll see y'all at lunch. Bye!"

Five minutes left, I better run...

"Chena, no running in the hallways!"

"Sorry, Miss Brown." Yes, I made it! "I'll take a plain donut and a chocolate milk, please."

"I thought we weren't going to see you today. Since we're closing up, go ahead and take the last two donuts," Miss Carla said in a warm, motherly tone.

"Thanks, Miss Carla!" Miss Carla was the head cafeteria supervisor. She had been working at Sal Valley High for twenty years, and she had seen my face bright and early every morning for the last two of them. In another five years she could retire. "See ya at lunch! Remember not to work too hard." Shit, I was about to be late to class, but I had to get a bite of my donut. Running holding a donut and milk wasn't easy. Oh, shit. I lost my footing on the wet floor. I began to fall forward.

Strategizing my fall, I quickly dropped my donut to break the impact with my right hand. Ouch, ouch, damn! The chocolate milk spilled all over my yellow Ralph Lauren puff coat. Laughter stirred behind me and as I looked up to see a crowd of boys, one of them began walking towards me. Oh, shit. It was Brandon. "Are you okay?"

Ignoring the hand he held out to help me up and the pain in my elbow, I jumped to my feet and blurted out, "I'm fine, excuse me, I'm running late for class. Got to go." I rushed past him without making eye contact. I just left the empty milk carton and donut on the floor to escape my humiliation and walked briskly to room 101.

While I walked to class I couldn't help but feel bad that I had left the garbage for Jose to pick up. He was hella cool and had enough on his plate being responsible for cleaning the entire school and all. The school just laid off two of his assistant custodians due to a major budget crisis, in addition to cutting the music program and not buying the Algebra II textbooks the sophomore class needed. And they wondered why kids were failing. The "crisis" was really a code word for embezzlement, hiding the fact that the superintendent had been robbing the district blind for years stealing hundreds of thousands of dollars from the district. They finally caught up with her ass, and now she's in jail. If Jose had more help I bet that wet floor would have been mopped up by now, or at least had a "Caution, Wet Floor" sign up.

Ring!

"What's going on?" I blurted in a startled whisper.

"Chena, were you sleeping?" Mr. Silverman asked in a hostile tone.

"No, I have migraines triggered by these flourescent lights, okay, and...uh, sometimes I have to put my head down until they go away," I said defensively.

"I'm sorry to hear that, Chena. I just can't have my best student sleeping in class, especially since within the last two years, she's never mentioned this condition before."

"Well, I just got it diagnosed and it's personal," I snapped back, looking down at my desk.

"I understand," Mr. Silverman replied, with an I-can-read-through-your-bullshit expression.

"Okay. I have to go so I'm not late for my next class." Mr. Silverman was a pain in the ass. Not only did he interrupt my sleep, just as I was returning to my dream man's arms, he had also refused to let me go to the bathroom so I could try and wash my coat before the chocolate stain sank in. Now I would have to be late to second period and we have a test today, but I had to save my coat.

Walking briskly to the girl's bathroom near the spot of my morning fall, I saw my boy Paul, also known as P. P was the coolest guy at the school—if you looked up the word "popular," his face would be next to it in the dictionary. P was funny, a good dancer, and most important, he was a good friend. P was "internationally known" within the school because he kicked it with every nationality there. P's friend list was like looking at a rainbow; he broke down segregation lines within the school. From staff to students, everybody knew P and loved him.

"Move, P, so I can get into the bathroom!" I yelled.

"Not till you give me your girl Becky's digits."

"Look, Paul, stop playing!" I said, agitated. "She got a man, plus you know she don't talk to high school boys, so move."

P was really getting on my last nerve. Was he really going to make me push him into the girls' room? Oh well....I gave him the hardest push I could muster my muscles to give. By the startled look on his face I could tell he wasn't expecting that push. He didn't realize that this 5'9" 120-pound carmel-brown beauty was so strong, until he fell backwards into the girls' room that just happened to be full of girls screaming for him to get his ass out!

"Damn, Chena, all you had to say was 'excuse me.'" He picked his red and black baseball hat up off the ground. Putting it back on his head, he completed his matched ensemble of red and black jump suit and red and black Jordan tennis shoes. He waved good-bye, but didn't exit the bathroom until he had flirted with at least two jailbait freshman. Up at the sink, I couldn't help but think those freshman girls were complete airheads. Both of these girls just gave P their phone number, and they call themselves friends. Well, I guess P just got game like that. I needed some soap to wash my coat. Dang, we were out of soap again, fucking budget cuts. Well, water would have to do. What? Surprisingly, the stain was gone. Maybe 'cause my coat was already wet from this morning's rain, no chocolate milk appeared on my coat, not even a drop. Cool, now I'd have enough time to secure my seat next to Brandon.

Looked like everybody wanted to be on time today. I saw Kindle up to her old tricks, writing little notes on the desk, and Sarah was making sure her pink and white Janssport backpack was in full view with a small index card poking out. What was this bitch Sheila doing sitting in my seat? I couldn't believe this shit, just when you wish you had assigned seating you don't! Fine, I'd just sit behind her, so I would still sit adjacent to Brandon. This seat sucked 'cause he couldn't look at me in my new ski pants, but I could look at him. I couldn't wait to finish my test so I could enjoy my eye candy.

"Hey, Chena, I heard you bit it this morning, are you okay?" I didn't know why this bitch was acting so concerned. She was just trying to front me off in front of Brandon.

As sarcastically as I could, I replied with a smirk, "Thanks so much for your concern, Sheila, you don't know what that means to me. Thankfully I didn't scratch my elbow or bruise my nose. I might have ended up looking ashy and hurt in the face...you know, like you look every day." Sheila sucked her teeth and quickly turned around to face the chalkboard, mumbling a word that sounded like "bitch," but I couldn't tell and I didn't care. Brandon never took his eyes off of his notes, but I know he heard me, and by the sound of Kindle and Sarah's laugh they heard me, too.

Brandon looked good. He was nearly eighteen, but he looked like he was twenty. He was 6'4" tall and all man. While some boys were just now growing peach fuzz on their faces, he had a full, neatly trimmed mustache and a small short goatee. Brandon had what was referred to as "good hair" in the black community. It was a dark silky black that would have been curly if grown out long, but since he wore it short it laid down with rippling waves all over. Brandon was the mystery man on campus, since he had transferred here from a school in town at the start of his senior year. Brandon was beautiful. Every time he was around I couldn't breathe; literally, I was out of breath. He made my palms sweat. I was so nervous to be in his presence that I would act like I couldn't stand him, to hide my feelings from him.

Brandon was the only man who made me feel this way, and I couldn't explain it. It was just something about him that made me feel safe. Brandon wore a Perry Ellis black and yellow jumpsuit, with the newly released all-black patent leather Michael Jordan tennis shoes. Brandon was not only handsome but also very athletic, artistic, and smart. I never saw Brandon's mother, but I suspected that she may have been white, 'cause his dad was the color purple and Brandon was carmel brown.

Brandon's fumbled for something in his bag. I wondered if he needed a pencil or something. This was my opportunity to make amends for being so mean to him this morning, I had just bought a pack of number two pencils that came already sharpened...

"Excuse me, Sheila, do you have an extra pencil?" Noooo! He didn't ask her! If I had had her seat that would have been me. Damn.

Batting her inch-long fake eyelashes, in a provocative voice she replied, "For you, I sure do."

"Thanks," he replied as he flirtatiously grabbed the pencil out of her hand, smiled, and turned back to his test. Brandon seemed to be flying through his test on the same pace as me, but of course I couldn't let him beat me, 'cause I needed to walk in front of him to hand in my test so he could admire my physique in my new tight-fitting ski pants.

Yes, finished! I thought as I looked over to Brandon, who was still working on his test. As planned, it worked! Getting up to turn in my paper, I could hear him getting up shortly after, and walking right behind me. I quickly moved through the narrow walkway between the crowded desks occupied by students and their backpacks, books, and binders. After handing my paper to the teacher, Mr. Robin, I turned around and bumped right into Brandon's hard muscular chest. He placed his hand behind my back to catch me so I wouldn't fall from the impact.

"Excuse me, I'm so sorry," I mumbled.

"It's alright, but you owe me 'cause you scuffed up my Jordans." As I looked down at his shoe, I noticed that my size ten lug boot was right on his shiny Jordan. I looked up at him with my dark brown puppy eyes and smiled, saying, "I don't see a scuff, but I'm sorry anyway."

"Break it up and get back to your seat, there's a test going on," snapped our irritated, underpaid teacher. Butterflies rushing to my stomach, I nearly fainted, mesmerized by Brandon's light brown eyes and gorgeous smile. Without taking my eyes off Brandon, I replied, "Yes, Mr. Robin." I slid to the left to let Brandon move past me, and I quickly took my seat. I had my Brandon fix for the week. I was going to have those butterflies in my stomach all night. Couldn't nothing mess my day up, not even Sheila's annoying presence.

As class emptied into the hall, I heard Tanisha's voice. "Yo, Chena, hold up!"

"Hey Nisha!"

"How you do on your history test?"

"I'm sure I aced it."

"Cool, how was your science exam?"

Tanisha looked at the ground and stalled before she blurted out with a smile, "I aced it." We gave each other a high five and started to laugh.

"Girl you had me worried for a minute, you should be an actress," I said. Tanisha was only five feet tall but she carried herself like she was seven feet tall. Her Timberland boots gave her three extra inches of height. Tanisha and I looked like twins today—the only difference was,she wore black baggy cargo pants and her Ralph Lauren puff coat and Timberland boots were a matching red. Tanisha and I both looked each other up and down, and we knew we were the finest, smartest things walking. Out of our clique we were the ones who were 4.0-honor and AP-class-taking divas. We managed both worlds, hanging with the geeks in class and the cool kids outside of class, members of everything social on campus, and holding down part time jobs outside of school.

"Guess who I bumped into? No girl, I mean I actually stepped on his foot."

"Let me guess...Brandon."

"Yes, and I touched his chest."

"Could you feel his muscles?" Tanisha asked teasingly.

"You know I could and they felt good."

"Girl, you hella stupid, let's go get something to eat." As we were walking I could see Sheila and her posse of rejects staring me and Tanisha down like we had shit stuck to our faces.

"Look, Nisha." I gave her a nudge and pointed. "They can't get enough of us. Let's pose so they can take a picture." Immediately Tanisha and I dropped our backpacks, turned toward Sheila and her crew and posed like superstars, and quoted a verse from Mac 10, "Take a picture, trick, one day it might make you rich." We looked at each other and laughed, ignoring Sheila and her clique's middle fingers with their jeweled-up four-inch neon-colored acrylic nails in the air. Grabbing our bags, we continued to head towards the quad to meet up with Bee and Becky.

To our surprise Bee was standing alone, which was odd since she and Becky had the same Spanish class with Miss Bird. Bee stood out like a sore thumb, looking like she was waiting for her limo to arrive. Bee was pretty and sweet, her 5'4" frame was petite but strong, and she had presence. Today she was styling hard—you would never catch Bee dressed down. She was rocking a pink London Fog trench coat and black leather stiletto boots. Bee never wore a backpack, only her oversized black Coach purse, which conveniently fit all of her books. Bee had green eyes and long jet-black hair that went well with her light ivory complexion.

"Where's Becky at?" I asked curiously.

"She probably couldn't make it to second period you know how she likes to cut school to be with her boo," Tanisha said in a sarcastic, jealous tone.

"No, she's still here. She actually headed to the lunch line before it got crowded," Bee said, filing her nails.

"Oh!" My eyes lit up. I excitedly realized that she was probably at the front of the line by now, and I could cut her.

"I'm going to go catch up with her and try to cut the line. I'll meet y'all back here."

"Alright, Nisha and me are going to get some pizza. See you in a minute," Bee said, carefully placing her nail file in the inside zipper of her Coach bag.

Running towards the cafeteria, I heard a deep smooth voice: "Be careful; try not to fall this time." As I turned to see where the mysterious yet familiar voice was coming from, my eyes immediately locked with Brandon's. He stood by himself with his hands gripped around the straps of his backpack. I couldn't help but notice how sexy he looks with the straps of his bag hanging slightly off his defined shoulders. He had one leg propped up against the wall balancing his other leg on the ground, and his back was up against the wall, smashing his backpack like a cushion. He shot me a smile.

Oh my God! He's smiling at me! Calm down...calm down... breathe. I stopped running, not wanting to fall again. Smiling back, I replied, "I'll do my best." I was so glad I wore my ski pants today! Blushing, I made it into the cafeteria. Becky spotted me and waved to me to hurry up and get in line. Becky was hard to miss, wearing her electric-blue leather Ralph Lauren puff coat, white ski pants, and black patent leather boots with three-inch heels that made her look like she was six feet tall. She truly looked like a supermodel. She was toward the front, with only five people in front of her. Stepping in line I noticed that the line held about forty hungry teens who didn't look pleased that I was cutting, but they knew better than to say something, 'cause we would have opened a can of whoop ass on them.

"Hey, girl, what's for lunch?" I asked hungrily.

"I don't know, looks like tacos. I'm glad you made it without falling," Becky said jokingly.

"How did you hear about that?"

"Jake was telling people in class this morning that he saw you fall. I told him to shut the fuck up before I got my boyfriend to slap his ass." I was surprised to hear that because I thought me and Jake were cool. But Jake loves being center of attention and he will do or say anything to get it.

Panicking, I asked, "What...who was he talking to?" I could feel my heart dropping out of my chest. I asked again, my voice rising, "Who was he talking to?"

Becky could see me getting upset and calmly replied, "Girl, nobodies, of course."

"Who?" I asked, now impatient.

Becky replied, "Sheila and her ugly-ass friends."

"Oh, that's how that bitch found out!" I whispered.

"Why you say that? Did she do something to you?" Becky asked with a look of I'll slap a bitch in her eye.

"Yeah, in second period she tried to front me off in front of Brandon."

Becky gasped, squinted her eyes, and whispered, "Let's slash her tires during lunch." I looked up at Becky, shocked that she said that. She wasn't known to be so devious.

Tempted by Becky's suggestion, I smiled. "Girl, it ain't that serious. I ain't tripping that much, plus I clowned her ass in front of the whole class and made her feel hella stupid."

"Good," Becky replied, grabbing her lunch tray off the counter. Becky paid $2.50 for her meal of one taco, fruit salad, refried beans, and chocolate milk. Growing up as a orphan had its perks; my meal was free. I just slid my student I.D. through the machine and we were off to meet up with Tanisha and Bee.

"Yo, Becky, when you gon' call me?" "Hey, Chena, you looking good today!" Waving and smiling like we were in a beauty pageant, we made our way past the jocks' table and headed to the center quad to our usual post, where Bee and

Tanisha were waiting. After updating Bee on the Sheila incident, I paused and told my girls that I needed their help with a very serious matter.

"Girl, what's going on?" Tanisha asked around a mouthful of food.

"Well, y'all know that I got a thing for Brandon."

"Oh, we know only too well!" Bee shouted and threw her hands in the air.

"Well, I know this sounds crazy but I think we have a connection and I want to tell him how I feel."

"Girl, are you crazy or just smoking crack? If you tell this man that you've been stalking him since school started he's going to freak out and laugh at you!"

"I'm not stalking him," I snapped at Tanisha. I didn't need her trying to make me feel stupid.

Becky put her hand on my shoulder and said, "What do you need us to do, you know we got your back."

Instantly I came up with a marvelous plan that needed to be executed immediately. "Becky, your grandma is going out of town this weekend right?"

"Yeah...why?" she asked, puzzled.

"Well, I think it's time to throw a party."

"What does that have to do with Brandon?" Bee asked.

"The party will give me an excuse to talk to him, and when he shows up at the party I'm going to make my move."

"Oh girl, what you gon' do?" Tanisha asked.

"If he comes to the party I'm gonna dance with him. If he's feeling me I'll know, and if he ain't I'll move on, but I have to find out cause it's driving me crazy!"

"So what you need us to do, girl?" Becky said, excitement in her voice.

"Tanisha, you know that Darien likes you, so I need you to sweet-talk him and convince him to get his brother to DJ the party. Becky, I need you to get the okay from your grandmother to let us have a sleepover this weekend."

"Girl, you know I got that under control," Becky said confidently.

"Bee, I need you to work your magic and design our outfits for the party. I'll buy the material."

"Dang, Chena, I wish you would have given me a little more notice," Bee snapped, sucking her teeth.

"Sorry, I just thought of this."

"Why does it have to be this weekend?" Becky asked.

"This Friday is our home game and it's a perfect time to plan an after-party, so you know everyone will come. So are y'all in or what?" I asked in desperation. Tanisha put her hand down first and we each laid our hands on top of hers like we were getting ready for a big game. We shouted "A.T.C.," which stood for the All That Club, which we had founded our sophomore year.

CHAPTER 3
LIL CHENA

Dear Diary,

I'm sad and I don't know why
I'm sad yet I cannot cry
This sadness is buried down
deep inside my soul,
A feeling that should cause
me to weep till I'm old
Why am I sad?

CHENA, THE MAKING OF AN ORPHAN

Something kept pushing me. "'top it," I muttered, rubbing my eyes, in a hazy sleep, trying to bury my face into my bear, curling up as tight as I could, fitting my little two-and-a-half-year-old, twenty-two pound body onto the cushioned seat of the small floral-patterned polyester love seat. Searching for air and peace I pushed my nose into the corners of the sofa, but something kept nudging my shoulder. The harder I curled my face into Mr. Bear the stronger the nudge became. Opening my sleepy eyes I looked around for my brother, he musta hit me and hid. I know what he wanted, he want to get to my Mr. Bear, its my bear. "Dominick, 'top it!" I yelled. I can't see nothing, everything is all fuzzy...

"Dominick...Dominick..." I called, smiling, but no one answered. The only sound and light came from the big ole TV in the middle of the living room. My smile slowly faded from my chubby cheeks as I sat up indian style on the couch, crying with a racing heart as my body filled with fear. It was hot, dark, and smoky, and nobody was there but me. I grabbed Mr.Bear and held him close to my chest so he could protect me, squeezing him tight as the tears fell.

"Wot you say, Mr. Bear?" I blinked my eyes and listened real good. I'm so happy, for the first time Mr. Bear talked to me like the Muppets on Sesame Street. But Mr. Bear had a girl voice. I opened my eyes, confused. He was supposed to sound like Teddy Ruxpin, the talking bear that comes with cassettes on the TV. Then I saw it...a shining light flickering in the middle of the room. It looked like a moving star.

Putting Mr. Bear down, I looked at the light. "Twinkle, twinkle, little star," I sang, still holding Mr. Bear's hand, as it came towards me. "Mr. Bear, look." It came so close to me its rays touched my nose, and my body started to feel all warm and tingly inside. Sitting in a trance, I enjoyed the tingles that shot through my body like a shock wave speaking to my insides, calming me down, telling me to not be afraid, I was safe. I felt something different wrap itself around me from head to toe; like when my Granny hugs me tight, I feel love.

"Wat you say?" I mutter in between the smiles that the gratifying light is giving me. Realizing it was the light was talking to me, not Mr. Bear, I put Mr. Bear safely on the other cushion and focused all my attention on the light. It told me to find my brother. It got bigger and bigger, turning into a womanly figure, but I couldn't see her face clearly. She had no skin color, just glowed a violet, yellow, white light. I felt the warmth of her hand take my hand and pull me off the couch, leading me through the dark hazy smoke-filled living room to the other side, where we found my brother sleeping in a cradled position, sucking his thumb on the long couch by the front window.

"Dominick.. Dominick wake up." He didn't move. "Brater! Brater! You gotta wake up," I whisper, nudging him with all my might, but he still didn't move. I looked up at the star lady with a defeated look in my eyes, figuring she gon' be mad at me, but she smiled and grabbed my hand, leading me towards the kitchen. The closer we got to the stove the stronger the burnt smell got. She leaned down with a smile, her lips didn't move but I heard her say, "Chena, you have to save yourself and your brother. You have to put the fire out."

Looking up at the stove, I saw its eye burning hot red under a pot. "I don't know how I'ma reach it, it's too tall and far up." I stand on my tippy toes trying with all my might to touch the hot pot, but I can't reach it. The harder I try the harder it is to breathe. Coughing my lungs out, I still tried with all my strength to stop the fire. "I gotta save my Bother and

Mr. Bear...I'm Wonder Woman," I yelled as my arm feels like it's about to fall off. I kept extending my right arm up above my head and standing on my toes, waiting for my magic power to kick in, and then I felt it, my feet lifted off the ground and I floated above the pot. I looked down and inside were two once-white eggs still in their charred shells, smoking, with no water in the pot. I took my right hand and swiped the pot off the stove with my palm. It crashed onto the floor.

My toes reached the floor again and I held my hand in front of me, feeling it stinging, but just as fast as it started stinging the pain just stopped. I looked up and saw the star lady moving away from me, smiling. "Chena, you're safe now."

I waved my right hand in the air. "Bye bye Miss Star Lady," I said as I ran towards her, trying to catch up with her like we were playing tag, but I stopped dead in my tracks in the middle of the living room, watching as Miss Star lady faded into thin air. "Pweeze...don't go...don't go...pweesz!" I yelled desperately as the thick cloudy air filled my lungs. Choking in between sobs, wanting to feel that warm safe vibration called love just one more time, I looked around for Mr. Bear.

I walked to the love seat and grabbed Mr. Bear, then headed towards the long sofa by the window and climbed up. Placing my left arm around the armrest, I lifted my left leg onto the cushion. With all my might I pulled myself up and Mr. Bear, who was pressed into my right armpit, onto the couch. Finding my way around the long sofa in the dark, I found my brother's foot and positioned my body to find his head. Then I laid real close to my brother to hear him breathing. I put Mr. Bear in between me and my brother to protect him. "I save you, brater. We safe now," I said, but he still didn't wake up. He just moved closer to me and nuzzled his face on Mr. Bear.

I laid there watching the smoke clear out the room, wait-ing for Miss Star Lady to come back until my eyes got heavy and closed. A little while later the early morning beams of sunlight woke me up by poking my face through the bars on the window, and a cockroach tickled me as it ran across my arm. I heard the jingling of keys in the door, the same keys that opened the door from the inside too. She was back, she usually left us and didn't come back for two or three morning sunrises. I closed my eyes tight and played sleep, wishing with all my might that Miss Star Lady would come back and save me and take me away from here forever.

CHAPTER 4
CHENA

Dear Diary,
How many nights
must I wake without him?
I can't erase him
from my memory...
He dwells on planted
unreal expectations...
I want to relocate
to that world, too.
He's perfect!
I can't stand
to be without him.
Narcolepsy, please.
Is there room for two?

CHENA, THE MAKING OF AN ORPHAN

Walking into Lacy's department store, where I had eagerly worked for the past year and a half, I immediately ran downstairs to my counter, unzipped my coat, and began buttoning up the hot pink smock that did nothing for my figure. The uniform designers obviously didn't take into consideration that small-chested, slender women did not look good in oversized pink pillowcases. I hated that damn uniform; it made me feel like I was wearing a sheet.

Laura was working on an elderly woman's face, softly applying eye cream with a cotton swab, attempting to rejuvenate her eyes. Laura didn't see me yet.

"Chena....Oh, you're here! Bless you, you always come to work fifteen minutes early...and get me home to my kids in time to make dinner!" Laura had been working for B.W.C. (Black Women's Cosmetics) for over twelve years. She constantly reminded me of the importance of this cosmetic line for our people. She would always say that before B.W.C existed, makeup for colored women only came in three shades: Dark Brown, Orange Brown, and Light Ivory. On top of that, it was rarely available in department stores.

Obviously women of color come in more than three shades, so B.W.C was a godsend to our people. I myself was not a big fan, 'cause B.W.C. has kept the same style and colors for over ten years. Although I would never tell Laura, when she left work I would buy my products from Girl Friends, a new and hip cosmetic line that made makeup for all nationalities and shades of women. They always had hot and trendy colors like plum purple and ice pink, which were my favorite lipsticks. Customers often asked which B.W.C. product I was wearing, so to double up on my sales I would lie and tell the desperate housewives that I mixed two colors of B.W.C to achieve the color on my lips. Like a charm they would eat it up and buy five of each color. I only worked three days a week, three hours a day, but including my commission, I proudly brought home one hundred dollars a week.

I loved my job; it was fun and most important it was easy. All I had to do was stand there and do what I loved most: play with makeup and make other women look beautiful. The job itself was really rewarding. I loved when I gave a person with low self-esteem a makeover and made them realize how beautiful they really were.

Once I made a forty-year-old woman cry. Her name was Tammy, and she came to my counter shopping for her mother. I asked her if she was interested in any of our new lipsticks, and told her that if she bought one she would get a free gift for our Mothers Appreciation promotion. Tammy bit her lip and mumbled, "This face can't be helped."

I immediately got into my salesgirl routine, not picking up that she wasn't fishing for compliments, but was in fact serious. I asked her if she had ten minutes to spare for a quick demo. She set her bags on the counter and said, "Why not? I can at least find my mother a good color." I knew I could make up her whole face in fifteen minutes, and once I started she wouldn't stop me. After applying blemish cream to cover the scars on her face (which I later found out were the side effects from her chemo treatments), I applied the Foxy Brown Power cream finish foundation. I didn't want to scare her with a dramatically made-up look, so I went for natural tones, using only brown, gold, and bronze colors for her eye shadow, lipstick, and blush.

When I was finished I handed her the mirror. Waiting in anticipation for her reaction, I said, "You look beautiful." When she pulled the mirror away from her face, tears were rolling down her checks. I rushed from around the counter and asked if she was all right, handing her a tissue. Carefully wiping her tears, making sure not to smear her makeup, she responded with a smile.

"Thank you so much. I never thought I would look like this again."

I put my hand on her shoulder and told her, "I didn't do anything but enhance what was already there."

She stood up smiling and said, "I'll take two of each thing you used, one for me and one for my mom." She thanked me again before leaving and said that I had changed her life. There are many Tammies out there, and I get to help them on a weekly basis. It really makes my job fulfilling and rewarding.

"Chena, I fully stocked the foundations, eye shadows, and blushes, I just need you to organize the display case and fill the liquid foundation drawers. And don't worry if you don't finish; whatever you don't get to I'll finish tomorrow."

"Okay. You better hurry, you know your train leaves in ten minutes."

"Bye sweetie, see you tomorrow," Laura said as she grabbed her purse out of the drawer.

"Oh, you didn't look at the schedule. I'm off Friday 'cause I worked Monday," I said with excitement.

"Oh well, I'll see you next week. Have a good weekend and be safe." Buttoning up the last button on her raincoat, Laura ran toward the exit in hopes of making her train.

"Hey girly, what's the latest scoop on your Brandon... crush?" Becky called over from her counter with a smile.

"Don't say his name to loud—someone who knows him might hear," I hissed. Becky is my best friend and I trust her with my life, but she has the biggest mouth ever. Becky worked at Girl Friends, right across from my counter. I wished

I worked there too, but I got hired first at B.W.C during my junior year, then GirlFriend's Cosmetics came to Lacy's my senior year and I convinced Becky to apply. Both Becky and I went to group interviews and were the only people asked to stay after the group orientation. We both were a little nervous because at both interviews we were competing against adults as old as thirty with way more experience then we had, but we each got a second interview. I'm sure it was because of my youth, and Becky's modeling good looks.

"I'm going to ask him tomorrow at lunch," I blurted out, looking around, paranoid that someone would overhear our conversation.

"You better not punk out...you want me to ask him?"

"Becky, I'm a big girl and I got major game. Remember, I taught you everything you know!" Laughing, Becky turned around to help a middle-aged lady wearing shorts and flip flops in the middle of winter try on lipsticks. Immediately Becky recognized money: rolling around in shorts in the winter means you got a car and just ran out the house to spend money.

Leaving Becky to her customer, I begin to stock the liquid foundations. That's when a familiar voice from behind me said, "Excuse me." Turning around quickly, I saw Brandon standing there.

Gasping, I squealed, "You scared me! How can I help you?"

"My mom's birthday is tomorrow and I wanted to know if you could help me, 'cause a brother don't have a clue on what mothers like." Damn, why did he have to see me in this pillow-case? Looking past Brandon, I could see Becky's face light up. She pointed to Brandon's back, giving me the thumbs up. "What you looking at?" he asked, turning to look behind him, but Becky quickly turned back around to face her customer, who was trying on every lipstick on the display case.

Taking my eyes off Becky, I slowly looked up at his ever-lasting height, searching for his gaze, until finally I reached his light hazel-brown eyes. Wow...his lashes are beautiful. "I'm sorry, I thought that customer might be shoplifting...we get paid a hundred dollars if we turn in a thief," I whispered nervously.

"Is she stealing?" he whispered back curiously.

"Naw, she just reached in her purse to match up a lipstick she already had." I cleared my throat and started over in a normal tone of voice. "I'm sorry, now how can I help you?"

"My mom," Brandon stated firmly.

"Oh, yeah! Well, you came to the right counter because with the purchase of one item you get a free gift, so it'll look like you bought her two things."

"Cool, that's what I'm talking about," Brandon said, smiling.

"Since your mom isn't here, I can't match up her skin tone with a color, so to play it safe, I suggest that you get her one of our fragrances."

"All right. I'll take the pink bottle." Brandon pointed through the glass of the display case behind me. Automatically I reached for the bottle, but then quickly turned back around.

"You can at least put a little thought into your mom's gift. Why don't you take the time to smell it?"

"What you trying to say, I'm not thoughtful? 'Cause for your information, I'm the most thoughtful man you'll ever meet."

"Really?" I said teasingly with a little smirk, indicating that I didn't believe him for a second.

"Give me the bottle, please." I handed the tester bottle to him and he read the label on the back. Then he said, "I need a pretty girl to smell it on. Do you mind if I use your wrist?"

"Why can't you use your own?" I said. Realizing the words that just came out of my mouth, I wanted to kick myself.

"Well, Miss Congeniality, I want my mom to be surprised, and if I walk in the house smelling like perfume she'll know!"

Realizing that this was a perfect opportunity for me to find out if he had a girlfriend at his old school, I responded, "Well, you could just say that your girlfriend accidentally sprayed you."

"Unfortunately that wouldn't work 'cause she knows I don't have a girlfriend."

"Oh, well then I guess I'd better help you out," I said as I extended my wrist towards him. He delicately held my wrist and sprayed the perfume lightly. Then he bent down and inhaled the scent on my wrist like he was smelling the sweetest smell in the whole wide world. Slowly brushing his noise against my wrist like he was playing Eskimo kisses with a flower, he took one last inhale of the rosy scent, and then looked up smiling.

"Thank you. I'll buy this one."

Smiling back, still tingling from his touch, I didn't want him to let my wrist go. I blurted out, "You know, there are five other perfumes if you want to compare."

Brandon looked up, fixing his hazel eyes on mine. "I know what I like, and when I find it I get it."

"Really?" I said, flirting. Turning to grab a new bottle from the display case for him, I asked in a sexy voice, "Do you have any plans this weekend?" I pulled out a sheet of wrapping paper from below the counter and quickly wrapped up the box.

"Not really. Me and my boys are going to the homecoming game. Why do you ask?"

"Me and my girls are throwing a homecoming after-party tomorrow and it's gonna be off the hook."

"Where's it going to be?"

"At my girl's house in the town."

A slight smile crept around the edges of Brandon's mouth. "Cool. Can I bring my boys?"

"Yeah, the more the merrier," I replied, trying to keep my cool.

Bee's talented designing ass had already printed over a hundred flyers in her third period class on Wednesday, and she had distributed them to the entire upper-class student body. I conveniently had three of them sitting by the register. Reaching over to grab one, I slid it across the counter to him. "The party starts at nine and directions are on the back. Your total comes to $27.59. Will that be cash or charge?"

"Cash. Thanks for wrapping it. See ya later."

"Bye. Hope your mom likes the gift—if not she can exchange it at any Lacy's," I babbled, trying to stay calm and collected. He smiled and gave me a short wave as he walked away.

The butterflies returned to my stomach, and I couldn't help but daydream about dancing with Brandon at the party. A big grin extended across my entire face, showing off my pearly whites. "Hey snap out of it! Earth to Chena...," Becky said impatiently, standing right in front of my counter. I sucked my teeth and looked at her, but I couldn't hide my ear-to-ear smile.

"Girl, did you see him all in my face? Girl, I had him eating out of the palm of my hands!"

"What happened?"

"Well, he said he was here to buy a gift for his mom, so I helped him and invited him to the party."

"Is he coming?"

"You know it, and he's going to bring some of his friends too!"

"I hope his friends are cute so we'll have some eye candy to look at."

"Girl, me too! Did Bee show you the outfits yet?"

"No, but she said that they were hella cute, and top secret. Oh, she also said to make sure I had Black Hills with Pink Frost accessories ready for our dress rehearsal tomorrow. And I think we're wearing skirts or dresses."

"How do you know?" I asked, speculating.

"'Cause she said that we better shave our legs 'cause we were showing them," Becky said with a huge smile. "I got a surprise too for all y'all."

"Really, what is it?"

"I'll show you at Bee's tomorrow," Becky said, looking over her shoulder like it was top secret.

"Come on girl, don't hold out tell me!" I whined.

"No, you're going have to wait," Bee stated, walking back to assist a customer pondering over the lipsticks.

"Attention all Lacy's shoppers! The store will be closing in fifteen minutes." I could tell the announcer was ready to go home by the rude tone of his intercom announcement. Whistling and humming "I like the way you comb your hair, I like those stylish clothes you wear, it's just the little things you do, that make me want to get with you," I balanced my cash drawer and headed upstairs to the employee room where I could drop my cash in the vault. Becky headed up with me.

"You need a ride?" she asked.

"Yeah!" I was glad she was driving today, 'cause I didn't want to walk to the train station in the windy cold rain.

Walking briskly to Becky's ride, I sarcastically asked, "Why did your mom let you drive today?"

"I didn't tell you, Mother left for Vegas yesterday," Becky said nonchalantly. I hated how Becky referred to her mother as "Mother." She should have been called "Bitch," since she was never a mother to Becky. She always put a man before Becky, yet Becky desperately held onto any sign of affection from her mom, yearning to just be loved. Thus she placed her on a pedestal, granting her the unearned title of "Mother."

Snapping out of my train of thought quickly, I blurted out, "No! So she left you the car?"

"Of course not; I took it. Who's going to tell her? Plus my grandma would say she was driving it if she got suspicious."

"Cool. When does she get back?"

"She isn't due back for two weeks." I was happy to hear that, 'cause that meant that I could get a ride home from work. Usually when her mom picked Becky up, she wouldn't offer me a ride 'cause she said I lived too far out of the way. The reality was she didn't like me 'cause I didn't kiss her ass. She knew damn well I only lived three blocks away from them.

Blasting music and jamming to the bass in her mom's 1998 BMW, we thought we were tight, shit we knew we were the shit. We rolled down the windows to clear the fog that begin to frost up the inside windshield from our hot breath as we sang as loud as we could. We were on top of the world, until the car hit something with a loud thump. Becky slammed on the brakes and we both screamed as we looked at the bleeding homeless man on the hood of the car. The windshield was cracked, but we could see the man struggling to get up.

"Oh my God, what do I do?" Becky screamed, trying to hold back tears.

"Calm down, he's moving so he's not dead!"

"Fucking bitches! I'm going to kill you! Get the fuck out the car you bitch!" The man crawled off the hood, trying to find his balance.

As the man staggered to her side of the car the fumes of alcohol reeking off his body rushed into the car through Becky's open window. In a shaky voice Becky yelled, "I'm sorry, I didn't see you, um...are you okay?"

Sensing something wasn't right about the look in his eye, I yelled, panicking, "Becky, get us out of here! Drive!" Right as she began to put the car in drive, the guy reached into the car, hitting her in her head and slapping her left cheek. Then he grabbed Becky's hair. Reaching over her to the driver's side door, I screamed, "Let her go, you fucking asshole!" I pressed the automatic window button upward, smashing the guy's arm against the top of the doorframe until he released Becky's hair. He yanked his arm back out of the car and tried to scrabble for the door handle. I slammed the control button upward until Becky's window was safely up as she smashed her right foot on the gas and took off. In the rear view window we could see the man giving us the finger before he picked up his bent-up grocery cart that had fallen over.

Relief poured over me as I put the scene together. Apparently Becky had hit his cart first and he had jumped on the hood of the car in retaliation. "Are you okay?" I asked, still trembling.

"No, that motherfucker almost pulled out a chunk of my hair." Becky couldn't hold back the tears. "Chena, for a minute there I thought I killed a man."

"Well, you didn't. Shit, he almost killed you." When we pulled up in front of my house I told Becky to park and come in to calm her nerves. She was in no condition to drive home by herself. Stepping out the car we could see that there was a slight dent in the front grille, the left headlight was cracked and the windshield had a crack in it too.

"How am I going to get this fixed? I don't have any money and I can't report it to my mother's insurance or she will know I stole the car." Becky looked at me, distraught and freaking out as if I'm supposed to magically make the dents disappear. I knew I should have been more concerned with her safety, as my gaze fixated on her swollen bottom lip, but I couldn't help but think, How this will affect my plan to get Brandon? "This is going to ruin our plans," Becky mumbled, causing panic to flash across my face. I tried to push down the anger that was building up, even as I thought, I hope this bitch doesn't try and cancel the party and ruin my chances of connecting with Brandon.

"Girl, we got two weeks before she gets back to figure it out. Don't worry, things will work out. We'll take care of it. Come inside; let's call your grandma." I tried to wipe the panic and irritation out of my voice. Walking up the stairs, Becky wiped the smeared mascara off of her cheeks and smoothed her hair down with her hands. "You can use the phone in the kitchen, I'm going use the bathroom," I said, reaching into the freezer to hand Becky a bag of frozen mixed vegetables to put on her eye and swollen lip.

"Chena, why do you have company this late? It's after nine p.m.!" Dena yelled out from her room in an irritated voice. I walked straight into Dena's room so she could see how distraught my face was. "Are you okay? Who's here?" Dena continued sternly.

"It's Becky. She's using the phone in the kitchen to—"

Dena cut me off midsentence. "You know I don't like when you bring people in our house without it being clean, and definitely not this late!" she snapped.

"I'm sorry, but we got into a little accident and Becky is too shaken up to drive right now." I looked down as I apologized. Throwing her book to the side of the bed and pulling off her glasses, Dena jumped out of the bed and hugged me. Not expecting a hug, I couldn't get my arms up fast enough to hug her back, and she squished my arms down along my sides. "We're fine, we didn't get hurt," I squealed.

"This damn weather isn't safe to drive in! What happened?" Dena asked. Shaking my head, I sat down on the edge of her queen-sized bed while she towered over me, waiting for a response.

Dena's legs look like they belonged to a WNBA player. She worked out and you could tell. She was 5'11" and had it going on; most people thought I was her sister, and couldn't believe I was her foster daughter. When people would gasp, she'd say, "That's right, I had Chena when I was young." Then she'd wink at me. She always managed to leave the "foster" part out when she introduced me as her daughter, and I guess I didn't mind. It was nice to feel like I belonged to a family; but deep in the back of mind I'd keep reality in perspective, Dena is a temporary mom, and will probably be out my life as soon as those foster care checks stop rolling in.

"We were driving home from work and at East 14th and 120th a homeless man was jaywalking, but we couldn't see him, and he pushed his buggy in front of the car, then he jumped on the hood and tried to attack us."

"You sure y'all didn't hit him?" Dena said, worried. I could see by the look on her face she thought we had killed him.

"We thought we hit him until he got up off the hood, reached into Becky's window, and started attacking her."

Dena gasped. "Oh my God, we should call the police." She reached for the phone on her bedside table.

I panicked. The police would report the accident to Becky's mom, and that would ruin Friday's party. A lie formed instantly on my lips. "We stopped at a pay phone and called the police already. Apparently an officer was patrolling the area, 'cause he got there in minutes. He took a report and left to go find the guy who attacked us."

"Good! Well, let's see if the child is all right," Dena said with a sigh of relief. My heart was pounding fast. I hated to lie to Dena, but luckily she hated Becky's mom too for be a fake snooty phony baloney , so I wouldn't have to worry about this coming up in conversation.

Despite the bag of frozen vegetables, Becky's face was starting to swell, so I grabbed another frozen pack out the freezer, wrapped it in five paper towels and handed it to her for her cheek. "Thanks. My grandmother is on her way to get me, and my uncle is with her, so he'll drive the car back," Becky slurred through her swollen lip.

Ring! Ring! I picked up the phone. "Hello?"

"Hi Dena, it's Becky's grandmother. Can you tell her I'm downstairs?"

"Would you like me to buzz you in?"

"No, I'm not feeling that well to come upstairs. My back is giving me pains."

"Okay, I'll send her right down. Bye."

Looking down at the floor, Becky mumbles, "Is it okay if I borrow the ice pack?"

"Keep it, we have plenty. Plus you're going to need it for tomorrow," I said as I wrapped my arms around Becky's limp body. She barely hugged me back. "Bye," I whispered as I closed the door behind Becky.

"I'm going to bed. If you need anything, let me know," Dena said softly as she kissed my forehead, then turns and disappeared down the hall into her room. What a crazy night. I hoped Becky's face wouldn't be too bruised or swollen at the party, poor girl. I'd pray for her...and that crazy drunk man too.

CHAPTER 5
LIL CHENA

Dear Diary,
I'm sad and I don't know why
I'm sad yet I cannot cry
My heart is empty, yearning
to fill a void
All I want is to be loved,
kissed ,and given a hug.
This feeling of melancholia
has taken over my body
Holidays go by and I remember
that I
... I am truly alone
I'm sad and I don't know why,
I'm sad yet I cannot cry.

CHENA, THE MAKING OF AN ORPHAN

We'd been walking for so long that the back of my ankles were bleeding as the blisters ruptured again. We walked from our house in Bezerkeley to Grannie's house in north Oaktown, so mother could borrow some money to get us some shoes at Payless shoe store. But I knew we ain't gon' get none, unless someone else give 'em to us. She always borrowed money and said it's for us, but she don't ever take us to get nothing.

I like seeing my Grannie. She's a short stocky woman with big dark brown oval eyes. Her eyes have a hint of navy blue in them. She say her eyes ain't always had blue in them, it be due to all them years of looking at the sun. She say that all old folks start turning back into babies as they get old, so when I asked her, "Grannie, why yo eyes got blue in dem?" she said, "I reckon my eyes was blue when I was a baby." She got a big round flat nose, high cheekbones, and the softest brown skin in the world. I asked, "Grannie, how come yo skin so soft?" and she said with a big ole smile showing off her gold-capped front tooth, "I'm turning into a baby, Baby."

I could tell she loved me 'cause she always gave me a big hug and a piece of peppermint and let me turn the channel on the big TV in her living room from the news to cartoons. She liked my brother better, though. She always gave him two pieces of peppermint. She said, "He handsome 'cause he light skinned. He gon' be so handsome when he grown up." Then she just looked at me with pity and said, "Thank God her hair ain't nappy." It's okay Grannie don't think I'm handsome too, 'cause at least she said something to me. My other Grandma don't even look at me. She's a little older then my Grannie, with long straight jet-black hair that she wore braided down to her butt. My Grannie said, "She be dyeing her hair, trying to look young and pass as white. But that alcohol gone and wrinkled up her pale white skin like prunes." Grandma was short like grannie too, but thin and hard. My grannie was soft and plump.

She told me not to dare call her Grandma, I could only call her Miss Evill'a. Then she told me I have to sit on the back porch and look after the chickens and ducks running around. I sat, and when she walked away I peeked in the back kitchen window at her giving my brother pie and ice cream at the kitchen table, while my little hungry stomach growled and growled. I hated Evill'a and she hated me. Every time Mother left the room she whispered to me, "You ain't my son's daughter, you ain't no grandbaby of mine. You too dark to be Creole." Then she gave me a pinch on my arm to make sure I know she meant it and sent me out to sit on the porch by myself till Mother came back for us. No matter how bad it was raining or how cold it was or how much I cried she left me out there and just turned on the porch light when it got too dark for her to see where I was at when she's looking out the back window.

My feet hurt real bad, my shoes were too small, and my tummy hurt, felt like a hole was growing bigger and bigger in it and sucking everything I got out. But I didn't say nothing 'cause the birds were singing to me and the sun was bright on my face. Me and my brother ain't ate for a couple days now, as Mother's been gone again visiting her special friends. Well, almost nothing except for the peppermint at my grannies and the raw bacon that was in the refrigerator; my brother told me to eat it and I'd get super powers. I ate it too, but then threw it right back up. He laughed at me.

Dominick said what I was thinking. "I'm hungry, Mommy!" He yelled and went straight into his usual tantrum, falling on the ground kicking and screaming like somebody was hurting him real bad. I was a couple feet behind 'em, watching my mother look around with embarrassment.

Mother was tall and skinny, but her brown skin glowed. You couldn't deny under the roughness of her life there lay true beauty. She had soft brown smooth skin, dark brown oval-shaped eyes, a flat forehead, and a narrow face with high cheekbones and slender round-tipped nose that went just right with her full lips. Her hair was in a curly afro with a stripe of grey in the front—looked like a lightning bolt hit her in that very spot. My Grannie said, "She use to be a model and was book smart, too." But Grannie say that was before she got on that aeroplane headed to Europe, a couple years before she gave birth to my brother and me. She went to be with them white folks, Grannie said, and she came back on a stretcher 'cause she got real sick in the head.

Wearing dirty, holey, tight-fitting high-waisted bell bottom denim jeans and an oversized dirty cream wool sweater cropped to her waistline that half hung off her bony shoulder, Mother held her head up high while she struggled to gather my malnourished brother to his feet. Picking him up, she shifted her weight in her flat white open-toe sandals. She cradled my brother's three-year-old body like he was a tiny baby, promising him some food. My two-year-old tummy was just as hungry, but she didn't care. She loved my brother, always saying, "You look just like your daddy." She said it over and over while she stroked his hair when he was sleeping. As they walked away she didn't even notice I was still across the street, standing on the corner. The light blinked red hand while she and my brother walked hand and hand in the crosswalk, so I stayed behind.

My Grannie taught me not to walk on the red hand, only on the stick man, or a big truck would come and run me over, smash my body into tiny bits all over the road and maggots would eat me up. She called it road kill. She pointed out the dead cats or dogs we'd see in the street, flattened and half eaten with white tiny worms coming out of their eyeballs and say they crossed the street on the red hand. I stood there waiting for stick man. I didn't want to become road kill.

Taking in the smell of the fresh air brought a smile to my face. I loved being outside, away from the roaches and out of our stuffy dirty empty house. I stood next to an old man who looked like Bruce Lee's grandpa. He was the oldest man I had ever seen, and old people usually scared me. I always thought they were going to eat me and turn me into a prune and take my youth. My Grannie tell me that old people don't smile no more 'cause they be missing their youth, and they'd take mine if they could. But this old man didn't scare me. His skin was yellow with soft wrinkles. He was hunched over and bald, with tiny bits of grey hair coming out in patches, and he had a black mole on his cheek like a raisin with one long hair coming out of it. His long grey and white skinny beard was stiff. It looked like my doll's hair after me and my brother put hair grease in it. He was dressed in Chinese pajamas: grey pants and a matching grey long sleeve jacket with Chinese writing printed on the fabric. He was old but still looked like he could turn into a ninja at any moment.

There was a red and green dragon on the back of his jacket with small gold Chinese letters. I stood there with a dumfounded look on my face, wondering if he would turn into that dragon on his back, and if he came out of a hole. My Grannie said that the Chinese could dig a hole in the dirt and make their way back to China, and if I didn't stop digging holes in her garden I'd fall into one of them holes and end up in China and no one would be able to find me.

He was wearing funny shoes, the same little black slippers that Bruce Lee wore, and some white socks that looks as thin as my Grannie's stockings. He was pushing a black fold-up buggy basket. My Grannie uses the same kind of thing to carry her clothes to the wash house, or her groceries on the bus, but he was using it to carry books. He had the whole basket full of all different kinds of books, big books, little books, old-looking books and new looking books. We both stood waiting on the light, not wanting to become road kill.

I stared at him, trying to see if he was breathing, and then out of nowhere the sound of the light beeping, telling us to cross, startles me. The old man looked at me for the first time, startled now too, 'cause he didn't even know I was standing so close to him, almost touching his leg. He grabbed at his heart, closed his eyes, then opened them again and smiled at me. I smiled back, showing all my little teeth. His eyes were small, slanted, and narrow, but they still revealed warmth.

We started to cross the street. I looked ahead at my mother and brother, now standing hand in hand. My brother was trying to break free from Mother's tight grip. Mother turned to face the crosswalk, just spotting me. When I was halfway into the crosswalk she yelled, "Come on now and hurry it up, Chena, we gots to get your brother something to eat!" in her high-pitched squeaky witchlike voice that could shatter glass. She narrowed her eyes at me as I got closer. Seeing Mother's angry face made me pick up my pace. I was about to run across the street until I was stopped by the sound of an abrupt squealing and a bump from something falling behind me. I turned around. The old man had been hit by an oncoming bicyclist, who had hit his brakes too late to keep from knocking the old man over backwards. The impact knocked the old man's basket over, too. All his books went flying, sprawled out all over the crosswalk.

"Ooh no, you made a boo-boo!" I said, walking towards him. He quickly jumped to his feet like the ninja I had imagined, with the help of the apologetic bicyclist, and together they lifted his buggy right side up. He dusted his pants legs off and began to slowly gather his books as if time were frozen. I ran as fast as I could, zipping past the old man to pick up a big book lying there behind him, not wanting him to become road kill if the red hand came back too soon.

I continued on picking up books as fast as I could, making a game out of who could try and pick up the most books. Almost all the books were picked up, but I continued placing them in his buggy, ignoring Mother's strident calls. Other people crossing the street, along with the owner of the bike who hit him, helped to collect the books and put them all back in the old man's buggy. Smiling from ear to ear, pleased with myself, I ran to put the very last book in the buggy, but before my hand could release it, the old man stopped me with the wave of his index finger. "You keep. You are good, you are a fighter, God watches over you, tiger child." He leaned down, looked at my screaming mother, then back at me and whispered, "You are love. Knowledge in books set you free." Then patted me on the head, before he walked past me as if we had never met. I became a little sad that the man was walking away. I wanted to go home with him and be a part of his family.

I looked down at the book. It had tigers on the cover. Opening the tiny paperback I could see letters that made no sense to me, Chinese writing and pictures of different animals in fluorescent colors. Maybe this is a magic book, with magic powers, I thought. It was the first book I had ever been given. I didn't know what lay inside it, but I knew it was something special, and at that moment I knew I wanted to learn everything inside of all books. I wanted to learn to read. I quickly closed the little paperback book, held it close to my chest, and ran across the street to meet my mother's dismissive eyes.

CHAPTER 6
CHENA

Dear Diary,

*I love being a woman; I am all
woman.*

*Baiting my eyelashes
The diva, the predator in the night
The rainbow in the sky
The eagle that takes flight
The phenomenon
The innovator
The trendsetter
The go-getter
The caretaker
The powerful woman I am*

*I love being a woman; I am all
woman.*

CHENA, THE MAKING OF AN ORPHAN

"Where are Tanisha and Bee? Damn, can they be on time for anything?"

"Chena, calm down. They'll be here soon," Becky said calmly.

"If Romonia catches us, we're busted!" Although we had gone to first period and had our excuse notes in our hand, I didn't feel safe, 'cause I knew that if Romonia saw us all leaving school together she'd know something was up. Then she'd go into detective mode and try to investigate the situation by calling all of our parents at work to verify our notes. "I got a bad feeling, Becky, and I have invested too much time for this party to be blown, 'cause people are running late. I'm going to walk to the 7-Eleven on the corner and page Bee and Tanisha. Stay here. If they don't show in fifteen minutes, start walking to the 7-Eleven."

Becky looked at me with uneasy eyes and paused before whispering, "Look behind you." Looking over my right shoulder, I could see Romonia approaching.

Turning back around, I whispered to Becky, "Turn around and walk back into the school and go out of the west wing. I'll meet you at the 7-Eleven. Hurry!"

"Where do you think you're going?" Romonia yelled out to us from the staff parking lot.

"Hi, Romonia. I was just saying good-bye to Chena. I'm headed to Mr. Robin's class," Becky yelled back with an award-winning smile. Winking at me with her left eye, she added, "See ya, Chena. I hope you feel better," loudly enough for Romonia to hear her.

Watching Becky walk away, my heart began to pound as I hear Romonia's footsteps stop right behind me. Sweat formed on my forehead. Turning around slowly, I went into what I hoped would be an Oscar-worthy performance. "Did you see a black Explorer parked up front?"

"No, why?"

"I'm waiting for my ride," I said in a low voice.

"Let me see your excuse slip," Romonia demanded as she snatched the note out of my hand. She began to read it, squinting her eyes and glancing back at me to ensure I wouldn't run away. She looked displeased that the note seemed authentic, handing the paper back to me with a slight grunt. "What's wrong with you today?"

Looking down, I mumbled, "I ain't got time for this, it's personal."

"Sure it is, it's a personal fake excuse to leave school. You don't have a doctor's appointment; what you've got is a test and Mommy wrote you a note to give you extra time to study."

"No, Romonia," I snapped, "I might be dying."

"What?" Her tone oozed skepticism.

Looking up with a tear I forced out, "I might have cancer you fucking nark, they found a lump in my breast, okay? So, uh..." I choked back a sob as my voice rose to the strength of a whining child's, "just leave me alone." I definitely deserved an Oscar for that performance. Romonia stood there speechless. After a moment, visibly swallowing, she walked towards me, put her hand on my shoulder, and said, "I'm sorry to hear that. I will keep you in my prayers. In the meantime, watch your language, okay?" The she walked away towards the back of the school. Oh my, I thought, looks like Romonia has a heart after all! I bet she won't be fucking with me no more. Ha!

Briskly walking toward the front entrance to the school parking lot I saw Bee's car a block away. I started walking towards her car, hoping to catch her attention before she drove in front of the school. She saw me waving my arms and pulled over. "Jump in," she said.

"Turn right down this street. Hurry." Tanisha let me in the passenger side and I slid into the back seat.

"Where's Becky?" Tanisha turned around in the front seat, looking at me with worry.

"Turn down your damn music! What do you want to do, get us busted?"

"Sorry," Bee said sarcastically, sucking her teeth and rolling her eyes at me.

I just went off, snapping, "Don't even try to have a damn attitude. Y'all are twenty fucking minutes late, and me and Becky almost got caught up by Romonia!"

"What happened?" Bee said in a low voice.

Ignoring her question, I turned my head towards the window and said coldly, "We have to pick up Becky from 7-Eleven so please just drive."

Keeping a low profile, we made it to 7-Eleven, where Becky paced nervously back and forth by the pay phones. Honk! Honk! "Becky, get in!" I screamed out the window. Becky ran towards the car. Tanisha jumped out of the front seat, leaned the seat forward, and I scooted over as Becky jumped in.

"What happened, Chena?" Becky asked, with worry.

"After you left I put on the waterworks for Romonia and told her that I had cancer."

"She bought that?" Tanisha said, astonished.

"Oh yeah—said she'd keep me in her prayers, how about that?"

"Damn girl, that was close," Bee said, looking at me in the rear-view mirror.

"Yeah, no thanks to you," I snapped.

"Well hold your fucking attitude, okay? I'm sorry you and Becky had to deal with Romonia, but you really need to drop your fucking attitude. For your information, I was late because I parked around the corner behind the school like we planned, and when I went back to my car it was being put on a fucking tow truck. I had to bribe the guy with a hundred dollars, which of course I didn't have on me," Bee said angrily.

"That's when I showed up and we walked to an ATM," Tanisha said, smiling like everything was hunky-dory.

"Oh," I said, calming down. "I'm sorry for yelling and having an attitude, Bee. It's just that y'all are always on colored people's time, and this time I needed y'all to be on time."

Laughing, Bee yelled, "We can't help being on C.P. time, it's in our genes!"

"Chena, take a chill pill and relax, 'cause we are going to have some fun tonight!" Tanisha said, grinning from ear to ear.

Rolling up to Becky's grandmother's house, we jumped out smiling 'cause we knew that the party was going to be off the hook.

"When did your grandma's plane leave?" Tanisha asked nervously.

"Don't worry, she ain't here. My uncle dropped her off at the airport this morning and she left her car for me to drive."

"Okay," Bee said, stretching her arms. "Help me with y'all's outfits." Running with excitement to the trunk of the car we each grabbed a bag.

"Y'all come upstairs to my room." We followed Becky into her room, which looked like it had been made for a princess. It had a canopy bed and plush pink wall-to-wall carpet. This room was off the hook! Becky had a reading sofa built into her massive bedroom window. The room had mirrored closet doors, a small private bathroom, and a beautiful white vanity table that actually had lights built in around the frame of the mirror. It looked like a room for a movie star. "I have a surprise for you guys. Come and look," Becky said, excitedly. On the bed we could see a pile of about five hundred dollars' worth of makeup and accessories.

"Becky, where did you get the money for all this stuff?" I said in amazement.

"Let's just say I used my five finger discount."

"What, are you crazy? Girl, you going to jail," I said, busily picking up all of the accessories that I wanted first.

"Thanks, Becky! I can't believe you took all this shit. When did you do it?" Tanisha asked, trying on a pair of silver sparkling earrings.

"I started slipping stuff into a purse that I hid in the back of one of the display cases since last week. Once we decided to have the party, I figured I better get y'all some stuff too."

"Slow your roll," Bee said, snatching the accessories out of my hands. "You have to wait and see your outfits first." Smiling with glee I agreed and turned towards Bee, who walked over to the window seat and began laying the outfits on the bed. They were beautiful. We all gasped with amazement that Bee had actually been able to put these outfits together literally in five days.

The outfits were all matching colors, but each outfit was designed differently. Mine had a medium-length black skirt made of spandex. Trying on the skirt I was excited; this skirt hugged my trim figure, showing off my thirty-five-inch hips, twenty-three-inch waist, and perky butt. My butt wasn't booty-licious but was just right on me, and it looked perfect in this skirt. The skirt flared slightly at the bottom with little ruffles trimming the edge, with diamond cutouts going down the side of the skirt exposing glimpses of the side of my legs. The top was perfect, too.

Bee really knew how to design a shirt that flattered the female body while still allowing you to wear a padded bra. The shirt was a shimmery frost hot pink. It was beautiful! Cut low to allow the cleavage produced by my padded bra to show, it was cropped at the bottom too to show off my six-pack. The extra-long sleeves hung over my ruler-like arms. Diamond cutouts exposed my shoulders.   Jumping on Bee and hugging her, I started to scream. "Thank you! Thank you so much girl, I love it! It's beautiful!"

"You're welcome! I'm glad you like it. Now get off me 'cause you're messing up my hair!" Bee pushed me off playfully, but I could tell she appreciated my reaction.

Becky walked around in her outfit like she was in a Lacy's catalog, smiling. "I love it...it's beautiful." Bee had made everyone's shirt out of the same material, but she made each one unique. Becky's shirt was sleeveless with a diamond cutout in the center of her chest exposing her cleavage. Instead of a skirt, she had on black capri pants that had diamond cutouts on the sides exposing her long, muscular legs. Tanisha's outfit was cut differently from the rest. Her top was just like mine, but her black capri pants were made like parachute pants, with drawstrings dangling at the bottom and carpenter-style pockets on the sides of the pant legs. Smiling and turning around to view herself in the mirror, Tanisha yelled, "I love it, I love it! Thanks, Bee. It's so me."

Bee's outfit of course outdid ours, but that was to be expected—she was the designer after all. Bee wore a hot pink backless halter top that tied at the base of her neck, in the middle of her back and at the shirt bottom, which allowed her to tie the shirt high enough to show off her abs. She wore a short black skirt with carpenter-style pockets on the sides. The back pockets of the skirt had diamond cutouts lined with the same pink material her shirt was made out of. As Bee turned around to show off her outfit we begin to clap, cheering. "Bee you look beautiful! I love your outfit!" Bee began to blush and we all just stood there looking at each other in amazement.

"Okay girls, jump out of your outfits. It's ten a.m. and we got less than six hours to cook, clean house, pick up the girls, and set up shop," Bee said sharply. Tanisha was the only homemaker in the crew, so she was in charge of making the spaghetti, potato salad, hot dogs, and hamburgers. Becky didn't know but I'd already talked to her grandmother, who agreed to report the accident as if she had been the driver and go through her own insurance to have the car fixed if we paid the five hundred dollar deductible, so we were planning on selling plates, coat check tickets, and charging five dollars at the door to help cover the cost.

"Bee."

"Yeah, Chena?"

"Don't forget to pick up our helpers—they get out of school at three."

"Girl, I can't 'cause I'm decorating the house, remember?"

"Oh yeah," I mumbled, a worried look on my face.

"I'll do it!" Tanisha replied, eager to drive.

"Tanisha, we need you here, you know we can't cook," I said. More importantly, Tanisha couldn't drive, but I didn't want her getting mad when I stated the obvious.

Looking at Becky in desperation, I said, "Can you pick up the girls?"

"No problem," Becky replied casually. Tanisha shrugged her shoulders and exhaled in disappointment. She really wanted to drive, but the truth of the matter is Tanisha and I were the only ones without a license, and Tanisha gets too nervous behind the wheel. Tanisha's mom ended her driving privileges and took away her learner's permit after Tanisha thought she'd put the family Ford Escort in reverse to back out of their driveway, and instead put it in drive and drove right into their living room window. And with Becky's accident hanging over our heads, I just couldn't afford to take any chances of anything ruining my big date with Brandon.

*****

"Hey girls, hop in!" Becky called, smiling. Tamika, Kelly, April, and Nina gladly jumped in. The girls were the A.T.C.'s eighth grade mentees, as well as little images of them. Their parents knew they were going to the football game with their older mentors and were going to sleep over after, but they had no idea their thirteen-year-old teens would be helping out at a party. Becky really felt protective of these girls, like a mother. She looked at them in the rear view mirror. "Make sure you all buckle up."

"I heard about your accident the other day," Tamika said, pausing, "and, uh...I was so mad at that homeless man I told my brother about it." He, of course, had a crush on Becky. "So we went looking for his ass."

"Watch your language!" Becky snapped.

"Sorry, but we didn't find him."

"Anyways!" Nina said loudly to get Becky's attention, "we're all glad you're all right."

"Thanks you guys. Don't worry, I'm fine. Just remember to always wear your seat belts and lock your doors," Becky said firmly as she glanced in the rear-view mirror and pulled out.

"Okay, okay," they all said, locking their doors and buckling their seat belts. As she pulled out she snapped her fingers, remembering. "Hey girls, hand me your permission slips." Tanisha's smart ass had decided that the club needed to get slips signed by the girls' parents stating they would not hold the A.T.C. criminally or financially responsible if anything happened to their children while in the older girls' care. The permission slip was very vague in describing the activities, saying the teens would be involved in sister bonding activities instead of listing what they would be doing.

The girls eagerly passed over their permission slips, except for April.

"Where's your permission slip?" Becky asked.

"I forgot to have my mom sign it, but she said okay."

Becky pulled the car over and shot a look at April, sitting in the back seat, fumbling with the tips of her extension braids and not meeting Becky's eye. "April, don't lie to me, we can get in huge trouble if you're not telling the truth, and we don't have a lot of time. Now, did your mom say you can go or not?" Becky snapped, knowing that this little hold-up could put a major glitch in Chena's plan to get Brandon.

"Yeah...uh, no. She said I could go to the football game, but I better have my ass home by ten."

"Okay, April, I will talk with you later about lying, but let's work on getting you to the slumber party first. Where does your mom work?"

"Are you going to call her?"

"No, I'd rather stop by to ask her in person."

Biting her lip in hesitation, April mumbled, "2121 Oakland Avenue."

The detour to the law firm of Johnson and Johnson, where April's mom worked, only took a few minutes. Becky instructed the girls on their roles before they walked in, then said, "Okay, let's go."

On the way up to the eighth floor, the girls comforted April and crossed their fingers in hopes that her mom would have a change of heart. When they walked into the office the girls quietly took a seat in the reception area, while Becky approached the counter alone. She had put on her reading glasses, pulled her hair back in a ponytail, and put on her brown

V-neck sweater, that she had hidden in her over sized hand bag. She not only looked older, but also very studious.

"May I please speak with Miss Johnson?"

"May I ask your name, please?"

"Yes, I'm Becky from A.T.C."

"Is Miss Johnson expecting you?"

"No, it's kind of a surprise."

The receptionist dialed Miss Johnson's extension and within minutes, Miss Johnson ran down the hall. "Is April okay?"

"Yes, of course, Miss Johnson. She's fine!" Before Becky could finish reassuring April's mom, the girls jumped to their feet, singing "Mama you know I love you" from the Soul Food movie soundtrack. April stepped in front of the girls, and with an angelic voice sang, "Mama! Mama! You know I love you," while the other girls harmonized in the background. They sang the entire song, until the end when April started changing the lyrics to "Mama! Mama! Please let me sleep over, you know I'll be good!" Smiling, April and the girls took a bow and sat down again. Everyone in the office came out clapping their hands at the girls' performance. Becky couldn't help but be proud of the girls; it wasn't even like they had had time to practice.

As soon as the girls finished their performance, Becky turned to Miss Johnson. "Can I speak with you for a minute?"

"Of course, sweetie, follow me. That was a lovely performance." Miss Johnson said. She looked Becky up and down with approval as she ushered her into her office.

"So I understand April isn't allowed to fully participate in our Annual A.T.C retreat, and I wanted to find out if it was due to something we did?"

"No, of course not. You girls are a godsend to my baby. You're all she talks about; she already told me that she has to go to Sal Valley High to take over your spots in the A.T.C. after you girls graduate. Her grades have jumped from Bs and Cs to As and Bs...I can't be more pleased with the positive effect you've had on my daughter," Miss Johnson said with a smile. Pausing for a moment, she put her fingers together under her chin before continuing. "I just did not agree with the permission slip that I received just this morning. I am not signing anything where I can't hold someone accountable for my daughter's well-being."

"I see. Well, if that's the only problem we could quickly rewrite something that you would approve of. You see, we wrote these slips to protect our organization. Girls, Inc. is sponsoring A.T.C., and if something happened to the girls, that would leave Girls, Inc. liable." Becky gave Miss Johnson her most winning smile, then tried another approach. "This A.T.C. weekend retreat is not only a retreat to allow the girls to bond and build each other up, it's also a reward." Becky began to embellish the lie. "It's meant to reward girls for their hard work in the previous school year, and out of twenty-five mentees these girls were the only ones invited, because they had the highest or most improved G.P.A.s and the most community service hours completed."

Miss Johnson gave Becky a stern look before she replied, as if she could read through the bullshit. "I understand, especially since I'm a lawyer, but I still don't feel comfortable signing the original permission slip. However I trust that my daughter is in good hands, so I'm going to have my paralegal draft another form that I will be more comfortable signing."

With a smile of success, Becky extended her hand to Miss Johnson and said, "Thank you for understanding how important this is to all the girls. They would have been very disappointed not to share this experience with April. I promise I will take good care of her."

Smiling back, Miss Johnson stood up. "I'll be right back with the revised form."

Becky couldn't resist the urge to keep the girls in suspense. With a serious face she walked out of the back office, concealing the new permission slip in her hand, and looked at the girls, who were waiting patiently on pins and needles. "Let's go," she said quietly.

Walking silently behind Becky, the girls huddled by the elevator as they waited for it to arrive. Looking up at Becky, they tried to read her expression.

"What happened, can I go?" April asked, near tears.

Becky couldn't hold back her grin anymore. "Of course you can!" High fiving each other and screaming, the girls all hugged April.

"Wait, I have to tell my mom something. I'll be right back!"

"Hurry, 'cause we got stuff to do!" Becky yelled out after April. Running past the receptionist, April disappeared into her mom's office. She reappeared a moment later. "Thanks, Becky," April said, nearly out of breath. I had to tell my mom I loved her." She grinned. "I told her that I'd still love her even if she said no. But I'm glad she didn't say no!"

"All right, girls, are you ready to have some fun?" Becky asked.

"Hell, yeah!" Nina said with excitement.

Running to the car, Kelly yelled out, "Shotgun!" and jumped in the front seat.

*****

When the car rolled up to Becky's grandmother's house, Becky yelled out the car window, "Tanisha, Bee, Chena! Come help us carry stuff!" Rushing out of the house I grabbed the grocery bags full of snacks and sodas and headed back inside. Happy to see the girls, I hugged each one.

"I'm glad you could make it. What took so long?"

"We had to pick up a permission slip from April's mom," Kelly said, unpacking the groceries.

"Oh?" I looked at Becky.

She winked and said, "I'll fill you in later."

"Hey girls, I got a surprise for you," I said with an uncontrollable smile encompassing my face.

"Really, what?" Nina said with excitement.

"We got you girls outfits to wear tonight. Come upstairs!" Running up the stairs one by one they stood in front of Becky's bed gasping and smiling.

"Are these really for us?"

"That's right! Try them on," I replied, full of joy that everything was working out as planned. Soon I'd be in Brandon's arms, I knew it. Bee had made simple black tube tops and pink capri pants for each of the girls. Their outfits were lovely.

"Thank you, thank you, thank you," the girls chorused with excitement while trying on each item.

"Okay, when you're finished change back into what you had on so you can help set up," I told them before I made my way back downstairs. It was time to put the final stages in motion for Operation "Make Brandon Love Me."

CHAPTER 7
LIL CHENA

Dear Diary,
My tears
build up
Reaching the
highest peak
Reconstruction of
my eyes begins...
From open
bright and deep
To closed
dark and blue
I'm sad
that this
reality is the truth...

CHENA, THE MAKING OF AN ORPHAN

Mother got us all cleaned up, fussing and making a big deal about us being clean. She was acting real different, like she was on her special medicine. Me and my brother could always tell when she was on her special medicine, 'cause she started acting real nice to us, especially to me. It was as if she saw me for the first time. If she was gone and come back on her special medicine, she usually brought us some candy. Last time she brought me back Mr. Bear. He was dirty and wet, but I loved him immediately, and after my Grannie washed him for me, he was brand new.

"Awwww! Eee aweee!" I cried, holding Mr. Bear real tight, hoping he could take away the pain. But Mother didn't seem to even notice; she just kept on combing through my hair and the pain continued. My hair hadn't seen a comb or been washed for weeks and had gotten all matted up. My hair only got fixed when we got a special visit from the white lady. Or when Mother was dropping us off at her special friends' houses, and she wanted to look like a good mother.

We had a visit from the white lady already last month. She was a studious-looking young slender-built white woman in her early twenties. Mother said, "She works at the welfare office and you are not to talk to her unless she speaks to you." She didn't come by often, and when she did come by she jumped when she walked in the house, as the roaches often surprised her when they fell from the doorway. She didn't like to sit down either, since the roaches tended to come out of the creases of the couch cushions. Now she just would just walk into the house, making sure to duck her head as she cleared the doorway, look around, ask Mother some questions from her notepad, call for us by name, take a good look at us, make notes on her notepad, smile at us, look around again, take more notes on her notepad, then leave. Mother would sit on pins and needles the entire time, trying to keep a straight face as she answered the white lady's questions. I would pretend not to listen and play with Mr. Bear quietly on the floor...but secretly I was hoping that this welfare lady would take me with her and never bring me back.

Mother finished my hair. She only ever styled it one way. First she'd comb all of my hair out, completely untangling each strand, then she pulled all my hair up and gripped it into a ponytail at the center of my head so my hair formed a tiny curly afro puff held in place with a rubber band. "Okay, I'm finished," Mother said as she took a good look at me. She smiled, but never made eye contact with me. "Go be a good girl and put on the clean clothes laid out on the sofa."

"O-tay," I replied, running to the sofa. I was excited to get to wear my favorite denim jeans with Ms. Pac-Man embroidered on the back pockets, my sky-blue Care Bear shirt, and the navy blue penny loafers my Grannie bought me for Christmas. We had to be going somewhere special, 'cause I never got to wear my penny loafers. My brother had already changed into grey corduroy shorts and a white T-shirt with a picture of his favorite Transformer, Optimus Prime, that his Grandma bought him for Christmas.

My brother and I ran out into the crisp night air as soon as the doors opened. "Come on now, and walk with Mommie," Mother yelled, reaching for my brother's hand. I lingered behind them as usual, skipping and hopping on one foot. "Chena, don't you mess up them good shoes scuffing them on the ground," Mother warned as we reached the bus stop and sat on the bench.

I started counting the cars going by. "One, two, three, four, five, six, seven...." I didn't know my numbers past seven, so

I started right back at one, two, while my brother joined me, "three, four, five," until Mother stopped us.

"Come on now, here come the bus." We stood up and watched the bus stop right at our feet. My brother and I ran onto the bus, smiling at the bus driver, and climbed into seats located on the right side of the bus directly next to the bus driver.

Mother stood in front of the bus driver and whispered, "I don't have any money, can you please let me and my babies ride? We just trying to get home, and it's too cold to walk." The bus driver was a sweet-looking black lady; she had brown skin with dimples. Her hair was in pin curls, and she wore a crisp uniform of navy blue slacks and a white long-sleeve shirt under a navy blue V-neck sweater. There was a patch on her sleeve with the same initials and colors as on the outside of the bus and some gold and silver pins.

The bus driver lady looked past Mother, took a good look at us, and smiled and nodded her head. She closed the bus doors and began to drive off. I sat still, staring at the bus driver lady. She was different from the other bus drivers I had seen before. She kept glancing at us, smiling. She looked at me like my Grannie looked at me. She kept asking Mother questions about us.

"Dominick, 'top hitting me!" I said as I slapped my brother's leg. Dominick was standing in his seat facing the window; he looked down at me and kicked my arm. "Awwwww!" I cried out, holding my throbbing arm.

"Ooh no! Is Mommie's Boo-Boo okay?" Mother crooned, reaching over me to grab my brother and place him in her lap. I sat there quietly sobbing, looking down at the ground.

"Are you okay? Don't cry, honey, you gon' be okay." I looked up to see who was being nice to me. The bus driver lady was smiling at me, and she reached over to pass me a piece of peppermint. I jumped out of my seat and took the candy.

"Thank you!" I said, then I held up three fingers towards her face. "I'm th'ee, I'm th'ee," I yelled, jumping back in my seat and forgetting the pain in my arm. Slowly opening the wrapper, I looked up at my brother, whose mouth was salivating at the sight of my candy. I quickly popped the candy in my mouth, smiling at him, and started sucking on it before Mother could make me give it to him. Mother kept talking to the nice bus lady and right before we got off the bus, Mother gave her a piece of paper with numbers on it.

Jumping down the steps of the bus, I turned back and waved bye-bye to the nice bus lady, secretly wishing she could take me away on her bus and take me home with her. She waved back with a warm smile before closing the doors and driving off. Mother grabbed my arm, "Come on now, you walking too slow."

"Where we going?"

"To one of Mommie's special friends," Mother said, a blank expression on her face. Last time she dropped us off at her special friend Nick's house, and left us there for four days. Nick was nice to us, and he had special powers. He could hear real good. When me and my brother asked him how come he hear so good, he said 'cause he was blind. Nick would touch a special bumpy book and read it to us, he cooked food whenever we said we were hungry, and we played all different games like freeze tag and Marco Polo in the dark. Nick would always win though. Me and my brother didn't believe Nick was blind until he took off his sunglasses and showed us his all-white eyes. Nick was the first person we met with superpowers. I wished we could've stayed at Nick's, but he said that he couldn't take care of us, and was only watching us till our mom came back. But she was on her special medicine and never came back. The police came and picked us up and took us to the police station. Later they brought us to my Grannie's until mother came for us.

It seemed like we had been walking forever. It was so cold I couldn't feel my toes or my nose anymore. We weren't going to Nick's house 'cause we were in a fancy neighborhood full of big houses and trees and he lived in a small house on a block with no trees.

"Okay, we're here now. Y'all be on your best behavior, and Mommie will bring you guys back a present," Mother said in her warmest voice, giving us a last look-over. She smoothed down the frizzies in my hair and tucked Dominick's shirt into his shorts. As I walked up the steps, I got that scared feeling— my stomach got tight and my heart started racing right out my chest.

"I don't wanna go, please don't make me go, I want to go to Grannie's," I cried, stopping rigid on the third step like I'd turned into a cement pole. Mother ignored me, grabbed me by the arm, and dragged me up the remaining four stairs.

"Chena, fix your face or else," she snapped at me as she rang the doorbell.

The door opened and an old white man in his late fifties stood there, wearing big ole glasses that made his eyes look huge. He had a big toothy nervous smile on his face. He frantically ushered us inside, and I looked back at him while I walked past. After we were all in, he leaned his head outside the door and looked left, then right, as if to see if anyone else was outside. Then he quickly closed the door, wiped his hands down his chest, and turned around to face us, with that big fake smile still on his face.

He looked like one of those scary clowns with makeup on their faces. His huge smile looked like it was painted on, it was so creepy and unreal. "Hi little girl, what's your name?" he said, bending down so close to me that his face is almost touching mine. He smelled of an old stale odor with a hint of pee. With his face so close to mine, his big brown glasses, which made his eyes look like they were popping out of his head, now revealed a wandering eye. He wore tan slacks, a white button-down shirt with brown suspenders, and brown penny loafers. His breath smelled of alcohol and his yellow teeth had brown gunk in the gaps. He straightened his crooked glasses so his wandering eye could focus on me. It rolled up and down as he stared.

"She doesn't talk," he said to Mother in an irritated tone, keeping his eyes on me.

"'top trying to take my youth, bitch ass whore!" I screamed, running behind Mother's leg, but not before stomping on his foot. My Grannie would say those bad words to the drunk women sitting on her front step and she would run away, but it didn't work because Mr. Bob didn't move.

"Stop acting out, Chena! Mr. Bob is a nice man, and he's being nice to you," Mother snapped, pinching my arm and pulling me from behind her.

"Hi, my name is Dominick," my brother said, reaching out his hands to the stinky scary old man.

"Hi, Dominick. Aren't you a polite young man! You aren't going to hurt me like your sister did, or use bad words, will you?" The man bent down toward my brother, and his voice got all bouncy like a cartoon character on the TV.

"Nope," my brother said, grinning as the old man shook his little hand.

"Would you like some candy, Dominick?"

"Yes!" Dominick yelled, a big smile on his face.

"And would you like to play with some of my grandkids' toys?"

"Yes!" Dominick's eyes were big as oranges, gleaming with excitement.

"Well, come on in here, I have some new toys that my grandchildren left over here for you guys to play with and plenty of candy for you and your adorable sister to eat."

Mother pushed me forward to follow Dominick and Mr. Bob as they went into the living room. It was indeed full of toys, puzzles, and coloring books. My brother and I both ran towards our favorite game to play, Hungry Hungry Hippo. Mother stood there for a moment in the doorway, watching us with a blank expression on her face. She whispered some words to Mr. Bob. They both turned and looked at us playing, and then Mr. Bob reached inside of his front pocket, pulled out a handful of money, and handed it to Mother. Mother took the money and put it in her pocketbook, and then they both stared at us some more. Mr. Bob put on his big fake smile, while Mother stood there emotionless, her empty blank expression making her look half-dead. Dominick and me got so caught up with playing we didn't even hear Mother leave.

Mr. Bob joined us in playing Hungry Hungry Hippo. Then we all played racecars, choo-choo trains, Go Fish, checkers, and Candyland. But when we started coloring in some Thundercat coloring books, Mr. Bob opened up a big book and begin reading us a story about a princess locked up in a castle waiting for her prince.

Mr. Bob stayed with us, never taking his eyes off us, like we were something special that he had never seen. He would only leave us to go get us more candy and popcorn out of the kitchen.

"Are you guys thirsty?" Mr. Bob said, his big scary smile creeping onto his face again. When we nodded, he disappeared into the kitchen again, but this time he came back with two cups of hot chocolate, one blue and one green. He carefully set them on the coffee table where we were coloring. Both my and my brother's eyes lit up.

"Oooh, hot cha-coooolate!" I hollered as I jumped up to grab the blue cup, but Mr. Bob quickly tapped my hand away from the handle as I reached for it.

"No, no, Chena, this one is made special for your brother," he said, and then he slid the green cup towards me. "This one is made special for you." I pulled my arm back, pouting. I couldn't see a difference: both had marshmallows and whipped cream on top. Since Mr. Bob was so funny about it I didn't want it anymore. I left it on the table and went back to coloring. My brother gulped down the hot chocolate from the blue cup.

Shortly after my brother finished his cup of hot chocolate, he fell asleep right there on the table, with his brown crayon still in his hand. Mr. Bob got up from his rocking chair, picked my brother up and put him on the couch. He covered my brother with a light green blanket that had been lying on the left side of the couch. Then he took off my brother's shoes.

"When is Mommie coming back to get us?" I asked. I didn't want to spend the night at Mr. Bob's house. He had been nice, playing with us and giving us lots of things to eat, but I still didn't like the scary smile that he kept on his face like a mask.

"Oh, she should be back very soon, but let's let your brother sleep in peace, okay?" He grabbed my hand and pulled me out of the living room.

"Nooo, I don't want to leave Dominick, I want to stay with him and wait, okay, Mr. Bob?" I begged, trying to squeeze my hand from his tight grip.

"No, I can't have you waking him up!" Mr. Bob said in an authoritative voice. He continued to pull me, half dragging my stiff body all the way down the hall into his bedroom. There he let his grip go. "Go on now. Have a seat on the bed. We'll watch some television until your mother returns, okay? She should be back soon, don't worry," Mr. Bob said in a soft voice, closing the door.

I didn't move. "I want to go home now, I want Mommie," I said as tears came pouring out of my eyes. He picked my stiff body up and put me on the bed. Then he turned around to the TV, turned it on, and twisted the knob to turn the sound up real loud.

"Stop all that crying! You're going to wake your brother up!" He came and sat next to me on the bed. He removed his glasses, and picked up a round object from his nightstand and handed it to me. My curiosity interrupted my tears. Not recognizing this new toy, I began to play with it, pulling a strip of sticky plastic out from the roll and sticking it to my pants leg.

"What's this called?" I asked as I put another piece of clear plastic on my arm.

"It's called Scotch tape," Mr. Bob said. "Do you like it?"

"Yes!" I said, smiling now. I had gotten the tape stuck on my eyebrow.

"Would you like to have it?" Mr. Bob asked, moving closer to me. I froze as I saw Mr. Bob's big fake smile fade into a serious look.

Mr. Bob started looking at me like he was going to eat me. He looked me up and down, his left eye wandering around as the right one stayed fixed on me. "Uhmmmm," he muttered. Then he slid off the bed and stood in front of me. "If you want the tape all you have to do is be a good little girl and play a little game with me."

"I don't want to play no more, I don't want this stupid tape! I want Mommie!" I said, throwing the tape on the floor, folding my arms, and turning my head towards his closed bedroom door. I hoped Mother would walk in right then and take me away. But Mother didn't come; it was just me alone and nobody to save me.

"Well, Chena, Uncle Bob is going to teach you a new game," he said firmly, placing his left hand around my tear-streaked face and using his right hand to remove his suspenders. I slapped his hand off my face, but he quickly grabbed it again as he unzipped his pants. I closed my eyes real tight and I wished with all my might that Star Lady would come and save me. I wished so hard my head hurt, but I kept my eyes closed and kept wishing until I couldn't hear the sounds of the TV or the words coming out of Mr. Bob's mouth, or feel Mr. Bob's hard hands on the back of my neck. I couldn't see the light shining through my closed eyelids, I couldn't feel anything, and I fell into complete darkness, fading far far away from where Mr. Bob could hurt me.

CHAPTER 8
CHENA

Dear Diary,
A kiss from him to me causes
heavy breathing,
heart pounding
for what could be...
Mind-blowing sensual chemistry
Enjoyable warm, pleasant
memory...
illuminates warm flutters of
euphoria inside of me.
The thought prolonged excites
me.
Thinking about soft, moist, sweet
kisses...

CHENA, THE MAKING OF AN ORPHAN

Everything looked great. The food was almost ready and the house was spotless. We blocked the stairwell with caution tape to ensure that no one would go upstairs, Bee and I took all the valuables in the house upstairs to Becky's room, and we covered the furniture with plastic tarp and put black sheets on top. The theme colors for the party were A.T.C. colors—black and pink.

"Becky!" I yelled.

"Yeah?"

I jumped. She was right behind me. "Can you please help me lay the tarp down?" I continued.

"Yeah, we have to get it out of the garage!" she yelled back sarcastically.

Walking to the garage, Becky filled me in on the April incident and scolded me for sending the permission slips at the last minute.

"I'm sorry, girl! I didn't even plan on bringing the girls at first. It was Tanisha's idea—she added it at the last minute. But I'm glad everything worked out."

We poked around in the garage, looking for the tarp to cover the carpet. Becky found it in the darkest back corner, next to a big chest.

I looked over her shoulder. "What's that?"

"I don't know, but it's got my uncle's name on it," Becky mumbled as she bent over to examine the chest.

"It's probably just his stuff from high school," I said, sneezing from all the dust in the air. "Girl, it's hella spiders and dust back here, gross!" I got distracted, brushing a spider web out of my face, as Becky opened the top of the chest.

"Oh my God!" Becky screamed, falling back.

"What is it, are you okay?"

"No!" Becky frantically pulled videotape after videotape from the chest.

"Girl, what are you doing?"

"Chena, look!" Becky said, panic in her voice. Looking into the chest, I saw pictures of nude boys and girls who looked no older then ten or eleven. Looking at Becky's shocked face, I fell to my knees speechless. Becky started crying.

"I can't believe my uncle is a big fag-perve! It would have been okay if he was just gay, but why does he have to be a fucking pedophile?"

This discovery couldn't have come at a worse time. With only hours to spare before the party was supposed to start, she might want to cancel it, damn. We'd have people showing up before we knew it. Scrambling for words, I blurted out, "Girl, we don't know the story behind this shit. For now put it back and wipe your face, before someone comes in here." Wiping her face dutifully, Becky grabbed the tapes that she had pulled out and placed one under her arm before throwing the rest back into the chest. Glancing at the stacks of pictures in the in the chest again with an uncomfortable knot in my stomach, I looked at Becky. "You sure you want to bring that in the house?"

"Yes." After an awkward silent pause, she added, "I have to know what's on it." She sniffled with all her might, trying to hold back her tears.

"Y'all need help or something...what's taking so long?" Tanisha asked, coming up behind us and smiling.

"The damn tarp was hidden under all this dusty shit, but since you're here grab the other end so we can shake it off before we put it on my Grandmother's newly cleaned carpet," Becky said as if nothing had happened. As we unrolled the tarp we noticed that its outer edges were dirty. Becky quickly volunteered to run in and grab a towel to clean it off. I knew full well that in the back of her mind, she wanted a chance to hide that tape before it got into the wrong hands.

Running back into the garage with an old funky-looking beach towel, Becky yelled to us five feet from the entrance, "Here, we can use this old thing." After wiping the tarp, we laid it down in the large living room that was going to be our dance floor. Tanisha set up shop in the kitchen, and with the help of the mentees, Bee put the last colorful touches in the house. She had borrowed a disco ball from the drama department at school, and balancing on her tippy-toes on top of a stool, she put it up on the ceiling over the dance floor like she was putting icing on a cake. It was clearly the final touch. As we all stood back, smiling and admiring the disco ball, I couldn't help but imagine dancing under it wrapped in Brandon's large protective arms...

"Okay girls, let's go through the rundown before we get ready for the game. Nina, I need you to serve the food. Remember, each plate is three dollars and water and sodas are a dollar each. Tamika, I need you to stand by the stairs with April to take care of the coat check. Make sure you give each person a ticket, and tape the matching ticket to their coat and charge them a dollar. Kelly, I need you to work the door; it's five dollars per person, no exceptions. I'll have you and April switching off. Girls, I just want to say thank you so much for your help, and if a song comes on that you want to dance to or you just need a break, get one of us to break you, okay?"

"Did you guys invite some of your friends?" Tanisha asked.

Kelly busted out, "April..."

"April invited George!" Nina finished.

"Ooh, who's George?" Becky asked curiously.

Tamika jumped up. "He's a sophomore at Sal Valley High that she likes."

"What?" I said, surprise all over my face. "Well, we'll be watching out for George. Now I must warn you: boys are stupid, so if he starts acting funny at the party, don't take it personal. It's because he's a stupid boy that's embarrassed to say he likes you in front of his friends."

April's face lit up as she spoke. "Well one thing I learned from y'all is that action speaks louder then words, and if he acts a fool, then I'm cool off him, 'cause I deserve the best."

The girls high fived April, smiling fiercely. "You go girl, that's what I'm talking bout!" Tanisha said with a grin.

"Okay girls, there are three bathrooms in this house and there are eight of us, so let's be fair and hurry. We got exactly one hour to get ready for the football game," I snapped, looking down at my pager.

Becky quickly ran into her grandmother's room. I knew she wanted to watch the tape in private. After waiting a few minutes, I decided she might need some support, so I knocked on the door.

"Who is it?" she snapped.

"It's Chena, can I come in?"

"Yeah! Close the door and check this shit out." I slipped in the room fast. She looked like a bull as she glared at the TV screen. She said, "I hope he burns in hell, I hate him, I'm telling the police!"

Shocked at Becky's expression and words, speechlessly I turned my head and looked at the screen. It showed Becky's uncle. He was thirty-five, but in the video he looked a lot younger. He was performing oral sex on a little girl who looked about five years old. After a minute the tape became even more graphic, and we had to turn the damn thing off before we puked our guts out. Disgusted, we both shook our heads in disbelief.

An uncomfortable silence filled the room. I couldn't stop seeing the image of that poor defenseless little girl in my head. "What are you going to do, Becky?" I asked, choked up, trying to hold in suppressed tears of sympathy.

"I'm going to mail the tape to a police station with a note where to find the rest of the incriminating trash in the garage." She hit the eject button on the remote and grabbed the tape as it slid out of the VCR.

Pulling myself together, I headed towards the mirror where Becky was standing. "All right, girl. Hurry, get dressed, we have to go...and if you need anything, let me know."

"Chena?"

"Yeah, girl?"

"Promise that this will stay between us, as sisters. Please don't tell another living soul," Becky mumbled.

"Okay, I promise. You know you're my best friend and you can trust me," I said, embracing Becky.

"I know. Let's act like this didn't happen and get ready to have some fun," Becky replied in my ear, attempting to add pep to overshadow the sorrow in her voice.

Four hours later, we had a house full of people excited to celebrate Sal Valley's winning game, and it was as if the discovery in the garage had been just a bad dream. "Glad to see you could make it to the party!" Bee greeted P with a hug as he walked in with half of the football team behind him.

"Hey girl, you looking good! Turn around so I can check out the whole package!" P said, licking his lips.

Jake made a whistling noise as Bee turned around, and his entourage copied him. "Damn girl, you looking good!" He said with a huge smile.

"Thanks, I do what I can," Bee said brightly.

Kelly made a rude noise in the back of her throat, then extended her hand. "Okay boys, I need five dollars each before we can let you pass."

"Uh, come on, give us a break. We did win the game and all," Jake whined.

"Congrats by the way for a great game, but this party is a fundraiser for our club, and we need the money," April said cleverly with a smile.

"Come on y'all, stop holding up these pretty ladies...pay up!" P demanded in a firm voice. The boys reluctantly dug into their pockets.

"Thanks! Enjoy the party," Kelly said as she collected the money from the boys.

"Okay girls, great job. I'll be back in a little bit to break you," Bee said before she turned and disappeared into the party.

"Girl, this party is off the hook and it's only ten o'clock," I said, dancing next to Becky. Pushing through the crowd, I could see Tanisha running from the front of the house towards me with a huge smile showing her entire front row of teeth.

"Chena, Chena! Guess who's here?" Tanisha said excitedly.

"Who?" I asked as my heart began to pound, hoping I would hear Brandon's name come out of her mouth.

"Sheila and her crew!"

"Oh," I said, immediately disinterested.

"Can you believe she showed up?" Becky asked, rolling her eyes. Without speaking, I nodded my head, signaling the girls to follow me. As we walked through the crowd, all eyes were on us: we looked good and we knew it. Near the entrance, Sheila and her crew stood with unease.

"Hi Sheila, Shermika, Tonika, Pam. We're glad you could make it," I said with a phony smile.

"Yeah, we thought we'd check it out before we hit up Club Six tonight," Sheila said with obviously fake enthusiasm.

"Oh, is that why you guys are dressed like that?" Becky asked in a rude manner, pointedly looking their cheap tight low-cut dresses up and down.

"Yeah, Sheila wanted to come to this little kid party, not us," Tonika responded, staring at Becky like she was ready to fight.

I stepped in between them to breaking the tense moment and interrupt the staring contest between Becky and Tonika. "Hey, you girls hungry? We're selling plates in the kitchen and our food is way cheaper then the food at the club."

"Yeah, thanks, we'll check it out," Sheila said, ushering her crew towards the kitchen.

"Hey Becky, what's up with you and Tonika?" Tanisha asked, amusement in her voice.

"That bitch thinks I stole her man."

"Did you?"

"No...Del is mine, he never would have touched that bitch," Becky said defensively.

"Hey, doesn't Tonika go to Cal State Haystack?" I asked, elbowing Tanisha in the side.

"Yeah, so what?" Becky said angrily.

"Well, it looks to me that your man and that girl go to the same college. What a coincidence..."

"She's probably just mad 'cause he's talking to a high school girl and dissing her," Tanisha said, smiling.

"She's just mad cause she's a ugly ass dick-sucking hoe!" Becky screamed. Honestly, Becky and I both knew that Del was fucking Tonika, just like he fucked the last three girls that Becky fought with. When will this girl learn? I thought.

From the other side of the room, excitement brewed as heads started turning towards a confrontation. "Chena! Chena! Come quick!" Nina yelled.

Pushing past a group of girls shaking hard to Luke's "It's

Your Birthday" remix, I rushed over to Nina, Becky and Tanisha right behind me.

"What's wrong?" I screamed over the music, which was blasting especially loud in the kitchen. My ears ringing from the DJ's loudspeakers blaring in the dining room, I leaned forward with my hand cupping my right ear to hear Nina's response.

"That girl over there spit in the spaghetti!" Nina yelled back to me, pointing to Tonika. Shocked, we stood there with our mouths open.

"Becky, wait!" I screamed as she headed after Tonika. Walking briskly up behind Tonika, Becky reached out and tapped Tonika on her shoulder before she could make it out the front door.

"Bitch, you better keep your hands off me!" Tonika yelled, knocking Becky's hand off her shoulder.

Shoving myself between the two girls, who were ready to go at it gladiator style, I faced Tonika. "Why did you spit in our food?"

"I didn't spit in your food," she replied with an attitude.

I could see the crowd forming around us, ready to see a fight. "Okay, let's step outside and clear this up." I looked over my right shoulder and spotted Kelly. "Kelly, run and get Nina and tell her to come here. Then you cover her post."

"Got it," Kelly replied dutifully, before running off.

"Tonika, we were told that you spit in our food, and we don't appreciate that," I said, taking off my earrings, gearing up to whip this bitch's ass.

Sheila walked in front of Tonika before she could take a step forward. "Look Chena, she ordered a plate, not knowing it was going to cost three dollars, and when she took a bite, the little girl demanded the money, so she spit the food out onto her plate and—"

"She knew the plates cost three dollars before she ordered, 'cause she asked me!" Nina said, cutting Shelia off before she could finish her sentence. Looking down at Nina, who had run up still holding the spit-in plate in her hand, positioned to throw it on Tonika, I pulled her behind me. Even though I felt relieved that Tonika hadn't spit into the whole dish of spaghetti, the way I thought when Nina had first told me, there was no way this bitch was going to disrespect me at my own party. Maintaining eye contact with Tonika, I calmly reached into the cash box that April was holding, and with a chuckle said, "Well, Tonika, since your cheap ass can't afford a three-dollar plate, you probably need this too." Letting a five-dollar bill drop out of my hand onto the ground, I took an emphatic, deliberate step backwards without taking my eyes off of Tonika.

"Go ahead and pick it up, bitch, you know it's all you're worth anyway!" Becky yelled.

Before Tonika could reply, I grabbed Becky's arm and said firmly, "Come on, let's go back inside. They aren't worth our time." With my other hand I kept hold of Nina and dragged her along too. Sheila and her crew walked briskly towards her Geo Metro, leaving the money on the ground. After they drove away, April quickly picked up the money, put it in the cash box, and took her post collecting at the front door again.

"That was some show you girls put on." Turning around, I saw Brandon standing right behind me, leaning against the wall near the kitchen.

"You sure know how to sneak up on a girl. I hope you didn't sneak in the party without paying."

"Naw...little shortie at the door took care of me and my boys. Why're y'all arguing with those rats?" Brandon said with a smile.

"Oh...where your boys at?" I said, pretending to ignore his rat comment but really just trying to control my smile.

"Getting something to eat over there." Looking behind Brandon, I saw four tall brothers. They were looking good! They all looked like ball players, but they looked a little older than Brandon. My girls had spotted them too, and were already introducing themselves while they helped make the boys plates.

"Well, don't you look nice this evening," Brandon said, looking me up and down like he wanted to eat me.

"You don't look half bad yourself," I said, blushing. I knew damn well that Brandon looked edible, good enough to eat, finger-licking good! He was wearing black Ralph Lauren jeans, with a snug red-collared polo shirt that hugged his muscular chest just right.

"It's like that, huh? I got all dressed up for you, and it's like that," he said disappointedly, shaking his head.

Putting my hand around his warm muscular arm, I leaned close to his cheek, pretending to talk over the music, and whispered in a sexy voice, "You know you look good, with or without clothes." Surprised at my unexpectedly sex-driven comment, Brandon started blushing.

"Word," he said, looking me directly in the eyes.

"Brandon, you know outfits don't make people like us, it only enhances what's already there," I said smiling.

Shaking his head, Brandon grunted, "Uhm, uhm, uhm... well, I guess you don't have to wear anything at all, do you?"

Trying to change the subject, blushing even harder, I pulled on Brandon's arm. "Come on, let's dance," I said excitedly.

"Uh...I can't," he responded.

"Why not?" I asked in a sad playful tone. I hoped my face didn't show my true disappointment; had he really just turned me down?

"I don't want to mess my hair up," he responded with a smirk.

"Oh, I see. You too good to dance, it's all good, I'll catch you later," I said, trying to save face. As I turned to walk away, he grabbed my arm to stop me.

"Hey, you want to run with me to the store real quick? I don't know the area that well."

"Okay," I replied eagerly. As we walked to the front of house, I could feel Brandon's eyes on my ass, so I gave it a little switch, like I was on a fashion runway wearing lingerie. Stopping at the door, I informed April that I was going to the store with Brandon, to tell everyone I would be right back, and to page me in case of an emergency.

"This is your ride?" I asked surprised, as Brandon led me to a candy-apple red Dodge Ram four-door pickup with double exhaust sitting on twenty-two-inch rims.

"Yeah, my father just bought it from his co-worker for my eighteenth birthday."

Trying not to seem impressed, I said, "Oh, must be nice to have such a great dad."

"It's all right, sometimes." Brandon held the passenger side door open for me, and I eagerly walked forward to take his extended hand for help stepping up to the passenger seat of his big-ass monster truck. Watching Brandon walk around the truck, I couldn't help wonder what he looked like naked, and how big his manhood was. Jumping in, he asked me if I was cold. Trying to be cute, I had left my jacket in the house and I was trembling.

"Just a little," I replied, hugging my arms for warmth. Reaching behind me into the backseat, Brandon grabbed a black leather coat and told me I could borrow it. "Thanks," I said, appreciating the fact he cared.

"Okay long legs, where to?" Brandon asked, touching my thigh.

My body was doing something very strange...it was actually warming up and yearning for his touch. Alarmed at the sensations flowing through my body, I placed my hand on top of his and slowly removed it from my thigh, saying, "Turn right at the corner." I'd never had a guy do that before, and I wasn't sure I was ready to move that fast, even with Brandon.

"I'm sorry, did I offend you with my hand? Bad hand, bad hand!" he shouted, holding his hand out in front of him.

Smiling and laughing, I grabbed his hand. "No, it's all right. I think you hurt your hand's feelings—you better kiss and make up," I said, smiling at Brandon. Brandon looked at his hand and mine together, and before I could let go he lifted my hand up and kissed it. My heart raced with excitement, the butterflies from my stomach rushed to my brain, and I grinned from ear to ear. I looked out the window the entire ride to the store to keep myself from jumping all over Brandon. At the store he spent more time giving me long soulful looks and finding reasons to touch my arms or rub my shoulders than he did looking for the candy he was supposedly there to get. By the time we got back in the truck to head back to Becky's grandma's house, I was about ready to grab him and tongue him down.

"So Chena, what are you going to be when you grow up?" Brandon asked sarcastically, parking the car in front of Becky's grandmother's driveway.

"I don't know just yet, but I know I want to help people, and be a star. What about you?"

"I'm gonna play ball," he said confidently.

"Do you have a plan B if that doesn't work out?"

"I can't imagine doing anything else. You know, I didn't really think about it," Brandon replied, looking at me with puppy-dog eyes.

I had to break the intense eye contact, but I immediately asked, "Do you know what college you want to go to yet?" to try to conceal my shyness.

"I want to stay on the west coast, but honestly, I'll go to any school that offers me a full ride. What about you?"

"I only want to go to UC Berzerkley. I've always wanted to go there since I was a little girl," I replied with a smile.

"Yeah, with your grades, I bet you'll get in, too," Brandon said, a warm soft smile forming on his handsome face. Brandon gently removed his right hand from my thigh, where it had somehow found its way during the ride back, and began turning the dial on the radio to KISS FM.

"What, you tired of the booty shake music?" I asked as I reached over to turn the music up. "Ooh, 'Kissin' You' by Total! This is my song!" I started to sing loudly and off key. "Kissin' you is all that I been thinking of...Kissing you is good!" Turning to look at Brandon, I saw him looking at me with a grin, as if he was planning something in his head.

"What you looking at?" I said in a flirtatious matter.

"You are too cute, with your bad-singing goofy self," he said, flirting right back. Blushing from ear to ear, I quickly turned to look out the window. "Hey, you know you still owe me from messing up my kicks," Brandon said, smoothly putting his hand back on my left thigh.

"Really, what do you want from me? Huh? What can I do to rectify the situation?" I asked, laughing.

Turning the volume down on the music, Brandon leaned towards me, smelling like a million bucks, and said, "I'll take a kiss and call it even."

"So one kiss and you'll never bring this up again?" I hoped my slightly shaky voice didn't reveal how nervous I felt. Having Brandon so close to kissing me took my breath away, but I didn't want him to stop.

"Just one kiss is all it takes," he replied in a smooth, sexy voice.

Leaning over with delight, I prepared to not only grant Brandon's wish of a simple kiss, but also to make my own wish of finding my true love come true. I could feel the warmth of Brandon's skin as his face inched closer to mine, and I braced myself for the moment I've been dying for since I first laid eyes on him.

As my eyes closed, a loud knocking startled me, and I pulled back abruptly. Turning my gaze towards this distraction, I saw Nina banging on Brandon's window. "Chena, come quick, hurry!"

Angered by the interruption of my dream moment, I shot Nina a look of death, but the panic in her voice brought me back to reality. I quickly softened my gaze and threw Brandon's coat on the back seat of his truck as I jumped out, throwing him a quick look of apology as I hurried away.

"What is it?"

"P and Jake are having a dance-off with Brandon's friends." Before I could get upset at her for the false alarm, Nina grabbed my arm and pulled me, and we rushed into the house. One of Brandon's friends was breakdancing in the middle of the floor, which was unbelievable, given his massive height. Looking to my left, I could see Brandon making his way to the corner wall near the patio.

Bee, Becky, and Tanisha walked up to me. "Girl, what have you been doing for the last two hours?" Tanisha asked with a stern look on her face.

"Oh...girl, I took Brandon to the store," I said, trying to hide my smile.

"It does not take two and half hours to go to the store and come back. You better give us details later, right now we got to show these niggas whose house this is." Tanisha grabbed my arm and jumped out to the dance floor, pulling me with her.

"Okay, ladies!" I yelled to signal the crew to start our dance routine. We were shaking it hard, and we looked good. Everyone started clapping and cheering us on, so we had to break it down, and we dropped to the ground. Before our dance routine was finished, P, Jake, and Brandon's friends Ibrahima, Michael, and Shawn approached us, and immediately we all started dancing together.

P was breaking Becky off, until he was interrupted by Del, who rudely cut in to remind P who her man really was. Becky and Del exchanged words. Noticing the commotion, I stopped dancing with Jake. Just as I was about to walk over there, Del slapped Becky across her head. Before Del could step back, my killer protective instincts kicked in, and I fired on his ass like he was a piñata. I wasn't the only one. I scratched his face with one slap and Tanisha kicked him in the butt, making him lose his balance. I swiftly dug my four-inch heel deep into the flesh of his left hand, which he was using to try to hold his balance.

As Del turned to grab Tanisha, Bee kicked him right between his legs, making him fall flat on his ass. Holding on to his crotch, he rolled into a cradled position. That was a big mistake, 'cause our little mentees went wild, kicking, punching, and slapping him.

"Break it up, break it up!" Brandon and his friends yelled, pulling Nina, Tamika, Kelly, and April off of Del's beaten body. Brandon grabbed Del by the collar and pulled him to his feet. "Look man, I don't know you, but what I do know is if you try and hit another lady at this party and I find out, I personally will whip yo' ass. Now get the fuck out of here," Brandon yelled furiously. I couldn't help the smile forming on my face as I watched Brandon take charge. His protective instincts proved to me that he was indeed the man for me.

Del's face was fucked up. Stumbling to the door, he looked back, and we could see his swollen lip, blackened eyes, and the huge scratch on his left cheek that looked like it had been given by Freddy Kreuger himself. Walking over to the DJ, who had been completely oblivious to the fight, I took my finger and ran it across my throat in a slicing motion to let him know to kill the music.

"All right folks, it's been fun, and y'all don't have to go home, but you got to get the hell out of here," I said with a smile. Tanisha, Bee, and Becky went upstairs, while the mentees ran to the coat check. After making sure people were moving out the door, I ran up to check on Becky myself.

Coming down the stairs from helping Becky put herself together, I saw that everyone had left except for P, Jake, Brandon, Ibrahima, Michael, and Shawn, who were helping the girls clean up.

"Thank you guys for staying, we really appreciate your help," I said gratefully.

"It's all good! Do you think a brotha can get a free plate of food?" Jake asked.

"Of course...I'll make you a plate," Tanisha interjected, leading him into the kitchen.

Walking over to where Brandon was pulling up the tarp from the floor, I asked, "Can I help you with this?"

"Okay, grab the other end." Reaching for the corners of the tarp, we rolled it up and put it away in the garage.

As we walked back from the garage, Brandon stopped dead in his tracks and turned towards me. "Don't you owe me something?" he asked with a smirk.

Walking toward where he stood near the oak tree to the right of the house, I said in a sexy voice, "How do you want it?"

"I want it however you want to give it to me," Brandon replied, lust in his eyes.

"Do you want it nice and slow, or fast and juicy?" I asked seductively. Brandon couldn't take being teased anymore with these word games; he was turned on and yearning for a kiss. Reaching towards me, he pulled me towards him with his left arm, grabbing my lower back. I moved towards him like a magnet. He laid his lips on top of mine and kissed me softly, and then paused, looking into my eyes.

Brandon could tell I was on cloud nine. Without speaking, I moved closer into Brandon's protective arms, and laying my body close to his, I kissed him deep and hard. Our tongues intertwined neatly together like they were dancing. My hands slid up around Brandon's neck and his were around my waist. The longer we kissed, the tighter we grabbed each other, causing our bodies to rub together. I could feel something hard poking my midsection. Stepping back, startled, I looked down and saw Brandon's lower body straining against his jeans. Embarrassed, I started blushing.

"I think we better go back inside now," I whispered shyly. I turned around to walk away.

Brandon grabbed my right arm before I could leave. "Chena, my body isn't the only thing that's interested in you. I just wanted you to know that, okay?"

"Okay," I replied softly. I thought to myself, Just maybe this man can be the one, who can give me the love I've been searching for all my life.

As we entered the house together, everyone turned and looked at me and Brandon with a huge I-know-what-you-did smile. "Did you guys find the garage okay?" Bee asked, eyeing us with suspicion.

Grinning from ear to ear, Brandon cleared his throat. "Actually, we got a little lost." Everyone laughed and continued cleaning the house. It seemed like the living room and dining room were spotless within minutes; the only trace of the party was the massive disco ball hanging over the living room floor. Brandon's friend Ibrahima was about 6'7", so he gladly volunteered to untie the ball from the ceiling.

While he did that, the mentees went upstairs and came back down with their PJs on. "Hey, lets play a game,"

Tamika said excitedly. Before I could respond, the doorbell rang.

Turning towards the door, Bee asked, "Who is it?" with authority in her voice.

"It's George." Bee opened the door, and George and three of his friends stood on the step waiting to be invited in. April jumped up and walked towards the door.

"What's up? Don't think 'cause y'all coming after the party that we ain't gon' charge you to get in," she said, her hands on her hips.

"Come on April, cut us a break," George said, a puppy-dog look beaming through his hazel Lebanese eyes, but April was not buying it.

"This party is for our fundraiser, and every dollar counts. So come on and pay up," April demanded, extending her hand for payment. George and his three friends each handed April five dollars before entering the house.

"Where's the party at?" George asked.

"It's right here on this Twister board," P replied. While they all started to play Twister, I went upstairs to check on Becky.

Knock, knock. I tapped on her bedroom door.

"Who is it?"

"It's me," I answered.

"Come in." Becky lay over her bed, crying.

"Hey girl, we about to play Twister...and, uh...Ibrahima wants you to be his partner."

"Really?" Becky responded, lifting her head and brightening.

"Yeah girl, and you know we can't play without you."

Looking down at the pillow, Becky put her head down again and said, defeat in her voice, "Tonight isn't my night, this week isn't my week...I just want to die, I mean it."

"Don't say that, girl. You have too many people that will miss you." Realizing that I was just feeding into her depressive mood, I decided to break the good news about the car. "Girl, stop feeling sorry for yourself. Everything is going to work out 'cause—"

Rudely cutting me off, Becky screamed at me, "You don't know shit! My mom's going to kill me, my relationship is over, and my favorite uncle is a pedophile!"

"No, you don't know shit!" I fired back. "First off, we already took care of your mom's car. Your grandmother agreed to file a claim through her insurance company, and from the money we made from the party we'll pay the deductible. You have a fine-ass good-looking man downstairs waiting to take that loser Del's place, and you can't blame yourself for your uncle, so get your ass up, wash your face and bring your ass downstairs." I stood up, annoyed, and stalked out before slamming her room door behind me.

Everyone downstairs was playing some kind of game. Bee and Tanisha were playing Twister with P, Jake, and Brandon, while Brandon's friends kept score. Our mentees were in the dining room with George and his friends, playing Truth or Dare. Everyone was having a great time. Walking into the kitchen to make some popcorn, I noticed the food was still sitting out, so I began to put it away.

"Can I help you with that?" I turned around to see Brandon with a tray of spaghetti in his hands.

"Yeah, thanks." We put all the leftover food in the fridge and took the trash out. Walking to the back of the house, I lifted the lid of the trash so that Brandon could put the food that we couldn't save in it. Brandon seemed uneasy, like he was worried he would scare me off. I couldn't stop thinking about our kiss, and I wondered if he was too.

Finally, after a long pause, Brandon blurted out, "How would you like to catch a movie tomorrow?"

"I'd love to, but I can't," I said sadly.

"Why not?"

"I know my mom won't let me go, 'cause she'll say I was gone all weekend, and I'll need to stay in and get ready for school."

"Oh. Well, can I get your number so I can call you, at least? Unless you're not interested."

Dropping the lid to the trash, I walked closer to him. "No, I'm definitely interested."

Smiling, he said, "I know I shouldn't ask, but it's your fault for being so fine...can I please have another kiss?" Immediately, I placed my arms around his neck and kissed him without bothering to tell him yes.

After we kissed for about ten minutes, Brandon stood back smiling, grabbed my hand, and led me over to the bench near the patio door. Brandon sat down and pulled me onto his lap, hugging me like I was a teddy bear. "Chena, I've had a crush on you ever since the first time I saw you."

"Why didn't you say something?"

"I didn't know what to say, and I didn't think you were feeling me...you never looked at me, let alone spoke to me."

"Well, I have a confession to make...I was so attracted to you when I first saw you that I couldn't speak."

"Really?" Brandon said, surprised.

"I didn't think you were interested in me until I stepped on your foot."

"I knew you did that shit on purpose!"

"Actually, it was an accident, but I'm glad I got your attention."

"I'm glad you did too."

Leaning out the patio door, Kelly yelled, "Hey Chena, it's you and Brandon's turn to play!"

"We'll be in a second, thanks!" I replied, eager to get rid of her and continue the conversation with Brandon.

"Chena, before we go back inside, I just want you to promise me one thing."

"What?"

"Promise me that you'll stay out of fights. You're too pretty to be fighting."

"Brandon, there is a lot you don't know about me. I've been fighting all my life, and I can take you out too if I have to," I said, punching my right fist down into my open palm as I imitated Mr. T's mean face. Laughing, we both got up and headed into the house, where we spent the rest of the evening playing games and having fun.

The after-party quickly turned into a sleepover, as people fell asleep watching Waiting To Exhale, starring Whitney Houston and Angela Bassett. I woke up with a stiff neck at about six o'clock to use the restroom, and found myself lying on the couch in Brandon's lap. He was sleeping sitting up. I tapped him on the shoulder to wake him up.

"Brandon, Brandon," I whispered in his ears.

"What's wrong?" he asked, startled as he jerked awake.

"Nothing! I'm going upstairs to stretch out. You want to come or stay down here?" He nodded and followed me up the stairs.

I opened Becky's door, but Becky was asleep in the bed with Ibrahima already. Judging from the looks of their clothes on the floor, they had gotten a little busy before they went to sleep. Quickly closing the door, I headed to her grandmother's guest room and found the bed empty. I jumped in the bed fully clothed, and Brandon followed. We pulled up the covers and drifted back to sleep. Wow, what a wonderful but crazy night, I thought. I can't believe I'm actually sleeping with Brandon in the same bed. Touching his chest for a reality check, I couldn't help but wonder if this warm, tingling feeling was a feeling I was supposed to feel with my real mother as a child. Tears formed under my eyelids, and I quickly shut my eyes to focus on my happiness in this moment and banish the past, drifting off into dreamland with a smile of contentment on my face.

CHAPTER 9
CHENA

Dear Diary,
The memory I have of him
I will hold as gold,
never spoken, yet never untold,
The unspeakable truth of
what...
one night
one intense, passionate,
romantic lovemaking night
can hold...

CHENA, THE MAKING OF AN ORPHAN

Three minutes of class left. Come on, ring, I silently pleaded with the bell. As it rang, I leapt out of my seat. Yes! Running out of the class, bumping into kids as they filled the halls like ants in a maze, I found my way to my locker.

"Hey Chena, what's up?"

"Hey Becky, what's going on?"

"Me and the girls are about to hit up the mall to shop for our outfits for the Black Saturday party, you coming?"

"Naw, I can't, sorry."

"Let me guess, you have a fucking date with Brandon again," Becky said bitterly.

"Yeah, it is Valentine's Day weekend. I'll catch y'all next weekend."

"You and Brandon been locked up at the hip for four months now. His dick must be good," Becky replied. I looked at her, confused. If I didn't know any better I would have said Becky was jealous, but why? She and Ibrahima seemed to be hitting it off.

"Look, Becky, I don't know what your problem is, but you really need to chill out. And I don't know what he's packing, 'cause we don't get down like that, and you know that," I said, slamming my locker shut and walking away.

"Chena, I'm sorry! It's just that I miss you, okay?" Becky yelled as I continued to walk away, ignoring her. She's obviously just jealous cause my boyfriend loves me. I haven't changed. I still hang out with my friends, make time to hang with my mentee's, participate in every school activity, go to work, train hard for track meets, and study hard. Nothing could ruin my day, 'cause me and Brandon had a date. And nothing was going to get in the way of my love for Brandon. I didn't know where we were going, or what we were doing—it was a surprise that I was counting down to.

I headed out to the front of the school to wait for Brandon, wearing a red cotton miniskirt and a baby white I-top tee. I had just flat-ironed my long jet black-hair the night before, and it bounced freely in the wind. My cute silver platform Skechers tennis shoes made me tower to at least 5'11". Reaching into my silver purse, I grabbed my bubblegum lip gloss and applied it over my lipstick. Honk, honk! Turning towards the noise, I saw that Brandon had pulled up behind me. Picking my backpack up off of the ground, I ran to his truck.

"Hey, baby, you looking good today," Brandon said, opening my door and grabbing my backpack out of my hand.

"I do what I can," I replied with a smile and a wink. "Where we going?" I asked him anxiously.

"It's a surprise, just sit back and enjoy the ride."

"Okay," I said dutifully.

"You hungry?"

"Yeah, I'm starving," I said, turning the radio station to KISS FM.

"Good, cause I'm starving, too. But you know what I have a feenin' for?"

"What?"

"A Chena kiss!" Brandon replied in a low sexy voice. With butterflies rushing to my heart, I jumped over and placed a fat kiss on his cheek, leaving a lip print on his face. "I wasn't talking about that kind of kiss, but it's cool. I'll steal one later."

*****

Brandon knew Chena was a virgin, but he thought he could change that, with his mack daddy skills. He liked Chena a lot, and he didn't want to cheat on her, but his body had needs too.

Every time he tried to go past third base with her he would strike out. Tonight, he wasn't striking out.

*****

"Why are we stopping at the Marriott Hotel?" I asked curiously as we pulled up to the big glass doors at the front entrance.

"We have to check into our room before we can start celebrating Valentine's Day." Brandon is too good to be true. I think I'm in love! Is this happily ever after? Thoughts of me walking down the aisle played through my mind.

"Chena, you did tell Dena that you were spending the night at your girls', right?"

"Yeah, I'm clear," I answered, looking out the window, impatient for our date to start. Jumping out the car, we valeted and walked in.

"Okay, sweetie—I need you to cover your eyes with this bandanna before we head upstairs."

"Come on...do I really have to?" I asked in a teasing baby voice.

"Yes. You're going to ruin the surprise," he replied in a firm tone. Tying the bandanna on, he led me like a blind woman up the elevator and down a long hallway. Opening the door, Brandon gently walked me into the room. I could hear the door close behind us. Rushing to snatch the bandanna off, Brandon interrupted me by clearing his throat. "Hey, no peeking just yet." I heard Brandon's footsteps stop right behind me, and then grabbing my waist, he pulled me towards him, hugged me from behind, and kissed my neck as he untied the bandanna.

"Um, baby, you smell so good you're driving me crazy." Turning around to face Brandon, I hugged him and kissed him hard. I wanted us to make out before we went to dinner. "I've been thinking about kissing you all day," I said teasingly.

"Word," Brandon replied as he spun me around. "Baby, check it out, you like it?"

"Wow...I love it!" Brandon had had balloons set up in each corner of the room, rose petals scattered on the floor leading to the bathroom, and best of all, Hershey's Kisses lined up in the shapes of hearts on the nightstand, desk, and bed. I'm not the typical girl; I usually hated flowers, balloons, and stuffed animals...but I loved what Brandon put into this room. Hugging him with all my might, I smiled and said, "I am so glad I stepped on your shoe."

"Baby, I would have eventually built up the courage to talk to you, even if you didn't," Brandon replied, hugging me back. "If you want, we can order room service and eat in," he suggested optimistically.

I loved the room, but not enough to miss out on going on our date. "Naw, baby I want to go out," I said, reaching for my purse.

"Okay," Brandon replied.

First Brandon took me to a movie. Afterwards, we went to a fancy restaurant on the pier called Kinskates. I had only been to Kinskates with Dena once. She took me there to teach me some proper etiquette for dining. She taught me to always place my napkin on my lap, to drink out of a straw, which forks to use, and most importantly, to always order something off the menu I would enjoy eating. I'll never forget her last piece of advice as we were leaving: "If you play your cards right, you'll be dining at places like this all the time." I guess I'm playing my cards right after all...

"I'll have a cheeseburger, well done, and a house salad with vinaigrette, please," I told our waitress.

"I'll have the same," Brandon added as he handed the wait-ress our menus. After she left, he leaned forward to stare into my eyes. "Chena."

"Yes," I replied with a sexy smile.

"How do you feel about me?" Brandon asked, his face serious.

Reaching across the table to grab his hand, I replied, "I really, really like you." I blushed from ear to ear and broke eye contact with Brandon.

"Well, I love you," Brandon said with a disappointed look.

Before I could respond, I was rudely interrupted by an annoying voice echoing from across the room. "Brandon, Brandon is that you?" Looking to my left, I saw a tall slim light-skinned attractive woman headed towards our table with a sly grin on her face. She looked about eighteen or nineteen, and I couldn't help but notice her huge breasts spilling out of her extra-small blouse. As she walked closer and approached the table, I could see that she may have had the body of a full-blown goddess, but her face was defi-nitely from Hell.

"Who is that?" I asked Brandon, jealousy in my voice. Before he could respond, she had already reached our table and was sizing me up. Studying Brandon's face, I could see he looked very uncomfortable.

"Hi Carmen," he blurted out.

"Oh, it's like that. Hi, I'm Carmen, Brandon's ex-girl-friend," she said, extending her hand to me. Cutting my eyes at her, I ignored her outstretched hand with its long red acrylic nails that were in desperate need of a fill. Turning my head slightly towards her, I pressed my lips together and shot her a phony smile. I glanced at Brandon, locking eyes with his as he squeezed my hand in attempt to assure me of his loyalty.

I replied, "Hi, I'm Chena, his new girlfriend, and if you don't mind we would like to continue with our romantic dinner; after all, it is Valentine's Day."

Carmen stood speechless, sucking her teeth and rolling her eyes. "Well, I must say, Brandon, you picked a rude one. Anyhow, call me sometime, okay? Bye," she said, winking at Brandon.

I know I shouldn't have, but I couldn't help it—this bitch was not about to disrespect me, right in my own face. It just came out. Before she could finish her wink, I snapped, "Look, bitch, can you stop looking desperate? Just pick your hoe act up and leave!" I rolled my eyes and threw my right hand towards the door as if I was sweeping away trash in the air. Gasps of shock stirred around the restaurant as couples' heads whipped around in our direction, shocked by my statement. I looked past the faces of judgment and disgust, not giving a damn what people thought or who was in the room. No one disrespected me, and defiantly not some stupid hoe trying to steal my one and only true love.

The waitress stopped dead in her tracks, listening in on the confrontation. She looked as if she wanted to speak, but the words wouldn't come out. Brandon looked at her with pure embarrassment, then cut his eyes to Carmen. "I think it's best that you leave, Carmen," Brandon confirmed with a firm, authoritative voice.

Embarrassed by the stares of the spectators, looking like she wanted to cry, Carmen mumbled, "You will call, you always do when you want some of this sunshine." She frantically made her way towards the exit and slipped out.

I looked around at the onlookers; irritation built up in me from all of the stares and whispers. I stood up. "Go on and finish your dinner! What the fuck are you looking at? Mind your damn business!" I said. Brandon grabbed my arm, forcing me to sit back down. I looked at him like I was the barrel of a gun and he was a target, ignoring the pain he was causing my arm with his tight grip. "Wow, so that's your ex, huh?" I asked, rolling my eyes and snatching my arm from his controlling grasp.

"We fucked, but she was never my girlfriend," Brandon replied nonchalantly.

"Well, if fucking makes you act like that, I don't want no part of sex. I'll be back."

"Where you going?" Brandon asked with panic in his voice as I stood up again.

"To the restroom," I snapped back, trying to mask the tears building up.

*****

Brandon really liked Chena, but Carmen's invitation sounded very tempting. The words "I don't want no part of sex" played over and over in Brandon's head as he waited for Chena to return. He caught a glimpse of Chena walking back from the bathroom. She looked good with her pretty long black hair, tight abs, sexy long legs, and best of all, her beautiful face. Chena was smart, goal-driven, and down to earth—she was everything he could want in a woman. Her innocence was not only a challenge, but also a turn-on. Chena was not easy, and didn't come a dime a dozen, but Brandon couldn't help but think about how much he wanted to be inside of her. Maybe I can get some on the side, and still be with Chena, he thought.

*****

"Hey baby, your food just came," Brandon spoke to me in a soft soothing voice.

I looked blankly at the food in front of me. "I lost my appetite." I looked up at Brandon, who was tearing his food to pieces. "I'm not hungry anymore, I'll just take it to go."

"What? But you said you were starving," Brandon replied, his mouth full of food.

"Sorry, but that bitch, the one you 'fucked,' made me lose my appetite."

"Chena, don't act like that. I'm with you and not her, so stop tripping," he said, reaching for my hand. I quickly pulled it away. "Chena, Chena! Look at me," Brandon demanded. Looking up, I shed a tear, and attempted to whip my face away, but Brandon had already rushed to my side of the table, kissing my cheek and hugging me before I could grab my napkin.

"Why you crying, baby?"

"I know that you want something I can't give you," I mumbled as I buried my head in his chest.

"Chena, I love you. Listen to me, I know we haven't been together that long, but I've never felt this way about a girl before, and I'll just wait till you're ready, okay?"

That was all I needed to hear. I quickly turned the water-works off, attempting to hide my smile. I looked up at Brandon. "You promise?"

"I promise." I knew that would work, men love to feel needed, I swear I'm going to be an actress someday. "Okay, eat up so we can go...I have a surprise for you at the hotel," Brandon said with a warm smile.

Entering the room back at the hotel, I could smell the fresh roses in the room and for a moment I felt like I was in a botanical garden. "Baby, close your eyes, so I can give you your surprise," Brandon said.

"Okay," I replied as I shut my eyes tight.

"Open them," Brandon said as he laid a beautifully wrapped gift on the bed.

"Can I open it?" I said childishly.

"Yes." Opening the box, I pulled out bottles of Victoria's Secret kiwi melon bubble bath, lotion, and body spray. Under the toiletries lay a beautiful red silk nightgown. "You like it?" Brandon asked, stroking my arm.

"I love it, thank you!" I said, reaching for my backpack. "I have something for you, too." I handed him a bottle of Pleasures for Men cologne by Estee Lauder.

He sprayed it into the air and sniffed. "Baby, I love it, thank you," he said as he walked towards the bathroom.

"Where you going?" I asked curiously.

"To run your bathwater," he yelled from inside of the bathroom. What? He wants me to take a bath, with him, oh no...I don't want him to see me naked yet, I'm not ready for that...

As my heart began to pound with anxiety, I yelled, "I took a bath this morning."

Walking out of the bathroom, Brandon grabbed the bubble bath off the bed. "But you didn't take a bath with this bubble bath. Don't worry, I won't peek," he replied with a smile. That was a relief to hear. I decided I could take another bath.

*****

While Chena was in the bathroom, Brandon laid back against the headboard of the bed with an erection, thinking about his promise. He knew that he couldn't keep it. He felt bad, but he didn't know what else he could have done—she was crying. I should break up with her, tell her I need to focus on playing ball and she's too much of a distraction, but I really like her. Damn, what should I do? he mused. Before he could finish his thought, Chena stepped out the bathroom in the new nightgown that hugged her body just right. She looked beautiful.

*****

Running out of the bathroom, I jumped on Brandon's lap. "What you watching on TV?"

"Nothing now that I've got you," Brandon said, kissing me deeply all over my neck and slowly laying me back on the bed. "I better put on my PJs too," he said as he stood up and took off his white T-shirt, exposing his rock-solid abs. He slowly unbuttoned his baggy pants, which fell to the floor, and jumped on me and started sniffing me from head to toe. "Girl, you smell so good, you don't know what you do to me," Brandon said, cuddling and holding me. "Can I give you a massage?" he asked as he reached over me to dim the lights.

"No baby, you've done enough. Let me give you a massage," I said seductively. Jumping on top of Brandon, I reached for the bottle of lotion on the nightstand and squeezed it firmly, causing it to pour into my hand. Rubbing my hands together, I commanded him, "Turn over." Rubbing Brandon's back was like a dream come true. I couldn't believe this was real, I almost expected my alarm to go off and pull me from this fantasy. I continued to rub his strong muscular shoulders, neck, and back, watching his face contort with pleasure into the pillow.

"Uhm, baby, that feels so good," Brandon moaned, before flipping over and tackling me. Pinning me to the bed, he laid his body on top of mine and kissed me deeply. The kiss was magical...I started to see stars. Slowly positioning himself between my legs, he laid his massive body on top of my tiny frame, carefully positioning his weight in an attempt to not smash me, and began to kiss my neck and collarbone.

Lying there, paralyzed with pleasure, I didn't know what came over me, but I started to moan. While I dug my nails into his back, Brandon kissed and sucked on my neck harder and harder. "Baby, you feel so good," I whispered in his left ear. He pushed his pelvis between my legs in an upward thrust, and I could feel his erection forming, making my panties moist. As he pushed his pelvis up and down harder and harder, I got extremely wet. Yearning to feel what was making me feel so good, I didn't fight Brandon as he carefully took my right hand off of his shoulder and guided it down toward his hard firm dick.

I had never touched a dick before, and I didn't know what to do; it was so big, long, and firm. Brandon held my hand and guided it up and down around the head of his dick all the way to the base. As I caught onto the motion, Brandon brought his left hand toward my stomach, and began rubbing it, lifting my nightgown above my thighs to expose my skin. He sucked and kissed my flesh until he reached my nipples.

"Auh...baby, not so hard," Brandon whispered in my ear.

"Sorry," I replied, embarrassed. I removed my hand from his rock hard dick.

"Baby, no, no, please don't stop, that felt so good," Brandon said, sucking my neck. Reaching again for his dick, I could see it was now producing a fluid from the tip. I begin to caress his dick like it was a delicate flower, spreading the moisture from the head to the base. Watching Brandon's reaction, I noticed he liked it when I rubbed up and down really fast, while playing with the head after each stroke. The more he moaned, the faster my strokes became. We were starting to become hot and sticky. Breathing heavily, I exhaled. My body was hot, tingling, and extremely horny. The faster I stroked, the harder he kissed and sucked my neck. The moment was really intense.

No man has ever made me feel this way, I thought. I wanted Brandon, and I wanted him bad. Seeing the pleasure on Brandon's face turned me on, and I continued to stroke faster and faster, until Brandon let out a loud moan and went stiff. Feeling the sticky fluid rush into my hand like water shooting out of a hose, I realized that Brandon had just climaxed. This was the big deal, the thing that guys wanted to do inside of a girl, that could make a baby, cause a girl to lose her mind... this was that special moment, sticking to my hand and dripping onto my thigh.

"Baby, you okay?" Brandon asked, nearly out of breath, bringing me out of my thoughts back into the moment with him.

"Yeah, but I got something of yours on my hand," I responded playfully.

"Let me get you a towel," Brandon replied, sliding off the bed. As Brandon walked into the bathroom, I laid there contemplating what had just taken place, replaying it quickly over and over in my mind. Smiling and blushing, I looked at my hand, which had thick white slimy sticky fluid wrapped around it. Noticing the faint unfamiliar smell coming from the fluid, I yelled, "Quick...it's dripping on the bed."

"Here," Brandon replied with a smile, handing me a towel. Wiping off, I got up to wash my hands.

When I returned to the bed, Brandon was waiting underneath the covers. Jumping in the bed, I snuggled next to him, and he gladly extended his arm and pulled me closer to his body. "Baby, did I make you feel good?" he asked curiously.

"Yes, I felt good, making you feel good," I responded shyly.

"Well, I want you to feel as good as I did," Brandon said, a devilish look in his eye.

"Baby, I felt great, trust me, I had fun," I replied and kissed his lips. "I want to do it again."

"Well, I know something I can do for you that will make you feel real good, and we don't have to have sex. Can I do it?" He asked brightly.

"What?" I asked suspiciously. Before I could say another word, Brandon disappeared under the covers. "Baby, what you doing?" I asked, in between giggles.

I could feel Brandon positioning himself on top of me, but only on the lower half of my body. Spreading my legs apart,

Brandon began kissing the inside of my thighs, licking them in a tickling motion. Slowly he made his way up to my panties and nibbled on them with his teeth, while he slowly pulled them off. All I could do was lay there, paralyzed with anticipation and curiosity. "Oh...oh...my!" I moaned as Brandon licked, sucked, and kissed my clitoris. Juices were flowing, and I couldn't control myself. Reaching under the covers I grabbed Brandon's head, which was occupied between my legs, and rubbed it fervently.

Overwhelmed, I attempted to pull upwards, away from the pleasurable stimulation caused by Brandon's tongue, but Brandon's right arm pulled me firmly down, pinning my pelvis into the missionary position. "Oh! Oh! OH!" I screamed, covering my mouth. I couldn't believe how good this felt...I couldn't believe it as my body shot an electrifying bolt of ecstasy down my spine, causing me to tense up. After I climaxed over and over and over again, I just lay there motionless, exhausted from the pleasurable roller coaster ride that Brandon had taken me on.

Peeking up from underneath the covers, covered in sweat, Brandon asked, "Did I make you feel real good?" Waiting for my response, he laid his head on my chest and held me tight.

My heart was beating fast, and I was still delirious and in shock from the pleasure I had just received. Rubbing my legs together I softly whispered, "Yes, thank you," and rubbed his wavy hair until I fell asleep.

Walking up the stairs home the next day, I couldn't help but think about my night with Brandon and what we did. As butterflies rushed to my head from my heart, I had an epiphany: "Oh my; I think I love him. I love Brandon, I love Brandon...Yeah, that's right I do!" Whistling with glee as I stuck my key into the door, I was greeted with a familiar unwelcoming stare-down from Dena. By the look on Dena's face, I knew immediately I was in trouble.

"Hey," I mumbled while closing the door behind me, trying to play it cool. Dena looked down at me sharply and suspiciously.

"Hey, did you have fun at Tanisha's house?"

"No, we got into it at school, so I didn't go." I replied, already catching onto where this was going.

"Really? How come you didn't come home after school then?" Dena asked, with her hands on her hips.

"I didn't want to have to sit in the house just 'cause Tanisha was tripping, so I hung out with Brandon, and then had him drop me off at Bee's house."

"Why didn't you call me when I paged you?"

"My battery went dead, see?" I said, handing my pager to her. Snatching the pager from me, Dena looked at the case and threw it on the counter.

"You ain't grown yet, and as long as you live in my house, you need to tell me where you're going at all times!" Dena yelled, pointing her finger in my face.

I sucked my teeth and rolled my eyes. "I'm sorry, but I thought if I called you, you would say no, 'cause I should have told you earlier, and you would have just accused me of planning this ahead of time like you always do when I change plans," I yelled in frustration.

"Chena, that doesn't matter! Don't you know I'm responsible for you? If something happens to you, I could go to jail! You belong to the state, not to me. Do you know how worried I was when I called over to Tanisha's house looking for you and you weren't there? I called the police, and they said I had to wait forty-eight hours before they would do anything. I was so mad at that little friend of yours, Tanisha. First she said you were at Bee's and then she pretended to lose Bee's number when I asked for it. Matter of fact, give me Bee's number right now," Dena demanded, picking up the phone and preparing to dial. Oh shit, I'm 'bout to get caught up...fuck...oh well, it was worth it.

"558-9132," I replied with an attitude. Dena turned her back on me as she waited for someone to answer.

"Hello, Bee, may I speak with your mother, please? Oh really, huh... uh-huh, okay. I'll let her know...thanks...you too. Bye-bye." Hanging up the phone, Dena turned around and stared at my guilt-ridden face. "You're grounded for two weeks, for not calling and telling me you were going to Bee's." I could tell by the way Dena was still glaring at me that she didn't really believe me, but she couldn't prove I was lying, either. I sucked my teeth and ran to my room, trying to conceal the smile that grew bigger the closer I got to my room door. What had Bee told told Dena? I turned the handle to my door. "I can handle two weeks, no sweat," I muttered as I shut the door behind me.

"I'm going to the gym, I'll be back. Remember, no phone! You're grounded," Dena yelled as she headed out the front door. Running to the front window, I watched for Dana's SUV to drive out onto the street from the underground parking lot. Once her black Explorer turned at the stop sign, I quickly jumped on the phone to call Bee.

"Hello?"

"Hey, Bee! What did you tell Dena?"

"I told her my mom was still out of town, and would be back this evening. I also told her to tell you that you forgot your makeup mirror at my house."

"Oh my God, girl, that was close! How did you know to cover?" I said with relief.

"Tanisha called me right after she got off the phone with Dena yesterday. We figured you were still with Brandon. By the way, what did y'all do all night?"

"Girl, words can't describe it! We had lots, and I mean lots, of fun." I heard a beep in my ear. "Hold on girl, I got another call." I clicked over. "Hello?"

"You better not be on the phone!" It was Dena's voice.

"I'm not!" I snapped with an I'm-right-and-you're-wrong teenage attitude.

"Good. Make sure you take the turkey meat out the fridge, 'cause you're cooking tonight," Dena snapped back.

"Okay, anything else?" I hissed in defeat.

"Yeah, make a salad too, and have it ready by seven," Deana said, irritation in her voice, before hanging up in my face.

Clicking the talk button, I switched back over. "Hey Bee, I got to go, Dena—"

Interrupting me midsentence, Bee asked, "Did y'all do it?"

"Naw girl, but I'll fill you in at school on Monday. Thanks again, I owe you big time. Bye!" I said with a big fat smile as I hung up the phone and lay out on the floor, closing my eyes and visualizing my time with Brandon.

Remembering the meat, I snapped out of my daydream and ran to the kitchen to grab the frozen meat out of the freezer. Carefully placing the package of meat in a bowl in of the sink, I turned the knob on the faucet all the way to hot and stood watching the bowl fill with hot water. After the bowl filled completely with water, I ran back to my room with a stomach full of butterflies and joy, reminiscing about my romantic night with Brandon.

CHAPTER 10
LIL CHENA

Dear Diary,
The rain begins to manifest
the formation
of realization
causing streams
of pain
to seep down
leaving a murky
trail of discovery
The levees break
and the water pours
flooding the heart...
I'm not going make it!

CHENA, THE MAKING OF AN ORPHAN

"Y'all get on outside—Miss Lucy is waiting!" Mother screamed to us from the front door.

"Yaaay! We on to the zoooo!" I hollered, running out of the bedroom towards the front door like a cheetah, wearing my blue and white Care Bear T-shirt and my denim blue jeans with Ms. Pac-Man on the pockets, but I had to turn around 'cause when I looked down at my bare feet, I saw I forgot to put on my navy blue penny loafers.

That nice bus lady had called Mother every day since she met us three months ago on the bus, and now she was coming to pick us up and take us to the zoo. Dominick had put on his grey corduroys, white Optimus Prime T-shirt, and his brown open-toed sandals last night before we went to bed so he would be ready when Miss Lucy arrived. He quickly ran past me while I put on my navy blue penny loafers and continued running all the way out the front door. Peeking at him from the front window, I could see he had jumped right through the open driver's side door. He started playing with the green steering wheel.

"Voom voom, beep beep!" Dominick yelled as he avoided all the pretend cars in front of him. Making my way outside in desperation, fearful Miss Lucy and Dominick would leave me behind, I pushed past Mother and dove into the yellow station wagon after my brother.

"Move ova," I said, pushing up my brother's butt with my left hand as I climbed into the car. He stayed standing on the seat, still driving and talking to his pretend cars and ignoring me. I crawled on the green leather bench seat like a soldier in a ditch until I made my way to the passenger side. I sat up, pushing my bottom off the seat with my hands to look at Miss Lucy and Mother over the dashboard. They were standing in plain view, and Miss Lucy was still talking to Mother. Mother looked like she was gon' drop dead right where she stood, but she just kept talking too. Miss Lucy occasionally looked our way and smiled, then looked back at Mother, who was standing there in her dingy grey bathrobe filled with cigarette burns from when she'd fallen asleep holding her long skinny brown cigarettes. Her white slippers were the color of burnt paper and too small for her ashy feet; her crusty heels rested on the asphalt driveway of our four-plex apartment building. Mother had been sick all week, and she said to Miss Lucy in her high-pitched squeaky voice, "Thank you for taking my babies, I just ain't been feeling well. I was waiting on the first when some money come in to get my medicine." Miss Lucy handed Mother some money, patted her on the shoulder, then walked towards us with a big warm smile.

I was excited to go to the zoo. I'd never seen animals outside of cats and dogs running in my neighborhood. I wanted to see a tiger, like the tiger in my magic book. The car ride felt like it was taking forever. Miss Lucy hummed along to a song on the radio, bobbing her head and smiling, "I heard it through the grapevine, not much longer would you be mine" as she checked in with me and my brother through the rear-view, mirror batting her smiling eyes.

My brother and I started to play our car-counting game. "One, two, d'hree, fo', five—" Dominick yelled out as he pointed to all the cars Miss Lucy quickly passed on the freeway. We count up to seven and start over at one until Miss Lucy turned down the round knob on the radio.

"Look up, we here," Miss Lucy told us in a sweet warm voice as she pulled into the parking lot. Jumping out of the car, smiling from ear to ear, I looked back at Dominick's smile, and my heart began to skip right out of my chest, I was so excited.

Miss Lucy hustled us through a big archway made of wood with different kinds of animals painted on it. Paths went off into all different directions, and I could smell a unfamiliar musty stinky odor in the air. Before I could yell out what animal I wanted to see first, Dominick had already broken free of Miss Lucy's hand and ran over to the ice cream stand. Miss Lucy smiled and bought us ice cream right away.

"This the zoo?" I said, looking up to Miss Lucy, who looked down and smiled and nodded at me. Still holding the big vanilla ice cream cone she had bought me in my right hand and keeping my left locked in Miss Lucy's hand, I squeezed her fingers a little tighter, hoping she would never let mine go. Lost in happiness, I released my left hand from hers and said, "I'm th'ee, I'm th'ee!" and held my hand up high, folding down my two end fingers, which made her smile and look at me with love in her eyes. My brother had finished his ice cream already, and he had double scoops! He was trying to pull away from Miss Lucy's hand every five seconds to run over to see the animals, but she just tightened her grip and told him, "Hold on; we'll walk over together."

We walked over to the tigers first. I had made Miss Lucy promise the whole ride here to show us the tigers first. I recognized them immediately from the special book Mr. Chinaman gave me. "Why these tigers gotta be locked up?" I asked.

"I suppose they'd escape if they aren't," Miss Lucy said, biting down on her bottom lip and staring dead-on into the tiger's cage.

One of the tigers with blue eyes and an all-white coat layered with black stripes stood up and gave a growl toward the zookeeper, who walked past the cage telling a group of kids, "Don't tease the animals please." He was a tall white guy, but he looked small compared to the tigers. He was wearing a green cap, a green short-sleeved polo shirt that had "Oaktown

Zoo" written in white letters on the front of it, khaki shorts, and brown hiking boots.

"They gon' eat us!" My brother yelled as he hid behind Miss Lucy's leg in fear.

While Miss Lucy comforted my brother and tended to his "I'm-scared" tantrum, I just stood there licking my ice cream, enjoying every lick. The sun was beaming down straight on my forehead, causing a river of sweat, but the cold vanilla ice cream took the heat away with every lick. That big white tiger must have known I was thinking how nice it would be if Mr. White Tiger could eat up Mother and her special friends, 'cause he came walking towards me, right up to the bars, and just stared back at me.

"You want some ice cream?" I whispered. Mr. White Tiger didn't move. He just licked his tongue out and smiled. "I share wit' you, Mr. White Tiger," I said, trying to climb on the bars to reach him. Resting my heels on the cement perimeter, I wedged my left foot into the black iron bars. I grabbed hold of the bars with my left hand and pulled myself up against them. I stretched my right arm out through the bars into the cage, holding the half-eaten ice cream cone in my hand.

People are screaming, "Get down little girl!" behind me, but I only vaguely hear them because all I see is Mr. White Tiger. I want Mr. White Tiger to be my friend and protect me.

"Come here, Mr. White Tiger! I share wit' you! Come kitty kitty!" I yelled, making kissing noises by puckering my lips and sucking them together. Mr. White Tiger locked eyes with me and walked towards me. Before I could breathe, he licked my ice cream.

His tongue was so strong he scooped the entire cone out of my hand with one lick. The ice cream and cone disappeared immediately and vanished all the way down Mr. White Tiger's throat. Then Mr. White Tiger started licking my hand. "You tickle, Mr. White Tiger!" I laughed with joy, enjoying the warm scratchy sensation of his strong tongue as it gently licked my hand. Mr. White Tiger and I were friends now, he could come home with me and protect me and my brother, maybe eat Mother and her special friends too. But before I could think of a way to free Mr. White Tiger or even pet him, Miss Lucy snatched me off the bars.

"No! Stop, I wanna play with him! Stop, stop...," I yelled, holding on tight to the iron bar with my left hand. Mr. White Tiger didn't take his eyes off me; his blue eyes stared without changing expressing. I couldn't hold on any longer, my last finger slipped off. "Noooo....I hate you! Fucking bitch ass whore!" I was so mad I yelled the meanest words I could, kicking and screaming, trying without success to squirm my way out of Miss Lucy's arms. My eyes filled with tears and snot pushed out of my nose. My heart beat hard, and I couldn't breathe. Every time I tried I just kept sucking in air and choking like having hiccups, but only in my lungs.

The harder I fought, the tighter Miss Lucy hugged me. She started slapping my back with her right hand like she was burping a baby. Tightly wrapping my body in her left arm, she walked away from Mr. White Tiger's cage at a fast pace. "Hush now, child, it's going be all right. That mean ole tiger could've ate you. Shhh...shhh...." Reaching my arm out over Miss Lucy's shoulder, extending my fingertips towards Mr. White Tiger as the distance increased between us and his cage, I watched him as long as I could. He followed us, walking the perimeter of his cage, until he reached the end. He never made a noise and I didn't take my eyes off him.

"Mr. White Tiger...save me," I mumbled in between sobs.

Mr. Tiger was finally out of sight and all I could see was Dominick looking at me scared, like he didn't know what was going on. "Sister, we save you," he said, grabbing my hand that was dangling over Miss Lucy's shoulder as we sat on a green bench next to the loud monkeys, far away from Mr. White Tiger. I continued sobbing, trying to stop myself from hyperventilating. Dominick looked up at me with tears in his eyes. He scooted closer to Miss Lucy on the bench, to get a better grip on my three tiny fingers, still sticky from the melted vanilla ice cream, with his left hand and started sucking his right thumb. We sat there in silence until I calmed down.

Then Miss Lucy stood me up in front of her and looked me in the eye. "Chena, why did you stick your hand in the cage?" she asked me, with a puzzled yet concerned look on her face.

Looking down at my feet, I wanted to tell Miss Lucy that I was sorry for calling her the bad names I had heard my mom and her special friends use. I mumbled instead, "So him can protect me."

"Protect you from what, Chena?" Miss Lucy said in soothing but confused tone.

"From...." I stopped and turned my head, looking at the monkeys, trying unsuccessfully to remember why I want Mr. White Tiger to protect me. I don't remember clearly, there are so many reasons—so many times, so many things, so many people. But I remember the feelings that won't go away, no matter how much I try. I remember feeling scared, alone, and pain, but I just don't know how to say it. I can't form the words to go with my little thoughts, because I haven't learned them yet.

"From what? You can tell me, Chena, I'll protect you," Miss Lucy said, waiting patiently for an answer.

Frozen deep in thought, I stared harder at the monkeys, noticing the details of their faces and the sadness in their eyes. I mumbled, "From Mother and her special friends. Them hurt me, and Mother let 'em." My voice rose into a yell. "I hate 'em, I hate her, I hate her!" I stomped my foot and folded my arms.

Angry and confused, I fell silent and stood there, never taking my eyes off the monkeys, as Miss Lucy scooped me up and wrapped me tightly in her warm loving arms. I started to cry again. "Shh. Naw...it gon' be all right, child....It's gon' be okay," Miss Lucy's mumbled in a trembling voice, as I sobbed in her arms.

CHAPTER 11
CHENA

Dear Diary,

A man who I love
a man
I
could marry,
not truly knowing
his full identity

First name Trickery,
last name Lies

Who is this
deceptive
causer
of
cries...

CHENA, THE MAKING OF AN ORPHAN

Ring! Ring! "Hello?"

"Hey Chena, you going to the Black Saturday party with us tonight?"

"Becky?"

"Yeah girl, it's me."

"I can't go. I'm on restriction for two weeks," Chena said in a sad voice.

"Why?"

"'Cause Dena found out I didn't spend the night at Tanisha's house last night," Chena said nonchalantly.

"Were you still with Brandon?" Becky asked viciously.

Irritated by Becky's question, Chena responded with an attitude. "Becky, what's your problem with Brandon?"

"Why you say that?"

"Every time I mention his name, you get a fucking attitude. I mean if I didn't know any better, I would think you liked him or something."

"Aw...it's not like that, you know me and Ibrahima are talking anyway."

"Then what is it, Becky? Why can't you ever just be happy for me?" Chena yelled into the phone.

"'Cause you always think you better then everybody else, flaunting your grades and now your new boyfriend."

"What?" Chena said, shocked at Becky's hurtful comments. "I don't flaunt shit, what are you talking about?" Chena yelled, rage in her voice.

Click...

"That bitch actually hung up in my face! It's cool, I'll check her ass at school on Monday," Chena said, slamming the phone down. Chena quickly picked it back up to call Brandon, and listened to it ring once, twice, three times. Come on, be home, dammit.

"Hello?"

"Hey baby, I thought you weren't home for a minute," Chena said, with panic in her voice.

"What's wrong? You sound upset," Brandon asked, his tone instantly patient and warm.

"I'm not sure, but me and Becky just got into over you. She's been tripping ever since me and you got together...I'm afraid she might like you."

"What? That's crazy, she's your girl...Aw, but she is a hoe."

"What do you mean by that?" Chena said in shock.

"Well, she let Ibrahima hit it the first night she met him, and she also fucked and sucked up Shawn and Michael in a threesome."

"What! Why didn't you tell me?" Chena demanded.

"I didn't think it was appropriate. We were just getting to know each other." Shocked by the news, Chena almost started to cry. She couldn't believe her friend, her sister, was living a double life. I thought I knew her.

"Hey baby, you still there?"

"Yeah" she mumbled. "And I got some more bad news."

"What?"

"Dena found out I didn't spend the night at Tanisha's, so I'm on punishment for two weeks."

"What? I can't see you for two whole weeks? What am I going to do?" Brandon pleaded in an adorable voice.

"I'll see you at school at least," Chena said, attempting to sound cheerful.

"Yeah, I just might have to climb up your fire escape and kidnap you one night," Brandon replied in a serious tone.

"Do you really think you can reach the fire escape?"

"Yeah, I'll stand on top of my truck."

"We might just have to meet up then," Chena said, playfully smiling ear to ear. "Baby, I can't stop thinking about you and our night together. I'm crazy about you," she confessed, butterflies filling her stomach.

"Baby, I can't stop thinking about you either. These two weeks are really going to suck."

"What you doing tonight?" Chena asked, hoping he would stay in and think about her.

"I'm going to go to that Black Saturday party with Ibrahima."

"Oh, that should be fun," Chena said sarcastically. "Well, baby, I'm going to jump off the phone so I can get dinner ready, have fun tonight and be safe."

"Wait! Aren't you forgetting to say something else?" Brandon asked.

"Uh, no? I'll talk to you later," Chena said, confused by his comment.

"Well baby, I love you too."

"Hey, you know this is new to me! I've never used that word before; it's going take some getting used to. But I know I really, really like you...no, it's more than like... aw, I think I'm starting to fall in love with you," Chena said, grinning and blushing, unsure in her vulnerability.

"Aww baby, I love you too! Talk to you later," Brandon responded joyfully, before hanging up.

Brandon couldn't help but think about Chena's comment about Becky. Shit, I sure wouldn't mind hitting that, she's a freak. Brandon knew that one night with Becky wasn't worth risking his relationship with Chena, but he also knew that Chena wouldn't be ready to lose her innocence until she decided she was ready, no matter how hard he tried. Brandon heard horror stories from his boys who had wasted months, even years, on virgins. Brandon was in his prime, and he had girls throwing pussy at him left and right.

Brandon knew if he went away to college, he would have to get some anyway, so he might as well prepare himself for the college life. Shaking the thoughts of cheating out of his head, Brandon took one last look in the mirror and headed out the door. He was looking good; he had just gotten a haircut, and his waves were looking tight. Brandon put on his Eddie Bauer jeans and a blue and white button-down shirt with his tan Timberland boots. Headed to his car, he hit the keyless entry and hopped in.

Arriving at Ibrahima's house, he turned the music down, not wanting to offend Ibrahima's mom, who had complained about the volume of his music just last week. Honk! Honk! He tapped the horn. Ibrahima came out the front door and headed to the car. Ibrahima was dressed to impress, wearing white Air Force Ones, khaki slacks, and a white polo shirt.

"Yo, what's up?" Ibrahima said as he hopped in the truck.

"What's up?" Brandon replied.

"Yo dogg, how did your big date go? Did you get some?" Ibrahima asked with excitement.

Looking down and shaking his head, Brandon replied, "Naw, but we did have some fun."

"Word," Ibrahima replied, a sympathetic look on his face. "What kind of fun?" he asked curiously.

"Not the kind of fun you and Becky had," Brandon replied with a fat grin on his face.

"Yeah well, Becky is a hoe, and hoes know how to have fun," Ibrahima said, a reminiscing look on his face.

"Yo dogg, Chena told me that she thinks Becky likes me, ain't that crazy?"

"What? Hey dogg, the pussy was good, but you shouldn't fuck with her," Ibrahima said firmly. "That girl is a nutcase. She's stalking Shawn, after he nutted in her face."

"What? Yo dogg, on the real?" Brandon asked in shock, as he pulled into a space in the club's parking lot.

"I know you horny as hell, but Chena's a good girl, and she would be hurt if you fucked with her partna," Ibrahima said, jumping out of the truck.

"Dogg, it's hard. I really like Chena, shit, I love her, and she turns me on...it's just so hard. I got needs, you know," Brandon said, catching up to Ibrahima, who was already near the entrance of the party.

"Dogg, I don't know what to tell you. You're just gon' have to keep your dick in your pants, or break up with Chena."

Walking into the club, Brandon and Ibrahima immediately noticed Bee, Tanisha, and Becky, who were breaking it down on the dance floor. "Speak of the devil, look who's here," Ibrahima whispered, tapping Brandon's shoulder and pointing. "Damn, dogg, I wish I would have fucked with the light-skinned one, what's her name?"

"Bee."

"Yeah, I'm gon' dance with her tonight," Ibrahima said, licking his lips.

"Dogg, they know you fucked Becky. They ain't hoes, they ain't going fuck with you. You can forget it," Brandon replied.

While Ibrahima headed to the dance floor, Brandon stood against the wall, keeping a low profile. He didn't want Chena's girls to take any gossip of him with another chick back to her. He stood there and watched Ibrahima dance with every girl in the room except for Bee, who was rolling her eyes at him, along with her crew.

"Hey, you want to dance?" He turned around to see which girl was asking him to dance this time. To his surprise and relief, it was Tanisha; he didn't want to have to hurt another girl's feelings.

"Hey, shortie! What's up?"

"What's up? You know you got my partna in trouble," she said, playfully hitting Brandon in the chest.

"I know. I can't wait till she gets off punishment," Brandon said with a smile.

Brandon had never noticed how pretty Tanisha was before. Tonight she looked very different, wearing tight clothes. The baggy clothes he was used to seeing her in disguised the fact she actually had a very nice figure, with nice round C-cup breasts and a nice round ass to match. "I can't dance," Brandon said.

"What? Why not?" Tanisha said, surprised.

"No, really. I don't dance, it's not my thing. I can't dance, never could, and never will," Brandon said, as he leaned back against the wall again.

Turning around and dropping her butt low to the ground, Tanisha smiled. "I'll just dance with you on the wall."

Laughing, Brandon stood back and let Tanisha dance. He thought it was funny until she did the unthinkable. Tanisha actually started rubbing her ass on Brandon's dick. Brandon's smile dropped off his face. His eyes widened and he watched as she bounced up and down, simulating a stripper. Brandon was shocked, but he was also becoming aroused. He couldn't stop his dick from gaining an erection; the faster she bounced, the harder his dick became. It was as if Tanisha knew she was turning him on, because she started to grind on him just a little harder.

Brandon could feel someone staring a hole in the side of his face. Turning to look, he saw Sheila and all of her friends in a circle, pointing and laughing.

"All right, that's enough," Brandon said, pushing Tanisha away from him.

"Aw, I'm not like Chena, you can't handle this, huh?" Tanisha said flirtatiously.

"Naw, you ain't nothing like Chena and you never will be," Brandon replied in disgust as he walked away.

Brandon's dick was hard, but Tanisha would never have the pleasure of seeing it. "Yo Ibrahima, let's go," Brandon said with anger.

"What's up? Why we leaving? We still got another twenty minutes," Ibrahima complained.

"Yo dogg, let's go."

Walking briskly behind Brandon, Ibrahima jumped in the passenger side of the truck. "What's up with you, man? Why we leaving?" Ibrahima asked furiously.

"That damn bitch Tanisha was grinding all on my dick, and Sheila saw the whole thing. She's going to blow it way out of proportion," Brandon said, screeching out of the parking lot.

"What?"

"I always thought Tanisha had a crush on me, always going out her way to speak to me and shit at school, but I never thought she would be a hoe! Fuck, what am I going to do?"

"Well dogg, you were looking for pussy. Looks like pussy found you first," Ibrahima said, laughing.

"This shit ain't funny! What should I do?" Brandon pleaded.

"Tell Chena before it gets back to her, or you won't have a chance," Ibrahima replied, patting his friend on the back.

Pulling up to Ibrahima's house, Brandon laid his head on the steering wheel and mumbled, "I can't 'cause she's on punishment, and I won't see her until Monday."

"Well dogg, I don't know what to tell you. Good luck with that," Ibrahima said, getting out of the truck.

At home, Brandon couldn't sleep. Tossing and turning in bed, he couldn't stop thinking about Chena and how she would react to the news. I shouldn't be worried, 'cause I didn't do nothing wrong, he thought. But he knew he did do something wrong: he allowed it to happen in the first place. He should have stopped Tanisha before she even started dancing.

Brandon realized at that point that he really loved Chena, and he made up his mind that he wasn't waiting till Monday to tell her. He was going to tell her right away. Brandon quickly jumped out of bed and threw on his sweats and Nike sandals. Before heading out the front door, he left his parents a quick note, telling them where he was going. It was two o'clock in the morning, and he hoped he wouldn't get mistaken for a burglar.

Jumping into his truck, Brandon went over his game plan in his head. Okay, I'm going to park my truck in the alleyway next to Chena's fire escape, and climb up and knock on her window. If anybody comes by and asks, I'll tell them that I'm locked out.

Arriving at Chena's building, Brandon turned his lights off and slowly backed his truck up, parking parallel to the wall right below Chena's fire escape. Quietly sliding out of the passenger side of the truck, he climbed onto the hood of his truck and pulled the ladder down. Controlling the weight of the ladder, he slowly lowered it onto the bed of his truck to minimize the noise. Climbing down off the hood of his truck, he climbed into the bed of his pickup and started climbing up the ladder.

Brandon had almost made it, with only five bars to climb, when he slipped and lost his footing. Hanging on for dear life, he looked down and watched the Nike sandal from his left foot hit the ground. Amazingly, it didn't make a sound, but his stumble on the ladder made it rattle, the loud noise echoing in the alleyway. Brandon's heart was pounding out of his chest, making him tremble with fear. The adrenaline gave him strength, though, allowing him to pull himself up. Reaching up for the bar above him, he lifted his body in a pull-up motion, brought his dangling feet onto the ladder, and continued to climb the final five bars. Reaching Chena's bedroom window, he peeked in and saw that she was asleep. Tapping lightly on the window, Brandon awoke Chena, who turned towards the window.

"Who the hell is it?" she whispered, reaching to turn on her lamp. Chena's first instinct was to scream, but she remembered that Brandon said he would climb up the fire escape. In the glare of the light, Chena made out Brandon's face. She quickly ran to the window and opened it.

Whispering in a low voice, Brandon told Chena to turn the lamp off.

"Hey, where's your other shoe?" Chena asked, pointing to his feet.

"It fell," Brandon responded. "Baby, I got to talk to you about something serious," he whispered, a worried expression forming on his face.

"What's wrong?" Chena asked, noticing the urgent tone change in Brandon's voice. Before Brandon could respond there was a knock at her door. Panicking, Chena pushed him in her bedroom closet, closed her window, turned the volume up on her television and lay back in her bed, pretending to be asleep.

Chena closed her eyes tight. Her heart was pounding out of her chest, and she began to pray. "Lord, please don't let Dena find Brandon in my room."

Brandon was cramped in the corner of her closet, trying not to hold his breath. Fuck, I hope this shoebox doesn't fall on my head. I can feel it slipping, Brandon thought, quietly trying to move his hand to hold the shoebox above his head. Chena's bedroom door opened and she heard footsteps in her room, stopping at the foot of her bed.

Just as Chena and Brandon thought Dena would walk right out the door again, a loud noise came from Chena's closet, sounding like something falling off the shelf. They heard the footsteps head over to the closet. "Get the fuck out of there! Dammit, Chena! What's going on?" Dena screamed, turning to face Chena. Turning on Chena's lamp, Dena stood there with her mouth wide open and eyes furious.

"I can explain, Dena. Please calm down, it's not what you think," Brandon said, climbing out of the closet.

"You better start explaining before I call the police for statutory rape," Dena said, putting her hands on her hips.

Chena sucked her teeth, looked at Dena, and rolled her eyes. "We weren't doing nothing!" Chena snapped.

"Why do I have to come in and catch him in the closet, if y'all wasn't doing nothing?" Dena asked, an angry look on her face.

"She didn't know I was coming. I have some bad news to tell her, and I couldn't call her 'cause she's on punishment," Brandon pleaded.

Turning from Dena to look at Brandon, Chena's heart dropped. Bad news? What could that be? Oh my...I hope nothing happened to my girls at that Black Saturday party... Snapping out of her anxious train of thought, Chena asked, "What's the bad news? What happened?"

Brandon hesitated. "It's Tanisha..." He paused and looked at Dena. "Can we please have two minutes alone?"

Dena looked at the hurt look on Brandon's face, and decided to give them a few minutes. Only after Dena walked out the room did he continue. "Tanisha came on to me at the party."

"What?" Chena said, trying to fight back the angry tears that sprang into her eyes, completely stunned by the betrayal. "First it was Becky, now it's Tanisha!" Chena murmured. She felt dazed, not quite sure what to think. These girls are like my sisters; they are my only family. But Brandon is my true love, and he could be in my life forever! Why would my sisters try and jeopardize my happiness?

Brandon cleared his throat. Attempting to speak in a calm voice, he slowly broke Chena out of her deep thoughts. "I was standing there, and she came up to me trying to dance. I told her I didn't dance, and she started dancing anyway."

Interjecting, Chena screamed, "Why didn't you stop her?"

"I didn't want to make her look stupid, so I just stood there letting her dance, until she started rubbing her ass all on my dick," Brandon said. He conveniently left out the details of his erection. "Chena, say something," Brandon demanded.

Chena immediately shut down, retreating to the safe place in her head like she often had as a child to avoid feeling pain. She couldn't be conveyed her thoughts into words for Brandon to hear, but they played over and over in her mind. Forgetting for a moment that Brandon was even in the room, Chena just stood in a trance with an empty hollow expression layered with deep sadness on her face. I can't believe one of my best friends in the whole wide world would do something like this to me, betray me, especially at such a public place, knowing it would get back to me. It's as if she wanted it to get back to me. But why? In that moment Chena decided that no matter what happened next, she would not let this betrayal or anything else ruin her one chance at real love.

After what seemed to be an eternity of silence, Brandon looked up from the floor, his hazel puppy-dog eyes locking onto Chena's narrow golden-brown face. Her expression hidden in the shadows running across her face from the moonlight through her window, Chena began to speak in warrior mode. "Did that bitch really think she had a chance?" Chena said, looking directly at Brandon with anger blazing from her slitted almond-shaped brown eyes.

"I don't know, baby. I'm sorry I got you in trouble, but I just had to tell you," Brandon replied, reaching to hug Chena.

In tears, Chena looked up at Brandon, then looked at her bedroom door, sure Dena would bust in at any minute. "Thank you for telling me. You better get out of here before you get put in jail." Opening the window, Brandon began to climb down. Looking up at Chena in the window, he blew her a kiss.

Dena busted in, as Chena expected, to see her leaning out her bedroom window. "Where the hell is he going? He could have used the front door, Chena," Dena said, closing the window firmly.

Standing on the edge of the fire escape, flattening himself to the wall like Spiderman, Brandon stood still listening. He couldn't leave until he knew Chena wasn't in any more trouble.

"I couldn't help but overhear the conversation, and I am sorry that Tanisha betrayed you," Dena said softly.

Sitting on the bed, Chena looked up at Dena with watery eyes. "I didn't know he was coming here tonight, I'm sorry I let him in," Chena said, before picking up her Care Bear pillow and burying her face in it.

Dena sat down next to her. "I will look past this incident, this one time. But Chena, I can't control your every move and I'm not going to, but I need to know that I can trust you," Dena said as she scooted closer and hugged Chena.

"You can trust me," Chena said extending her arms to hug Dena back.

"Okay, get back to bed. We'll talk some more tomorrow."

"Dena?"

"Yeah?"

"Thank you for being like a mother I never had."

"Thank you for being the daughter I always wanted," Dena replied as she turned off Chena's lamp and closed her bedroom door.

Brandon tapped lightly on the window, trying to be as quiet as he could. Apparently he was too quiet, since Chena just turned in her bed and cuddled her pillow. He quietly watched her drift off to sleep, then made his way down the fire escape and quietly drove off.

CHAPTER 12
CHENA

Dear Diary,

I Fight

Holding Back the tears,
thinking of all my fears.
Will somebody hear,

A cry for Help

Strangled by the reality of truths,
Trampled for being the condemned
aloof

I scream

Hoping for the arm of the savior
Please Get to me sooner then later

Begging

In the darkness of hope
Until light fades away
For Survival to see another day

CHENA, THE MAKING OF AN ORPHAN

Two months later, I was walking the long way to school down S and L Boulevard, in hopes of avoiding Bee and Tanisha. They had still remained friends, even after Tanisha stabbed me in the back. As I scanned the traffic, I spotted P, who just gotten off the 821 bus.

"Hey P, wait up!" I screamed, crossing the street. Turning around to see who was calling his name, P waved and started walking towards me.

"Hey Chena!"

"Hey P, what you doing catching the bus?" I asked, nearly out of breath from my short run across the street.

"My car's in the shop."

"Why?"

"I got into an accident this weekend," P replied nonchalantly.

"What happened?" I asked with urgency.

"A homeless guy threw his shopping cart in front of my car on East 14th Street, and made me run into a pole."

"Well I'm glad you're okay," I said sincerely, remembering what happened to me and Becky.

"So what's up with you and Tanisha?" he asked me.

"I haven't spoken to Tanisha in a month, fuck her," I replied, rolling my eyes.

"Damn, y'all tripping. Y'all been friends way too long to let some nigga come between y'all."

"First off, P, you need to get your facts straight. It ain't about the nigga. It's the principle of the whole thing," I said angrily.

"Well, I think y'all just tripping. It ain't that serious, to be mad at your girl for dancing with your man," P said as he pressed the crosswalk button.

"Well P, if it was just a dance, that would have been all good. But it was more then that, P—she was actually trying to fuck him on the dance floor," I said, sucking my teeth.

"How do you know? From my understanding, you wasn't even there."

"Because everyone saw her grinding on him! And he told me what she said too."

"Well Chena, before you throw four years of friendship away, at least hear her side of it first," P replied as he crossed the street toward the school.

Walking briskly behind P, attempting to catch up with his fast pace, I demanded, "What did she tell you, P?"

"She said that she was just dancing, and it wasn't that serious for you to be tripping."

"Well I don't know, but what she did was still out of pocket, and even if Brandon is putting the two on the ten, I would have never disrespected her like that."

Opening the door to the west wing of Sal Valley High, P just replied, "Y'all should talk."

"All right, P. See you later," I said, heading to the cafeteria to get my free breakfast.

"Hey Chena, wait up!" Becky screamed, running down the hall toward me as I left the cafeteria.

"Hey girl, what's up?" I asked, biting my plain glazed donut.

"Hey, did you hear about Tanisha and Sheila?"

"Naw, girl what's up?" I asked curiously, hoping that Becky was still not talking to Tanisha too.

"Jake said that Tanisha was going to fight Sheila at lunch today."

"What? But why?"

"'Cause Sheila's been going around telling people that Tanisha tried to take your man, and that she was a hoe," Becky said with excitement in her voice.

How ironic—my enemy has just become my biggest supporter...or is my enemy really not my enemy? I thought. "Well I guess we'll see," I said, my eyes fixated on Brandon, who was placing books into his locker, oblivious to the fact that I was right across from him.

"All right girl, I'll let you holla at your man, see you at lunch," Becky said with a sincere smile.

"Bye, I'll meet you at my locker," I mumbled, still focused on Brandon, hoping he would see me.

Becky's attitude towards Brandon had done a 180-degree turnaround, once she found out how scandalous Tanisha had been to me. I guess Becky realized good friends were hard to find. She had confessed that she was not really jealous of me, but more of my new friendship with Brandon. Still, I had my guard up. Tanisha's betrayal made me doubt who I could really trust.

"Hey baby," I said, tapping on Brandon's locker.

"Hey," Brandon mumbled.

"What's wrong? Are you okay?" I replied, noticing that he wasn't his usual joking self.

"Nothing, I'm just tired." Brandon had been tired a lot lately, ever since he started playing on the YA area's semi-pro basketball team. The past two weeks had been killing me. We hadn't spent much quality time together; he was always too busy to talk on the phone and I was at track practice or at work when he did have time to talk. All the alone time left me plenty of time to wonder if he was with someone else.

"Hey, you want to hear something funny?" I asked with a smile.

"No, not really, Chena," Brandon answered without even looking at me.

"Okay, what's up? I know something's up. You haven't returned any of my calls, and now you're talking to me like I don't exist!"

"Look Chena, there's a lot going on in my life right now, and I don't have time for this shit!" he yelled in a firm voice. Hurt, I turned and started running down the hall to the girls' bathroom.

I couldn't hold back the tears anymore. I was having a meltdown; the person I loved was treating me like shit, a former best friend was my new enemy and my circle of friends was broken, I came in fourth at three different track meets, and on top of all of that, I had gotten two rejection letters from colleges I had applied to. I can't believe this shit, Brandon ain't even gon' run after me, what did I do? Why doesn't he care about me anymore? Crying for almost thirty minutes, I finally realized I was actually cutting Mr. Silverman's class. Sitting in a toilet stall with the door shut, I started to compose myself. Wiping the smeared mascara off my swollen red eyes, I started to cry again, but I was interrupted by the sound of the door opening to the bathroom.

"Hey come in, ain't nobody in here." A familiar voice echoed in the tiled room. It was Sheila, but who was she talking to? Wiping my nose, I quietly picked my feet up and stood on the toilet seat, crouching, hoping to conceal my presence in the stall.

"Sheila, we can't keep doing this." My heart dropped. I did not want to recognize the sound of his voice, but I knew immediately who it was.

"You know you like it when I suck your big-ass dick," Shelia replied, trying to sound sexy.

"Word," he replied, moving towards the handicapped stall. I could hear them walking in, but I couldn't see them though the one-inch crack between the stall and the door. They had walked by too fast. The stall door closed behind them, and I could hear his zipper go down, the shuffling of clothes, and then smacking and sucking. Quietly walking out of the bathroom stall, I could practically feel steam coming out of my nose, like I was a bull who wanted to see only blood. I balled my fist up, creeping towards the handicapped stall, and set my backpack down. Unzipping it, I grabbed the fat-free chocolate milk left over from my breakfast and opened it.

These motherfuckers were so busy getting it on, they never heard me coming. As the sucking, smacking, and moaning continued, I became furious! I kicked the stall door with all my might and it flew open, hitting Sheila in the back and knocking her forward. As the door opened I threw the chocolate milk. In fury and near tears, I watched as the milk landed all over Sheila, looking up with a fat one in her mouth. With the word "bitch" about to fly out of my mouth, I was instantly silenced with relief when I saw that Sheila wasn't sucking Brandon's dick. She was giving head to Jake. Even through my shock, I couldn't help but notice that little annoying Jake was actually packing a log in those pants.

Chuckling and covering my eyes, I yelled, "Oh my God, I'm so sorry! I promise I won't say nothing." I backed out of the bathroom as fast as I could, followed by the screams of Jake and Sheila.

Once out the bathroom I busted out laughing. I couldn't stop laughing; I couldn't remember the last time I had seen something so funny. I was laughing so hard, I forgot why I was upset to begin with.

"Chena! What are you doing out of class?" Romonia snapped.

Contemplating whether or not I should bust Sheila and Jake out, I decided not to, and instead put on my Oscar performance. "I'm too happy to go to class!" I responded with a smile.

"What, are you trying to be funny?" Romonia responded angrily.

"Actually, Romonia, I just found out that the cyst in my breast was benign!" Running towards Romonia, I started jumping up and down in the air like I had won the lotto. I hugged her and shouted, "Romonia, Romonia, I'm gonna live, you hear me? I'm gonna live!"

Turning around and releasing Romonia from my grip, I started walking away down the hall. Looking behind me, I could see Romonia standing there speechless, with a warm motherly smile on her face. "Make sure you get to the library until your next class!" she yelled after me, before she headed upstairs to patrol the halls.

I was so happy to see that Sheila wasn't with Brandon I didn't know what to do with myself. Walking past Room 108, I saw Brandon sitting in the back of the class. I stood in the doorway waving my hands to try to get his attention. I not only got his attention, but also the teacher's. She kept turning back, trying to look at what was distracting her students, but I was faster then her. Each time she would turn, I would dash behind the doorway. Finally Brandon looked up and saw me. Immediately, he asked to go to the bathroom.

Walking towards the door, he turned right, away from the boys' room, to meet up with me near the stairs. I had a glow of happiness, and it showed in my face. I was happy, and I wanted to tell Brandon about Sheila.

"Hey babe, guess—" Before I could finish my sentence, Brandon's lips were covering mine, and he was kissing me passionately. I was taken off guard, especially since we were still in the hallway. Reaching behind me, Brandon opened the janitor's closet and pushed me in. Closing the door behind him, he placed his fingers on my lips and whispered in my ear.

"Baby, I'm sorry for talking to you crazy this morning, I'm sorry for not spending time with you, I love you." And then he kissed me deeply. Taking his lips off mine and moving them towards my neck, he kissed my ear and whispered, "Baby, I need to talk to you after school, about something serious."

"Okay, I'll meet you at your truck," I replied, after stealing another kiss. Enjoying the hardness that bulged out of Brandon's pants rubbing on my abdomen, I wrapped my hands around his butt and pushed his pelvis onto mine, letting out a slight moan. We didn't want to let each other go, but an internal alarm within Brandon and I went off, alerting us that any longer in the closet and we would either be caught or naked. Releasing each other without words, we gathered our flustered selves. Brandon cracked the door to ensure the coast was clear, and we snuck out of the janitor's closet. I speedily walked towards the library, all hot and bothered and on a natural high of happiness, while Brandon headed back to class.

Later, leaving second period, I couldn't help but wonder what could possibly be the bad news Brandon needed to tell me. It has to be bad, 'cause he seems so hesitant to tell me. I wonder if he cheated on me? No, no, that's not it, he loves me. He probably didn't get his scholarship to USC...oh shit, maybe he wants to break up with me! No that couldn't be it, then he wouldn't have made love to my mouth in the janitor's closet. Oh well, I guess I'll find out after school.

"Hey, Chena!"

"Hey, Bee," I said nonchalantly as I continued to walk past her, towards my locker.

"Chena!" Bee yelled.

"What, Bee?" I said turning around to walk towards her.

"Girl, we go back too far to throw our friendship away," Bee said, a sad look in her eyes.

I placed my hands on Bee's shoulders. "Bee, I told you I would still be your friend. I just can't talk to you as long as you're hanging with backstabbing Tanisha."

"Tanisha is your friend too! She's sorry for what she did, but she wouldn't have taken it any further than dancing! Chena, you're the one who always said 'friends before niggas for life.' Now you're being a hypocrite," Bee replied in a softened tone.

"I'm sorry, Bee, but friends don't stab their friends in the back. I have nothing to say to Tanisha, in addition to the fact that she still hasn't admitted what she did, and as long as you remain friends with her, I will not have anything to say to you either." Turning around I continued to walk to my locker to drop my backpack off.

Walking down the stairs towards the cafeteria, I walked past Shelia, who still had the chocolate milk stains on her white jean jacket from this morning. The first thing I noticed was Shelia's friend Tonika standing out like a sore thumb amongst us teenagers. She was in college, why is she on our campus? Was she here to help jump Tanisha? But before I could put two and two together, Sheila and her fat ass friend Pam started punching me and slamming me against the wall.

"Now what, bitch?" Pam screamed, while Sheila kicked me in the shins. Before I could respond, Shermika and Tonika jumped in and started kicking and punching me, hitting my face and stomach. I fell on the floor near the trashcan, hitting my head on the floor. Lying there dazed and in pain, I saw a glass Snapple bottle on the ground. With anger and fear rushing through my veins, I instinctively reached for the bottle, cracked it on the ground, and started swinging, slicing any ankles or hands that reached for me.

"Ooh, this bitch cut me!" Tonika screamed. Straightening up to wipe the blood off her wrist, she was met by Becky's fist, which knocked her to the ground. Bee was pulling Pam by her braids with one hand and scratching her face with the other. Looking to my right, in disbelief I saw Tanisha, my enemy now becoming my savior, charging towards me like a bull, pushing through the crowd. She dropped her books on the ground and jumped on Shermika's back, who was in the process of kicking me in the head.

Gathering my strength, I got up off the ground and headed straight for Sheila, who was pulling on Bee's hair. Not realizing I had the Snapple bottle still in my fist, I hit her across the head, causing a deep gash across her temple that started gushing blood immediately. Off balance from the pain, I fell to the ground and was rewarded with another kick to the head from Sheila.

"Break it up!" "Break it up!" sounded along with the blowing of whistles. Romonia and her squad patrol of narks had arrived on the scene, and were pulling the fighting mass of girls apart. As they handcuffed the girls, I looked into the massive crowd that had formed and saw Brandon attempting to break through. He was blocked from reaching me by Romonia.

"Chena, are you okay?" Brandon yelled. As I lay on the ground, limp and bleeding, I couldn't move or respond—no sound came out of my mouth. I tried to keep my swollen eyes open and focused on Brandon, but everything became blurry, and in a flash I had blacked out.

The next thing I was aware of was Dena's voice crying out to me, "Chena, Chena come back to us." She was lying on the side of my bed, her face buried into my stiff right arm. Opening my eyes, I realized I couldn't move, my body ached, and I had a splitting headache. Clarity started to come to my confused, now-conscious brain; as I looked around the room, I smelled an aroma like a botanical garden, mixed with a stench of staleness. The stinging pain from the lights quickly faded as my watery eyes adjusted with each blink. The cloudy grey blur in front of me began to dissipate and I could see big bouquets of flowers, handwritten "get well" posters decorated with glitter on the walls, foil balloons, and a big brown stuffed bear wearing a navy blue shirt with "UC Bezerkeley" in gold yellow letters on the front.

My brain began to frantically search for the memories of how I had gotten here. Forcing myself to turn my stiff neck to the right, I saw Becky, Tanisha, and Bee sitting in chairs on the other side of the room near the bathroom, asleep and leaning on each other's shoulders. Staring at my friends, who were here and had been there for me through thick and thin, a tear started to fall from my right eye, wetting my pillow. I made an attempt to speak, without success. I tried again, and this time a groan came out. It startled Dena, and she quickly popped her head up. Her watery bloodshot eyes met mine, and she gasped with joy.

"Chena, take it easy; don't try and talk," said a cool, unfamiliar voice. My eyes flickered to the source, a man in a white coat standing near the foot of my bed.

Ignoring the doctor's request, I whispered, "Where am I?"

"You're at Saint John's Hospital, and you've just woken out of a coma."

Clearing my throat, I croaked, "How long?" in a groggy voice.

Smiling and jotting down notes, the doctor looked up and responded, "One week." The noise from our conversation woke up Tanisha, who then woke up Becky and Bee. Apparently they hadn't left my side since the fight. The doctor later informed me that every day after school they would come and visit until the nurses forced them to leave.

"Chena is going to need her rest now that she is conscious, so please keep your visit brief," the doctor said as he set my chart on the foot of the bed and walked out.

Looking at my friends, tears started uncontrollably to slide down my cheeks. I realized in that moment that true friends were hard to find, and that these girls really loved me. They were my only family and I was so grateful to have them in my life. I also realized that fighting with Tanisha over Brandon was stupid. I had almost lost a friend, one who has proven she is a true friend who would fight for me, and die for me, out of fear of losing what I thought was the only love who wouldn't abandon me.

"I love you all," I whispered with all my might.

"We love you, too!" they said in unison, taking turns hugging my stiff body as I begin to drift back off back to sleep. As my eyes shut, the image of Brandon's face began to fill my brain.

"Where is Brandon?" I mumbled, right before losing consciousness again.

CHAPTER 13
CHENA

Dear Diary,
I can't go back in time
And take back what he took.
I know it's time to say good-bye.
But I want a second look

He made a fool out of me
On top of betraying tables!
I won't let him close enough to hurt me!
And I won't let him go far enough to abandon me.

I know it's time to say good-bye
But I'd rather we linger in the past instead
Enjoying love

I'm my own savior keeping my heart at bay.
I'm not brave enough to ask him to stay away,

But the time has come and gone,
Coming back to finally say
Good-bye

CHENA, THE MAKING OF AN ORPHAN

It was so good to be home; that hospital food sucked! "Dinner's ready!" Dena yelled from the kitchen.

"Okay!" I yelled back, applying cream to the three stitches on my forehead. I wondered impatiently when my bruises would go away. My left arm had been fractured in three places during the ambush, forcing me to wear an ugly brown arm brace. Quickly putting the brace on, before Dena caught me with it off, I headed towards the kitchen. "Oh, something smells good," I said, licking my lips. Dena had outdone herself tonight, preparing a full homemade meal of fried catfish, collard greens, hot water cornbread, and potato salad. Dena had even made my favorite desert, sweet potato pie.

Sitting at the end of the dinner table, I noticed that Dena had laid down three plates, rather than plates for just the two of us. "Why are there three place settings?" I asked, confused.

"Oh, I wanted to surprise you. We have a special dinner guest tonight," Dena replied, opening the oven to check the pies. There was a loud knock at the door.

"I'll get it!" I yelled, eager to meet this mystery guest.

"No, I'll get it," Dena replied as she took her apron off and headed towards the front door. Peeking down the hallway to see who was at the door, I could see Dena at the door talking to Brandon. "I'm glad you could make it, Chena's in the kitchen waiting for you," Dena said to him as she closed the front door.

Running out of the kitchen I jumped on Brandon, knocking the box of chocolates right out of his hands. Brandon picked me up and hugged me tightly. "Baby, I missed you," Brandon said as he kissed me on the cheek.

"A-huhm!" Dena made a rude noise in the back of her throat to get our attention as she headed towards the kitchen. "Come and eat before it gets cold," she said as she walked away. Following behind Dena and clasping hands, we walked into the kitchen and took our seats at the dinner table.

Something seemed different with Brandon; as I watched him devour his meal it seemed like his body was there, but his mind was not.

"Brandon, would you care for some dessert?" Dena asked as she placed our dirty plates in the kitchen sink.

"No thanks," Brandon replied with a sad look on his face. Dena disappeared into her room with her piece of pie, I guess to give us some privacy.

Reaching across the table with my good right arm, I grabbed Brandon's hand. "What's wrong?"

"I have some bad news to tell you, and I wanted to tell you sooner, but I didn't have the heart, especially since you were in the hospital and all." My heart began to pound and my hands were trembling. I tried to calm down, but I couldn't.

"What is it Brandon? Just spit it out, okay?" I shouted.

Brandon's face lit up in anger at my tone of voice. He looked down at the table, then back at me, shrugged his shoulders, and placed his hands over his face. Lowering his hands, he looked at me with the saddest eyes. "I might have contracted HIV."

"What?" I shouted, my mouth wide open.

Brandon saw the fear and sadness in my eyes, and reached for my arm, but I quickly snatched it back. "I received a letter from the doctors stating that I may have contracted HIV from a person who was intimate with."

"Who?" I asked, staring at him wide-eyed.

"Carmen," Brandon mumbled. Before I could respond he quickly continued, "I got tested already, but the results haven't come in yet, and I always used a rubber with her." He couldn't quite meet my eyes as he spoke. Was he just embarrassed or was he lying to me?

Processing Brandon's words, I stood up, and before I could even think about the words coming out of my mouth, I yelled, "Leave my house before you infect me!" Without speaking Brandon looked at me with disgust and shook his head. He headed towards the front door, and opening the hallway closet and grabbing his coat, he walked out, slamming the front door behind him. Sitting back down on the kitchen chair, I wondered angrily if he had slept with her since we'd been together, and if I could get AIDS from kissing...

I could hear Brandon's truck tires squeal away, and at that moment my heart fell out of my chest. That could very well be the last time I would ever see Brandon. My whole life felt like it came crashing down in that moment. My teenage mind didn't know how to process all of the emotions I was feeling. My true love, my best friend, my lover, my everlasting love, had betrayed me. The one person who I thought would never abandon me, could abandon our love with a premature demise.

Before the numbness could wear off, the phone rang. On its fourth ring, irritated that Dena didn't pick up, I answered. "Hello?" I yelled with an attitude.

A shaky, squeaky voice responded, near tears. "Chena, I need to talk."

"What's wrong, April? Why are you crying, are you okay?"

"No."

"What's wrong? Where are you?"

"I'm at home. I'm pregnant! I missed my period, I know I'm pregnant."

"What! When? No, more importantly, with who?"

Choking down tears and snot, April mumbled, "George."

"Stop crying, April, everything is going to be okay, don't worry. Did you tell your mother yet?"

"No, I can't, she'll kill me, I don't want her to know, please help me."

"Okay April, calm down. I won't tell your mom, calm down. I'm going to get off the phone with you so you can think about what you want to do. If you want to keep this baby or have an abortion, this is a serious decision either way, so really think about it, and when you decide, I will help you, okay, April? So don't worry."

"Okay."

"And April?"

"Yes?"

"Stop crying, if you don't want your mom to find out."

"Okay, I'll call you tomorrow."

"Okay. If you need to talk later, just call me, okay?"

"Okay, bye," April replied, hanging up the phone.

Mind reeling with the bad news from both Brandon and April, I hid in my room. Pacing back and forth, I finally couldn't keep it in any longer. I grabbed the phone and started dialing my girls. "Hey Becky, it's Chena."

"Hey girl! What's up?"

"I need you to call all the girls, and I need you guys to come over so we can talk. It's serious. April's pregnant, and Brandon might have HIV."

"Oh my...are you serious? We'll be right over," Becky replied before hanging up the phone.

Rushing to the door before their loud knock disturbed Dena's sleep, it opened it and placed my finger over my mouth to caution Becky and Bee to be quiet. Slowly closing the front door behind them to insure it didn't slam, I ushered Becky and Bee towards my room.

"Be quiet. Dena's asleep," I said in a low whisper.

"Okay," Bee responded as she tiptoed towards my room.

"Thanks for coming. Where's Tanisha?"

"She couldn't come. Her mom was tripping about letting her out the house on a school night," Becky said, sitting down on my bed.

"Girl, what's going on?" Bee asked, sadness in her voice.

"Brandon came over earlier talking about how he might have AIDS from that bitch Carmen."

"Who's Carmen?" Bee asked, confused.

"She's his ex-girlfriend or ex-booty call, depending on who you believe."

"Do you think he had unprotected sex with her?" Becky asked in a sharp whisper.

"He said he didn't, but I don't fucking know," I said covering my face with my hands in an attempt to hold back my tears.

As I sobbed, Bee and Becky rushed towards me with open arms, attempting to console me.

"Did you have sex with Brandon?" Becky asked softly.

"No!"

"Then why are you worried?"

"Brandon might die! And we did kiss and fool around on Valentine's Day," I whispered with anger.

"Brandon's not going to die. Look at Magic Johnson! He got HIV and he's healthy," Bee said.

"Magic Johnson is rich, and Brandon's not. How is he supposed to pay for the medicine Magic Johnson uses?" Becky said, sucking her teeth at Bee.

"Well, I don't think you have anything to worry about, he said he used a rubber," Bee said in a calm tone.

"Yeah, he said he used a rubber, but he was freaking out like there could be a chance he got it."

"Maybe she sucked his dick without a condom, and that's why he's worried," Becky said nonchalantly.

Attempting to be strong, and wanting to change the subject, I blew my nose and then mustered the strength to speak. "Well, I don't want to think about Brandon right now. What are we going to do about April?"

"Do you think she wants to keep the baby?" Becky asked with a disappointed look in her eyes.

"No, but she wants to keep the whole pregnancy from her mom."

"I think she should tell her mom," Bee said, moving closer to the mirror to apply lipstick.

"What the hell you getting all glamorous for?" I asked, irritated.

"My lips are chapped, okay? And I don't have anymore lip gloss, so I'm using my lipstick. Is that okay with you?" Bee responded in an angry whisper and rolled her eyes.

"Whatever," I said as I blew my nose like it was a horn.

"Do you think April got pregnant the evening of our party?" Becky asked with anxiety.

" No, that was over five months ago, and she told me she just missed her period...but this still could ruin A.T.C.," I said, shaking my head.

"Shit, we better get April tested for HIV as well," Becky said.

"Okay, first thing tomorrow I'll make an appointment for April and myself at Planned Parenthood" I said.

"For yourself?" Bee said in shock. "But I thought you didn't have sex with him!"

"We did kiss, and he went down on me. I want to make sure I don't got nothing either, plus April won't feel like she going through this alone." Feeling emotionally drained, I cut a quick look at my digital alarm clock on my nightstand and noticed it was almost midnight. "Thanks for coming over you guys... you truly are my sisters." Trying not to tear up, I looked up at the celling then back down at them. "Y'all better go before the wicked witch wakes up and raises hell..."

*****

"Girl, I think Chena did have sex with Brandon," Becky whispered as the elevator doors closed.

"Naw, she didn't, she would have told us. Ain't no shame in her game," Bee replied.

"Then why she wanna get tested then?" Becky said, a confused look on her face.

"Maybe she just want to make double sure that while they were fooling around kissing and stuff she didn't get it. I heard this one lady got AIDS from her dentist while he was working on her tooth, so you just never know; you gotta be careful!" Bee said as she pressed the lobby button.

Damn, I hope I don't got AIDS. I slept with guys without protection before. What if Brandon do got AIDS? Becky thought.

"Are you okay?" Bee snapped at Becky.

"Ooh yeah, I'm cool. Just thinking 'bout the whole AIDS thing, you know..."

"Yeah, it's some deep shit," Bee replied. Silence surrounded the elevator and it seemed for Becky that a decade passed before the elevator arrived at the lobby floor. The thought of her having AIDS, and all the guys she had slept with without protection, weighed on her shoulders like bricks. Becky's heart pounded harder and harder and she started to become short of breath. As the elevator doors open she fell out, hitting her head right on the ground.

"Oh my God, Becky! Becky, are you okay?" Bee yelled. It was the last thing Becky heard before she passed out.

"Wake up, sweetie!"

"Grandmother?"

"Yes, baby?"

With a puzzled look and groggy voice, Becky asked, "Where am I? Why am I here?"

"Baby, you collapsed last night in the elevator. The doctors say you'll be fine. They think you had an anxiety attack...I'ma tell your uncle to come in and sit with you a bit, I gotta check on my turkey cookin' in the oven at home." Becky had avoided her uncle ever since the discovery of his secret life, and she did not want to see him now. "No, Grandmother, I just want to be alone. Can you send the doctor in? Just have Uncle take you home."

With a confused and concerned look, Becky's grandmother nodded, kissed her, and left. Becky noticed her uncle talking to her grandmother through the curtain. He seemed bothered and saddened receiving the news that she didn't want to see him. In defeat he looked back one last time towards Becky's room and walked away.

The doctor walked in twenty minuets later with Becky's chart in hand. "Hello, Becky!"

"Hi, Dr. Sims." Becky thought, Damn, why couldn't I get a doctor I didn't know, a doctor my family didn't know...

"Your grandmother said you wanted to see me?"

"Yeah, I was hoping you could run some tests on me since I was already here."

"Oh, there's nothing to worry about. You're fine! Your blood pressure is normal, and you don't have a concussion—you're as healthy as can be," the doctor said, staring at Becky's chart without making eye contact with her.

Nervous and stuttering, Becky choked out, "Uhmm...ah...I want to be tested for STDs...uhmm, like AIDS, if that's okay."

Caught off guard by Becky's request, Dr. Sims immediately looked up at her. "No problem, I'll send in a nurse right now to draw blood for the HIV test, and I'll set you up with an appointment on the fourth floor with an ob/gyn in a few hours to examine you and collect samples for the other STD tests. Now you lay here and rest; we'll be releasing you tomorrow."

The next morning when the nurse wheeled Becky to the front entrance of the hospital for pick-up, Becky had her head buried in her hands, dreading getting in the car with her grandmother and uncle or worse, her mother. She could hear a loud noise around the corner, increasing in volume as the source drew closer. Finally, she could clearly hear a familiar rap song: "Expect the Unexpected" off of the Cell Block Compilation.

"These ignorant teenagers! They got no regard for other people in this hospital, playing this loud noise!" the nurse complained under her breath. Watching the purple Camaro pull up and stop right in front of her, Becky felt a smile begin to form at the corners of her mouth.

"Hey, Becky, wake up!" Chena shouted, jumping out of the front seat to pull up the back seat for her to jump in. The nurse's face turned cherry red. Embarrassed by her earlier remarks, she stood speechless and gave a faint smile, waving to Becky as she jumped out of the wheelchair and into the car.

"Hey y'all! Thanks for picking me up."

"You know we missed you," Bee yelled, looking at her in the rearview mirror.

"Yeah, girl! Don't be scaring us like that," Tanisha said, leaning over to give Becky a hug through her seatbelt.

CHAPTER 14
LIL CHENA

Dear Diary,
I am sad
yet I cannot cry
buried inside
an empty collapsed
building,
sleeping on a cloud of
loneliness,
layered with images of
hugs from a mother,
to awake to the reality
of untouched stillness,
lying in a pile of dirt,
daydreaming for
a better tomorrow...

CHENA, THE MAKING OF AN ORPHAN

Mother rushed around the house trying to clean up, but ain't nothing to clean with and ain't no cleaning gon' change this pigsty. She had to be cleaning 'cause the social worker lady was coming. That was the only time she moved from her dented-in spot on the dirty unmade mattress that lay in the middle of her bedroom floor. Abandoning her attempt to clean an unclean house, she sat back down on her mattress. She propped her frail, malnourished body up against the wall, dressed in her usual dingy off-white robe, with an ashtray and a red pack of long skinny dark brown cigarettes next to her.

She looked like the dead body with wide-open eyes that me and my brother saw one time in an alley. She barely blinked her eyes, and she didn't move from that spot or talk. She just sat there staring into space, smoking her cigarettes one after the other.

Both bedrooms in our house were the same size, with closet doors that had been taken off their tracks, propped against the wall, and turned into slides. Dominick and I had made decorative murals on the walls with Mother's nail polish, crayons, markers, pencils, and anything else that would leave a mark. The floors were covered with stained light brown carpet. It was ruined beyond recognition from water damage, dirt, and cigarette burns. The bedrooms were bare except for a mattress laid out on each floor and six-drawer dressers, one in each room. Both dressers were full of mold from water damage, since Dominick and me turned them into big submarine boats.

On one visit, the social worker lady bent down and asked me, "Why did you destroy the furniture with water?"

I replied, "Me and my brother be playing shark boat and we...we in the ocean."

Confused by my answer, she just shook her head, mumbled, "These were just donated," and continued writing notes on her folder as she finished inspecting the house. The closet doors were dented in and cracked from being turned into slides. The remainder of the doors lay halfway against the wall and half on the stain-filled carpet.

All of our clothes were in black garbage bags lying in the closet. They didn't keep out the roaches though, and they weren't even full of clothes. Empty hangers hung in both closets; sometimes Mother would hang up her faded, torn elastic bras after she washed them in the tub. My brother and I had about three outfits between us, and three pair of PJs, all stuffed in one bag. The other bag was filled with Mother's clothes, but she mostly wore her dingy bathrobe and slippers. She even wore them to the corner store.

Mother turned the couches right side up, destroying the forts we made last night with throw pillows to block the entrance. "Get up from under there and get in that bathtub like I said!" Mother screamed in her high-pitched witch voice, clearly irritated.

"My booty still hurting," I yelled, laying in a cradled position, irritated by the moistness of the diaper I had to wear. Mother continued as if she didn't hear me, and I lay there watching the roof of our fort disappear as Mother finished turning the couch right side up.

"Fine. Go and get dressed then," Mother snarled, looking down at me.

The doctor had told us I would have to wear a diaper for three weeks and apply cream four times a day just three nights ago. Mother had left us for the night while me and my brother were still in the bathtub. Mother never told us when she was leaving, to avoid Dominick's tantrums when she deserted us. She'd just slip right out the front door and lock it behind her. We were playing in our bubble-gum-smelling bubble bath with the rubber duckies my Grannie gave us for Christmas. My Grannie got us the Mr. Bubble bubble bath, too. It was a pink liquid that even looked like bubble gum. I liked to sit and watch when Mother poured it in while the water was running, and magically the bath filled all the way up with bubbles.

Me and my brother played with our rubber duckies, we played submarine, and then we played mermaid until the water got cold and the bubbles faded away.

"I'm cold, I'm getting out," my brother said, climbing out of the tub.

"You gon' get in trouble," I said, still listening for Mother to come in and yell at us.

"Mommie ain't here no more."

"Yes she is," I said, trembling in the cold water. I sat back down in the tub, waiting for the water to warm me and peeking up to see when my brother would come back, but he didn't come back.

"Dominick, Dominick, Dooooommminiick!" I yelled.

"What?" Dominick yelled back with irritation. I stayed still, not sure what to do. "Mommie gone! Come in here, sister," he yelled from the living room, so I started to crawl out of the tub. Laying my upper body on the side of the tub, I grabbed the tub from the inside with my left hand while my face rested on the edge. I reached over and grabbed the outside of the tub with my right hand and leg. As I shifted my weight to the right side to ease myself to the ground, my left hand slipped down off the tub, making me hit the floor hard; my right butt cheek broke my fall. Still dazed from the fall, deciding if this moment required tears or not, I mumbled, "Aweee," and got to my feet, holding onto my right butt cheek and shivering. Water dripped off of me and chilled in the cool air of the room, forming a puddle on the floor and taking what little warmth I had with it.

Walking towards the living room in search of warmth, I saw a brown towel on the floor in the middle of the hallway. "Towel," I said, smiling as I picked it up and wrapped my body in it. "All better now," I said, squeezing the towel tight in my hands. Warm and reenergized, I ran full speed into the living room, holding the towel tight to my body. Dominick was sitting indian-style on the long sofa near the front window staring at the TV. I ran straight in front of the steel wall heater.

The warmth from the breath of the heater immediately warmed the towel and my little three-year-old body wrapped inside of it. A smile of satisfaction formed on my face from ear to ear while I enjoyed the euphoric rays of heat rushing through my body, heating me up from head to toe.

Dominick noticed the pleasure on my face. "Gimme the towel, I'm cold," Dominick whined.

"No, it's mine, I found it first," I said, ignoring his request. Dominick jumped off the couch and ran towards me. Pulling the towel off me, he headed back toward the couch.

"Give it back, poo-poo head!" I yelled, grabbing the bottom of the towel.

"Let go, stupid!" Dominick yelled back as he pulled the towel with all his might.

"No! Give it!" I pulled right back with all my might. I pulled the towel so hard I snatched it right out of my brother's hands and fell back onto the steel heater. A crisp sound came from my butt landing onto the face of the heater's grille.

"Awweee aweee...awwwwwww! Awwwwww!" I screamed, in full tears. The stinging intensified and engulfed my entire twenty-four-pound, three-year-old body with a burning pain. I lay on the floor crying. My brother lay next to me, holding my hand and crying too. He carefully laid the towel over my body.

"Here, sister, it okay, I'm sorry," he mumbled in a fearful and sincere tone. We laid still until we both fell asleep.

I was woken by Mother, who had moved the towel and seen the crispy bloody scabs that covered my entire bottom like a zebra print. "Come now and get up, Boo-Boo, we gotta take your sister to the hospital," she said to Dominick, shaking him awake. She didn't say a word to me and didn't make eye contact, just stood me to my feet, slid my long-sleeved flannel My Little Pony nightgown over my head and put my navy blue penny loafers on my feet. She told Dominick to put on his PJs, a jacket, and his brown open-toe sandals, and we walked out of the house. It was still dark; the sun was just peeking out. It was never-ending walk, with only the sound of crickets breaking the silence. My feet gave way halfway into the journey to the hospital, and Mother was forced to pick me up and throw me over her shoulder, carefully avoiding the blood-soaked area of my nightgown covering my bottom. She held the back of my legs for support instead. I stayed backside-up all the way through the emergency room doors of Alta Bates Hospital.

As Mother finished trying to straighten up the sofas, when I heard the doorbell ring, I dashed out of the room to see who was at the door. Mother quickly turned to me. "Get yo' ass back in the room," but I couldn't move, not today, and so I just stayed there, ignoring Mother's evil eyes and hisses. Mother rolled her eyes and turned back to the door, turning the knob and opening the door slowly. Standing in the doorway was the social worker lady. She looked like she was ready for rain, but it wasn't raining. She was wearing a clear plastic scarf over her head, smooshing her straight brown hair down. A thin shoelace connected both sides of this plastic scarf and tied under her chin in a tiny bow. The brown Isotoner gloves she wore went with her long yellow London Fog coat. Her coat was so long it almost fully covered her black slacks and brown three-inch high-heeled boots. She ducked her head frantically as she entered the house.

She still looked scared from the last time she came and was greeted by our "roommates," the roaches. Last time she had come in the front door, she had interrupted the freeway of roaches traveling above her in the doorway, and a dozen roaches immediately rained down on her. Mother had stood there with a blank expression as the social worker lady screamed and started jumping up and down. My brother and me had thought she was putting on a show, so we moved closer, sitting indian-style on the floor and laughing and clapping till our tummies hurt. After she had composed herself she continued through the house, but when she opened the hallway closet she was greeted by another dozen big black and light brown roaches on the inside of the closet door. They must have been as surprised as she was, 'cause when she opened the door, they jumped right on her arm. Guess to them it looked like she was part of the door. Today she was ready for them.

Mother was acting awful strange on today's visit, kind of how she got when she needed her medicine. She was acting real nice to this lady, offering her something to drink and inviting her to sit down. Usually Mother just let her in, gave her some fake smile, and stood motionless until the lady did her fifteen-minute sweep through the apartment. "Y'all go on now and play while I talk to the nice lady," Mother said in a nice warm voice. My brother and I got up off the floor, I grabbed Mr. Bear, and we headed towards the hallway. My brother ran forward into our room, jumping on the mattress on the floor like it was a trampoline, but I stopped halfway down the hallway. Hiding behind the wall, I hugged Mr. Bear real tight and listened.

The social worker lady cleared her throat. "Anna Mae, today's visit is serious—"

Mother cut her off frantically. "I have been trying to look for work, Miss Shelly, it just real hard with the kids being on break from preschool—"

"Anna Mae, this isn't about work. There have been some complaints about child neglect, and possibly child abuse," Miss Shelly said in an authoritative voice. There was a long silent pause. "Have the children been left alone in the house?"

"Ooh, no, never," Mother quickly lied.

"Have the children been left in the care of others, outside of their grandmothers?"

"No ma'am," Mother mumbled.

"Anna Mae, witnesses have called social services, stating that these things have happened."

Mother lost it. In her high squeaky voice, she cried out, "Well, I don't know why these people would go out they way and lie on me! I don't know why somebody wanna take my babies from me! They lying, Miss Shelly! I love my babies, they all I got! They lying, Miss Shelly!"

"Okay, calm down, Anna Mae. We just want what's best for the children," Miss Shelly responded in an unsympathetic tone. "Anna Mae, is there any food in the house for the children to eat?"

"No ma'am, I haven't had a chance to get to the super-market yet. I've been sick all week," Mother said, sounding as pathetic as possible. She even managed to squeeze out a cough.

"You received your monthly food stamps and WIC two weeks ago. There should be food here for the children," Miss Shelly said, her tone going from cool to fully irritated.

Out of nowhere I felt something pushing me from behind. I moved forward, then took a step back, trying to stay hidden behind the wall. But the push came again, and my body bolted forward. I looked behind me to see if it was Dominick, but nobody was there. "Miss Star Lady?" I whispered, trying to avoid Mother hearing me, but the Star Lady didn't appear.

I gasped at the insistent movement of my legs, startled and confused. And before I realized what was going on, the pushes from nobody and my own legs had carried me to stand right in front of Miss Shelly, still holding Mr. Bear's arm. Miss Shelly sat on the very edge of the couch with the notebook in her left hand resting on her left leg and her pen in her right hand. She quickly turned her eyes on me, making Mother spin around in the chair that she had placed in front of Miss Shelly. Mother cut me a cold chilling look, but before she could get a word out, I opened my mouth and yelled, "She be story telling! She went to the store and bought grown-up food." Miss Shelly looked at me with a puzzled look. I ran to the open kitchen and opened the refrigerator to show her a twelve-pack of silver cans with a blue bull on them. "See! She got grown-up food," I squealed.

Miss Shelly immediately stood up. "Anna Mae, this visit is over. Shame on you! I've seen what I needed to see!" She started to head for the front door. Miss Shelly was in such a hurry to leave that she didn't wait for Mother to open the door, as she usually did to avoid having to touch anything in the house. She turned the knob, swung the door wide open, and walked out, leaving the door ajar. Mother just sat in her chair, squinting her eyes from the bright sunshine that rushed in, filling up the living room with its rays.

Mother slowly got up and walked towards the door in silence. She closed and locked it, then calmly gave the door a pull to ensure that it was properly locked and closed. Then she headed into the open kitchen, which was only about three feet by three feet. It contained a sink with two cabinets underneath it, next to a narrow gas stove and a refrigerator. The refrigerator was wedged in between the stove and the edge of the square table that seated two, but only one chair could fit in the tiny space.

The kitchen was literally two feet away from the front door, allowing Mother to reach its threshold with two steps. She stood over me, piercing me with an evil grim look. All I could do was look up at her and smile, 'cause I thought we were going to the supermarket now, but before I could say a word, Mother hauled off and slapped me with her open palm, whipping my face all the way to my right shoulder. "Get your little fast, fucking ass outta my damn face!" Mother yelled at me, her voice screeching so high that I wanted to cover my ears.

All I wanted was her to get some food for kids too, instead of just grown-up food, I thought, quickly running past Mother and into the bedroom closet. I crawled under the dented wooden closet door until I felt securely hidden and shielded. It stood leaning against the wall, halfway on the carpet. Crying to myself, I stuffed Mr. Bear close to my stinging face to block the sounds of my cries so I wouldn't be discovered. I stayed crunched under that closet door for rest of the day and night, crying and wishing Miss Star Lady would come and take me far away, far far away to my real mommy, my mommy who loved me...

CHAPTER 15
CHENA

Dear Diary,
An Unwanted Seed

Forced to walk a path of thorns
She keeps her will alive
Dying day to day to survive

A flower with no sun

Has a stone in her heart
Enables her to be brave
As she scrapes for hope
On the roadside called life

A stem who grew from concrete

Wearing her concrete shoes
on a lonely path
paved with the love of God
Lifts her head up high

An orchid in full bloom

CHENA, THE MAKING OF AN ORPHAN

After our monthly A.T.C. meeting, Bee dropped Becky off at some boy's house. Fifteen minutes later I got a page from a number I didn't know with Becky's code at the end.

"Hey Bee, pull over to the next pay phone, I need to make a call."

"Okay, but it's gon' be by Eastmont mall where it smells like piss. You sure you don't want to wait till we get to Tanisha's?"

"Yeah, it's important." As Bee pulled over by the 43 bus stop, I jumped out, fumbling in my purse for my calling card. Here it is...

"Hello?"

"Hey girl, what's up? You paging me with 411."

"Oh, it wasn't nothing urgent. Uhmm, I got some tests run when I was in the hospital, and I've been too scared to go in by myself to get results, and I wanted to know if you would roll with me next week to get 'em. Did you ever get yours?" Becky asked, fear in her voice.

"Oh yeah, no prob! I already got mine though."

"When?" Becky asked with a sense of urgency.

"Right after we found out April wasn't really pregnant. Turns out she just has irregular periods 'cause she's so young. But George didn't use a condom, so she freaked out. We both got tested for STDs while—"

"Where did y'all go?" Becky asked, cutting me off midsentence.

"We got pap smears at Planned Parenthood, and they gave April a whole bunch of free condoms. She came back negative on everything except for this thing called HPV."

"HIV?" Becky yelled frantically.

"No, pee-vee. It's the Human Papilloma Virus. Lots of people get it and don't even know they have it, but if it continues to produce these antibodies it can cause cancer. But she got it treated, she's fine. Oh, and I'm fine too."

"Hurry up, Chena, we ready to go!" Tanisha yelled out of the car window.

"Uhmm, I hear Tanisha's loud-ass mouth, so I'll just hit you later when I get the date to go. Oh, and can you not tell the girls, 'cause I—"

Before Becky could finish her sentence, I responded, "My lips are sealed, I'll talk to you later."

As I jumped back in the car, Tanisha immediately asked, "So what did she want?"

"Who?"

"Yo momma, fool, you know she the only one paging you," Tanisha said, hitting me in the back of my head.

"Ooh yeah, she's just fussing at me for not doing my chorus, you know, same ole shit—"

"Hey, ain't that Brandon's truck?" Bee blurted out, cutting me off in midsentence.

Looking past the pay phone into the movie parking lot attached to the mall, I spotted it. "Yeah it is," I mumbled in shock.

"Who do you think he's here with?"

"Shut up Tanisha. Just 'cause he parked at the movies don't mean he's here on a date," Bee said, sucking her teeth and rolling her eyes at Tanisha. "It's been three weeks since you talked to Brandon. You know you want to see him, Chena," Bee continued as she made a right turn at the stop sign and headed in the direction of Brandon's truck. Brandon had gone on home study shortly after the news from Carmen. I hadn't spoken to him, and I did want to see him. There were so many things I wanted to say. I wanted to tell him I was okay, and find out if he was okay. I still didn't know if he actually had HIV, all I knew is that I didn't.

"Uhmm, what if he is on a date?" I said as my hands started to form a waterfall of moist clamminess. The more vividly the buried memories of Brandon's love returned to my thoughts, the faster my heart raced. The beat was so powerful I thought my heart would pop right out of my chest.

Walking up to the movie theater, I paused at the door, not sure if I was really ready for the truth. Before I could back up and walk away, Tanisha pushed the door open and grabbed my arm, leading me inside. "So fuck her, you know he loves you," she said in a comforting tone. "I say let's act like we have to use the bathroom and chill in the arcade while we wait for him to walk out. By the looks of the show times, the movie should be out in the next twenty-seven minutes." Tanisha grinned, obviously feeling clever that she had figured out the timing perfectly.

"Okay," I said, blood rushing to my head, my hands moving into a full on sweaty, clammy waterfall. I knew I was nervous. I didn't know what to say or what I'd do if he was with another girl; I might punch her in the face...

Standing at the edge of the arcade near the main exit, where I could see everyone, I focused my eyes on the people exiting the theaters, my heart was pounding fast. I desperately searched for Brandon's tall, muscular frame in every direction from top to bottom, with no luck. I felt that time had just frozen still. I couldn't move, I no longer heard the whispers or wisecracks from my friends, and the sound of oncoming voices slowly went silent, leaving me with just the noise of my deep thoughts, wondering if my heart would be broken, or if my love would see me and remember our bond.

My eyes searched and searched, and I caught my breath seeing any man that resembled him, but I didn't see him. I turned around, ready to give up.

"There he is, girl!" Bee exclaimed. Doing an about-face, I saw him walking out smiling with a white woman.

"Wow, he's moved onto a cougar, a cougar with a bad wig on...haha...his loss," Tanisha said, sucking her teeth.

"Girl, that looks like his momma! He ain't dating her...go say something." Bee pushed me forward, but I couldn't move, I couldn't breathe, I didn't know what to say, so I just stood still like a frozen snowman melting in the burning sun, hoping he wouldn't see me.

"Hey Brandon, Brandon! Over here!" Tanisha yelled out, standing on her tippy toes with her right arm high in the air fanning back and forth. Before I could punch her in her mouth, Brandon's eyes locked with mine and I gasped. He whispered something to the white woman and handed her his keys, then headed right toward me.

I saw Tanisha and Bee walking away in my peripheral vision, but I couldn't move. It seemed like an eternity before Brandon reached me. I couldn't help but admire his tall muscular build. He had shaved off all his facial hair; it made him look a little younger, but he still looked good. As he stopped in front of me, I looked at his hazel brown eyes and how intently they were looking into mine. Still speechless, all I could do was reach my arms around his neck and hug him. To my surprise, he not only hugged me back, he picked me up off the ground and spun me around.

"Chena, baby, I missed you so much!" When he releasing me, I just looked at him and silence took over. "Well, say something," he said with a confused look at my weird behavior.

"Ummm...ahhh...who was that white lady?"

Caught off guard by my rude question, Brandon's face twisted up into a confused, irritated expression. "That was my moms."

"Oh," I mumbled, quickly looking down at the ground in embarrassment. "Well, I'm glad I ran into you, I...wanted to call you, but your number was changed and you stopped coming to class, so I didn't know what happened...If you had H—"

Brandon cut me off before I could complete my nervously delivered sentence. "No, I'm fine, no HIV," Brandon said, looking around to make sure our conversation was private. Clearing his throat, he looked back down at my vulnerable eyes. I hung onto his every word. "Let me get you my number. We have so much to catch up on. I don't want to rush this conversation," Brandon's said in a sincere comforting voice, then looked up towards the exit, "and my moms is waiting."

Brandon scrambled for a pen in his back pocket, and looked behind him. "Be right back," he said, then ran over to the concession stand. Returning with a big smile on his face, he passed me a napkin with his number written on it. He smiled, put the napkin in my hand, then gave my hand a tight squeeze. "Call me," he whispered, and walked past me shaking his head. Frozen still and speechless, I watched him until his image became a blur. My eyes never left his tall figure...

Carefully folding the napkin, I placed it in the inside pocket of my purse, next to my calling card. The hazy daydream of happily every after began to wear off and reality crept back into my brain. Okay, he may have a new number, but mine hasn't changed. I haven't moved and I still work at the same damn department store....Why is he acting so excited to see me when he didn't reach out?...I'm not calling him!

"Hey zombie girl, stop daydreaming and tell us what happened!" Bee yelled out behind my head, scaring the hell out of me.

"Where did you guys go?"

"Uhmm, spill it, what did he say?" Tanisha asked, ushering me towards the glass doors of the theater.

"We really didn't get to talk 'cause he was with his mom, but he did give me his new number."

"That's it, that's all he said?" Bee said, sucking her teeth.

"Yeah, but he did give me a big ole hug, spinning me around like he missed me. But I don't get why he just went M.I.A. on me."

"Well, the last time y'all saw each other you told him not to infect you. Maybe that's why he kept his distance."

"He said he didn't have it, so I don't know...well, I got his number now," I said, shrugging my shoulders.

"Well, when we get to my house you should call him," Tanisha said, still filled with excitement.

"I can't," I mumbled, still pondering the fact that he had just disappeared without a word, just abandoned me without a second thought.

"Duh, she needs her privacy," Bee said, pressing the unlock button on her clicker four times so everyone could see she was the owner of the tightest car in the parking lot.

At home I busted in the front door and spread the mail out over the kitchen table to sort through it. Okay, today is the last day...either I'm in or I'm not... Oh God, please let me get my acceptance letter to CAL Bezerkeley...okay, here goes nothing. Bill, bill, bill, oouee, East Bay magazine, mine! Bill. Mine—UC Santa Claus, UC LALA...My heart began to race as I tore open the letter from UC LALA. My eyes narrowed in as I begin to read each word as if my life depended on what was on the page in front of me: "Dear Chena Johnson, Thank you for your application to our College of Letters and Science. We regret to inform you—" Tears building in my eyes, I crumpled the paper in the palm of my hands. I don't know why I even fucking opened it, I get it by now, the small envelopes are rejection letters, and the large ones are acceptance letters...no need to open UC Santa Claus or UC Division's large envelopes,

I already know I'm in...Fuck, if I didn't get into UC LALA, chances are I didn't get into CAL Bezerkeley...

My self-pitying thoughts were brought to a screeching halt by the alarming sound of Dena's bitching voice. "Hey, what did I tell you about leaving the door open?" Dena yelled from the living room. Irritated by her comment, abandoned my mission to run into my room and bury my tears into my pillow, did an about-face, and headed toward the front door, where I slammed it shut with all my might. Fuck her rules, I thought, but before I could hit the hallway towards my room, she blocked my path with her tall frame, staring down at me with angry green and hazel eyes. "What the hell is your problem, slamming my door like you grown and pay bills in here!" she said.

Rage and frustration crept up in me, quickly spreading through out my body; dropping the crumpled admissions letter out of my tight grasp, no longer able to hold back my tears, I exploded. I pushed past Dena's tall stick figure, yelling, "Fuck, I don't have time for this shit! I didn't get in...I didn't get in! I got another rejection letter, okay?" I made my way into my room, slamming the door behind me.

I put my head down on my pillow and cried for over twenty minutes. When I finally looked at the clock, I realized I had only thirty minutes before I missed my Fremont train. I have to get ready for work! Where's my black tights? Where's my B.A.R.T. ticket? Shuffling through my purse for my Hello Kitty wallet, I pulled out my B.A.R.T. ticket from where I had carefully placed it behind my bus pass. Okay, cool, I got three dollars left on it. That saves me ten minutes, I won't have to go to the ATM. Quickly I threw on my black ski pants with my black tight-fitting wife beater and my knee-high black boots.

Dressed and ready to go, I grabbed my long black and orange FUBU windbreaker and headed out the door, but before I could turn the handle on the front door I was stopped by Dena.

"Hey, come here."

"Yes," I mumbled, as I released my hand from the door handle and headed into the living room to face Dena, who surprisingly was looking at me with caring eyes.

"Don't you leave this house mad. God has a plan for you, and no matter what happens, it is in his plan." Nodding dutifully at Dena, trying to smile without tearing up, I thought about how I'd heard this saying over and over my entire life, and how God has never left my side. I moved towards Dena's open arms and hugged her.

I rushed out the house, now with less than fifteen minutes before I missed my train. Briskly I walked down S and L Boulevard, and almost out of breath, I managed to make it. Right on time...I saw my train pulling up as I slid my B.A.R.T. ticket through the terminal. The machine sucked it in the front and quickly popped it out again at the top, next to a little light that turned from red to green as the flaps on the doors retracted inward to let me pass. I briskly walked through, the flaps closed behind me, and I ran up the escalator.

"Fremont train!" announced the computer-generated voice over the intercom system. I walked into the train and sat right in my favorite window seat. Reaching into my purse for my lip gloss, I felt a napkin. Pulling it out, I realized I had forgotten to call Brandon. I'll call him tomorrow.

"Hey baby!" Sarah greeted me as I arrived at the counter.

"Hi Sarah. How was your day?"

"It was slow. I'm sure glad to see your pretty face, though. You get your dress for prom yet?"

"No, I'm not sure if I'm gonna go," I replied with defeat.

"Baby, you have to go! You only get one senior prom."

"Well, I guess I gotta find a date first."

"Well, I'm sure the boys are lined up around the corner for you," Sarah said as she grabbed her purse and walked out from behind the makeup counter. Looking past her, I suddenly noticed Becky leaving her station with two security guards and heading upstairs. Sarah paused, noticing my wandering gaze, and looked back to see what I was staring at. She turned back to me with a disappointed expression, shaking her head. As she walked away she mumbled, "Can't bite the hand that feeds you. That child just lost her job..."

I immediately turned to use the phone by the register and paged Becky to see what was up. I waited and waited but she didn't come back downstairs. Then Evelyn, the cosmetics manager, a sweet pretty petite Filipino lady, came down the escalator and started walking toward me. She wore six-inch-high white stiletto heels that matched her two-piece white and navy suit. Oh shit, gotta look busy! I immediately started reorganizing the shelves and dusting the display cases.

"Chena."

"Hi, Evelyn."

"Hi, sweetie, can you please come into my office? I need to speak with you."

I swallowed, a big lump in my throat. My heart started beating fast. "Sure," I replied with a fake smile painted on my face. Am I in trouble? I've never been late, I've never missed a shift, I wonder what's wrong. Following her into her office, I sat down immediately. Evelyn closed the door behind me, and put her hand on my shoulder.

"I have some good news, and I have some bad news. First, we've terminated your friend Becky's employment with Lacy's. She's had quite a number of missed shifts due to her modeling work, and recently we've also come to suspect that she has been stealing from the store. As I'm sure you realize, theft cannot be tolerated. I'm afraid we had no other choice but to let her go." Wow! I can't believe this...poor Becky. I kept my face absolutely still. If they didn't have proof Becky was stealing, then maybe they wouldn't be calling the police on her.

"That means we're looking for a new Girl Friends sales associate, and we think you would be perfect. The position pays three dollars per hour more than your current position, and you would receive an instant three hundred dollar gratis of Girl Friend products." Silence filled the room as my brain tried to process both the benefits of this offer and the reality of Becky's actions. Just as I was about to respond, Evelyn abruptly sat down at her desk and looked at her computer. "I know you and Becky were close friends, and I could hire from outside, as I have five qualified candidates available, but I'd much rather hire from in-house, so please think it over and let me know by tomorrow."

Speechless and confused, I stood up and began walking towards her office door. Turning around to meet Evelyn's piercing slanted eyes, I smiled at her. "Okay, thank you," I said gratefully.

Standing back at the counter and looking into the mirror, I wiped the eye boogers from my earlier tears out of the corners of my eyes, then began to apply a little blush to my cheeks. I was interrupted by Rosa, a pretty Hispanic lady in her early thirties. Flattening her red Lancome cosmetic smock with her hands, she reached inside her front pocket and pulled out some liquid eyeliner.

"You want me to do your eyes mija?" Rosa asked in her heavy Spanish accent. Rosa always did my eyeliner; she said it made my big almond-brown eyes pop.

"Yes, please!"

"Okay, sit right here." She patted her makeup chair. Placing the blush back on the display case, I came from behind my counter to sit at the Lancome counter.

"Damn, this light is still out." Rosa beckoned me to move over to the Girl Friends counter. Everyone knew that Girl Friends had the best everything; since they sold the most product, they had top-of-the-line everything, from chairs to lights. They even had their own surround sound, where they controlled their own music. Their sales associates didn't even have to wear uniforms, they just had to be trendy and stylish. "Sit still, mija, or I'ma paint your nose." With both my eyes tightly closed and holding as still as possible, I sat and let Rosa do her magic. "Okay, almost done," Rosa whispered, putting on the last touches. She always included a little glitter in my creases; she knew I loved glitter. "Okay, all done. Take a look." I grabbed the hand mirror from Rosa and a fat grin ran across my face as I looked. I love it! Wish I had somewhere to go to show it off...

"Thank you, Rosa! You always make me look pretty."

"Hey mija, isn't that your mom over there?"

Before I could answer, Dena stood in front of me with a large envelope in her hand, laughing and looking like she had just won the lottery.

Confused as to her giddiness, I asked, "What are you doing here?"

"You got in!" Dena said with the biggest smile on her face I had ever seen.

"What are you talking about?" Irritated and confused, I batted down the damn large gold and blue envelope that she kept pushing in my face.

"It was put in 103's mailbox by mistake, she brought it over after you left for work." Rolling her eyes at the confused look on my face, Dena yelled, "You got in, silly! Into CAL!"

My face instantly filled with joy. I looked down at the envelope and finally realized what she was talking about. It was a fat envelope from CAL...UC Bezerkeley... which means...

"I got in!" Screaming at the top of my lungs and jumping in the air, I ran from behind the counter and jumped into Dena's arms. I couldn't hold back the tears. My legs almost collapsed at the news. Emotion took over my whole body. I was so so so so happy! All my hard work paid off, all those honors classes, the late night studying for tests, the tutoring sessions...it all paid off. I was going to the best college in the world! It was the happiest moment of my life. I made it out the 'hood, I'm gonna make it! I screamed in my thoughts. Overwhelmed and crying, Dena hugged me tighter and we both sobbed with joy for what seemed an eternity. We made so much noise that Lacy's department store shoppers and employees stopped to inquire what was wrong.

"Oh my God mija, that is wonderful news! Chena is going to UC Bezerkeley!" Rosa shouted for onlookers to hear. With tears streaming down my face, I turned to look at Rosa and the proud look on her face. I hugged her too. As happy as I was feeling, a homeless man who hadn't bathed in six months could have gotten a hug from me...even the homeless guy who hit Becky's car.

CHAPTER 16
LIL CHENA

Dear Diary,
Is anyone there? Does anybody care?

Did I exist in her world
Or was I just make believe?
Just a seed spawned from ecstasy
Is anyone there? Does anybody care?

I'm looking for some reality
That I can touch, feel
Without pain

Is anyone there? Does anybody care?

Am I a figment of her imagination
Is she even aware
Her blank eyes, her cold stares

Is anyone there? Does anybody care?

To her I'm an abomination
Who just won't die
I'm crying
I'm screaming
I'm fighting for help

Is anyone there? Does anybody care?

CHENA, THE MAKING OF AN ORPHAN

Mother hadn't spoken to me or even looked at me since Miss Shelly had left two days ago. I didn't leave my hidden place, not even to go to the bathroom. I just went in my diaper. Laying on my stomach, I felt my soggy diaper full of poo poo and pee pee.

"Sister...sister," Dominick whispered as he entered the bedroom. "Sister!" he whispered louder as he looked behind the dresser.

"Here, brother," I whispered.

"Sister, you stinky," my brother mumbled as he slid into the darkness under the dented closet door, nearly bumping his head into mine. As he entered my wooden cell, Dominick coughed and held his nose. He handed me a piece of bread that was carefully rolled up into a ball.

"T'ank you," I said, as my eyes widened with the realization that this is food.

Dominick quickly crawled out on his knees, still holding his nose, but once he reached the light, he filled his little lungs with air, like he was a vacuum. Squeezing Mr. Bear real tight with my right arm, I sat up and positioned myself indian-style and began to eat the moist and doughy ball. Enjoying the cool moist meal in my mouth, I began to chew quickly from hunger, until every bite of the rolled-up slice of bread was gone. My tummy was so empty, and it was still growling. It gave off a growling bubble that got so loud that I thought Mother would hear it and find me in my hiding place. I began to lick my fingers, which still had the residue of the sticky dough on it, until there was no more flavor left. My bottom began to sting real bad, making me quickly unfold my legs and stretch forward back onto my stomach.

Lying now on my knees with my chest on the ground and butt in the air, with Mr. Bear under my head as a pillow, I suddenly remembered. The doctor told Mother to put some medicine on my bottom four times a day. Mother hadn't put any on, she just put it behind the mirror in the bathroom. My Grannie always said, "If you don't put rubbing alcohol on them cuts, splinters, and blisters after you get 'em, you can get an infection called gain green, and die." I don' wanna die wit' gain green butt, I thought, trying to build the courage to move.

A noise in the hallway startled me, and my heart started racing, for fear Mother was looking to punish me again, but the footsteps stopped short before the entrance into the bedroom and moved towards the living room. I laid as still as a mouse, not wanting to be seen or heard. I held my breath, and only released it after I hear the front door open and close. When I heard the lock being turned by keys from the outside I knew immediately that Mother had left the house. Not yet sure if she was tricking me, I crawled backwards on my knees out of my hidden space, making sure to leave Mr. Bear tightly hidden. I stood up and tippy-toed to the bedroom door. When I peeked out, I didn't see anybody, so I crept out into the hall-way far enough to see the living room, where I saw Dominick laying on his back in his birthday suit, with one leg propped up and crossing the other, forming a T. His hands clasped behind his head, he stared at the Thundercats cartoon on the big ole TV.

"Brother...brother!" I whispered, catching Dominick's attention. "She gone?" I asked, hugging the wall like Spiderman and creeping my head forward just two inches toward the edge of the hall doorway.

"Yep!" he said with excitement and a smile, then he quickly turned his head back to the TV.

"Brotheeeeer, watch for she be at the door," I said.

"Okay," Dominick replied, keeping his eyes focused on the TV. Turning around slowly I walked into the bathroom, and immediately pulled down my soggy diaper and kicked it to the side. I put the toilet seat lid down and climbed on top of it to reach the sink. I turned both knobs on the sink, and then turned my body around to face the celling and grasp ahold of the sides of the sink, like I was holding the toilet seat to make sure I didn't fall in the bowl as I scooted my booty towards the sink. My legs hung over the sink and my ankles rested on the toilet paper holder. The warm water hit my tailbone first, before sliding down my butt cheeks.

"Awweeee! Aweeee!" I screamed in tears. But I didn't want to get gain green, so I kept ignoring the pain and moved my rear end around, with my arms holding my bottom up and my legs securely pinned down onto the side of the sink. I moved my booty forward, backwards, right, and left to let the running water clean all the poo poo and pee pee.

"What you doing, sister?" my brother screamed from the living room. Except for screams of agony, I didn't answer him, and within a blink of an eye, he was running toward me from the living room, stopping dead in his tracks by the awful smell as he entered the bathroom. "Ooh, you stinky...you smell like ka-ka! Yucky!" my brother said, backing up and holding his nose with both his hands. Before Dominick could say another word, we heard a knock, and quickly turning his head, he looked toward the front door. "Who is it?" he yelled.

A woman's voice replied, "Hello, hello, Anna Mae?"

Dominick wasn't sure what to say, so he just turned and looked at me, still sitting on the sink with my butt in the bowl, and shrugged his shoulders. We heard the sound of keys turning in the front door.

"Mommie at the door!" my brother yelled.

There was another few hard knocks. "Open up, it's the police!" a man's voice screamed. Then we heard the sound of both locks being unlocked, and a creak as the door swung open. I managed to climb down from the sink, leaving the water running. But just as I was making my way off the toilet seat, I got caught looking like a deer in headlights, watching the sunlight usher Miss Shelly, two men dressed in green pants and tan shirts with gold metal stars on the right side of their chests, and the Chinese man who lives upstairs who Mother calls "the landlord" into the apartment.

Their eyes all looked at me with contempt as I stood with one foot on the edge of the toilet and the other leaning towards the floor. They took a quick look into the living room as they moved into the apartment.

"I told you, she no here with her kids, and she no pay rent!" the landlord said, frustrated, throwing his arms in the air as he turned around and walked out the front door.

"Who are you?" my brother asked, with fear in his voice.

"It's going to be okay. We're the good guys, and we're here to take you away," one of the officers replied with a warm gentle smile on his face.

"Oh my God," Miss Shelly gasped, clenching her nose with her hand as she peeked over me into the bathroom, looking down at the soiled diaper.

Miss Shelly managed to locate my My Little Pony fleece nightgown and put it over my head as I slid my arms into the sleeves. She told my naked brother to put some clothes on too. He grabbed his Transformers T-shirt and some green flannel pajama bottoms. "Okay children, let's go. Make sure to grab your favorite toys," Miss Shelly said, as she looked around the empty room that was supposed to be ours. I walked past her, exposing my nude burned bottom as I held my nightgown up so that the back of the rough material would not rub against it.

Falling to my knees, I quickly crawled under the closet door into my former prison cell and grab Mr. Bear with my left arm. My brother grabbed his red and blue Transformers toy truck and an oversized seashell that Mother gave to him and told him she got from a mermaid. After Miss Shelly and the officers shuffled back and forth between the two bedrooms to find matching pairs of shoes and coats for us, we went out the door and climbed in the back of Miss Shelly's brown Nissan Sunny. Miss Shelly placed a brown bath towel that she had grabbed off our sofa on the back seat for me to sit on. After securely tucking the length of the towel into the crease of the brown bench seat of her compact Nissan sedan, she picked me up and carefully placed me on top of the towel. "This is for your burns, sweetie," she said in a neutral tone.

Dominick squealed, laughing, "Sister stinky butt!" Ignoring Dominick's advances to play with his pokes to my side and pulls on Mr. Bear's arm, I sucked my teeth and turned my head.

"'top it, brother!" I screamed as I snatched Mr. Bear's right arm from Dominick's grip. Holding Mr. Bear tighter to my face and resting my chin on the top of his head, I looked out the car window with relief and joy, as Miss Shelly drove us away from a home that we would never again have to call our own.

CHAPTER 17
CHENA

Dear diary,

On the church steps
Of the last supper,
Looking at the sunlit sky,
Listening to trains go by.

I see love sculpted in the clouds like a
detailed lie.
Words are crafted and painted by
pure lust,
Displayed as musical notes to the
naive ear.

I should have known from the start
This union would fall apart
But I was bound with hope

An architectural vision of eternal bliss
Blown to bits!...

Dumbfounded as to why,
The sudden destruction of me over and
Over again is

Caused by good-byes....

CHENA, THE MAKING OF AN ORPHAN

Happy to have the house to myself for the weekend while Dena was off for a girls' weekend out at a spa in Napa valley, I sat on my daybed staring out the window at the B.A.R.T. trains going by at an unreal speed. Dena wouldn't be back until Sunday; what would I get into this Friday night? Blue sky and white clouds completed the image of a perfect bright sunny day. Sitting here with the sun tingling on my face and warming my hands, I was having a nearly out-of-body experience, reflecting on my life.

The memories of Miss Star Lady rushed into my head, and for the first time in a long time, I thought about Dominick. What happened to him? Miss Shelly tried to keep us in touch after we were separated as children, but it never seemed to work out. An unpleasant update from a newspaper two years ago, featuring a teenaged gun shot victim is all I had on him, leaving me to wonder Why he choose such a destructive path for his life? I can only hope getting shot in the neck and chest, after a failed home robbery would set him on a straighter path.

Memories of Mother and all her special friends flooded my thoughts like a rushing tide. It was just too painful, it was starting to feel surreal. I started rubbing my hand over my forehead as if to wipe those thoughts and memories out of my head. Weird!...I don't hear the noise of the train, or anything for that matter. Is there something wrong with my ears? My eyes began to fixate on the smoothness of the trains sliding by. My heartbeat slowed and my breathing became virtually undetectable. My calm mediative state was abruptly disturbed by the obnoxious ring sounding from my alarm clock.

"Five p.m. already!" I slapped the top of the alarm clock with ease. "Thank God I don't have to get ready for work today!" I should have felt relief, but instead I felt uneasiness. This familiar feeling was the same feeling I got before every track meet, or when I had to get in front of a group and speak. My heart pounded harder and harder as I scrambled to control my thoughts. I'm not ready to say goodbye to life as I've known it! Damn, time flies...two weeks ago I got my golden letter, and I graduate next month. It's too soon! I'm going to be an adult; yes, legal to do as I please, but how will I survive? I got into the college of my dreams, but I'm alone with no support and I still haven't told my friends...

I grabbed my purse and started searching it. Digging frantically through an empty purse, unzipping and re-zipping, emptying the contents from the side pockets, I can't find anything that looks like a napkin.

"Oh no, it's gone!" I yelled. "Fuck! Where would I have put it? Think, Chena! Think!" Completely frustrated and mad at myself for losing it, I kicked my trashcan and watched it fall over, screaming. The contents hit the ground and infuriated me even more. I had just dumped all the ashes from two weeks of incense burning, along with the dusty contents of the vacuum bag, all over my white carpet...staring at the mess got me more upset by the second. Feeling like the Incredible Hulk as the rage built inside me, I yelled, "I hate this fucking small-ass room! I hate this stupid-ass room! I can't find shit in here!" I simultaneously turned into a maniac, throwing papers and books in every direction.

In the midst of creating this startling tornado of destruction I instantly regretted it as I watched the pencil holder that I had made of paper-mache when I was eight shatter as it bounced off the wall and landed on the floor. Inflamed by the destruction of my summer camp creation, I kicked over my thirteen-inch all-white television with built-in VHS player. I felt gratified at the resulting loud thumping noise it made as it landed on the floor. Returning my attention to my desk, I saw the CDs that were stacked neatly on the corners, like the fake stories of my perfect childhood I fed to strangers and friends. At a distance they looked perfect, sitting perfectly neatly on this small white wooden desk, but at a closer glance, one could see the cracks in the cases, and the scratches on the discs.

"Fuck these CDs!" I screamed, allowing a sense of release to take over my body as I watched them all crash to the floor after one quick swipe of my right hand. The cracks on the cases widened as the CDs flew across the room, landing upside down and sideways. Sweating, breathing hard, and in full tears, I fell to the floor. I searched for my breath, unable to find it. Hyperventilating, I began to black out. What's wrong with me? Am I having a nervous breakdown? Fuck, is it hitting me, am I going crazy like my mother? Am I schizophrenic?

Twenty minutes later, sprawled out on the floor with dried tears crusting my eyes and trails of dried saliva at the corners of my mouth, I began to calm down. Exhausted, I felt like a child who had tired herself from a temper tantrum. My heart rhythm began to slow, and the hard thumps that had been beating out of my chest slowly faded into a soft quiet peaceful stillness. Taking in full long inhales, now completely calm, I freely allowed the tears to fall from my eyes, releasing the strain to hold them in.

I realized that my body was yearning for a hug, a gesture of love. I felt so alone. Laying in stillness, listening to my heartbeat without blinking, put me further into a mindset of loneliness and abandonment. Trying to pull myself out of this pity party, I rehearsed the speech in my head that I had always given myself over and over again my entire life. Chena, things could be worse. You could have been an orphan in Africa like those kids on the "Feed the Children" commercials. So what if you don't have parents? You have your health and a roof over your head and clothes on your back. Suck it up! And so I did. In full realization of how blessed I truly was, I laid there in stillness, feeling a little silly at the tantrum I had just thrown.

My eyes focused on the trash flowing over the floor like lava flowing from an island volcano. The sight of the grey-brown colorful mess irritated me. Squinting to clear my sight and pushing the last tears out of my eyes, I focused in on something white poking out of the dusty gray particles that engulfed the carpet like a mud bath on white skin. It was the napkin with Brandon's number! I wanted him to be the first to receive the good news.

Wiping the smeared dust off of the napkin, I positioned myself indian-style on the floor with my back against the drawers of my daybed. Hesitating to move for fear of bring-ing on another panic attack, I managed the strength to reach for the phone to call Brandon, but I couldn't dial. What's wrong with me? I just saw him two weeks ago. Am I afraid of rejection? No! I'm just bitter at the fact that he did not reach out to me for two fucking months and just fell off the face of this earth. Shit, he still ain't called. Fuck him, I'm not calling him!

Pulling the long silver antenna out of my ancient cordless phone, I began dialing Becky, trying to call to mind the right words to break the ice. I can ask her when she wants me to go to the doctor with her. I don't know why she still salty that she got fired from Lacy's and I got asked to be promoted to her position. I don't know why she's tripping, it's not like I didn't ask her if she would be okay with it before I accepted! Shit, I have to save all the money I can! I had to pay for my own senior pictures and my prom dress.

Ring! Ring! Ring! Twirling my hair with anxiety, I decided I would hang up on the fourth ring, but Becky picked up.

"Hey girl!" I said.

"Hey, who is this?" Becky replied with annoyance in her voice.

"It's Chena."

"Oh. What's up?" Becky said. I could hear her sucking her teeth on the line, most likely mad that my number comes up blocked in her caller ID.

"Is this a bad time or something?" I asked, hurt by her response.

"No, it's all good, I just don't feel good. But what's up?"

"Oh, ummm, I was calling to...see when you wanted to go to pick up your results and to tell you that I got into UC Bezerkeley," I said, failing to hold in my excitement.

"Oh, well I went already and got them, thanks!" Becky said sarcastically.

"Yeah, that's cool. So I take it everything is all good?"

"Yep, all gravy," she said nonchalantly. Silence filled the line. I pulled the phone away from my ear to see if the power light was showing green. I can't believe this bitch still hasn't told me congratulations yet, I thought.

"So did you hear what I just said?" I replied with as much attitude as I could muster.

"Yeah,...that's great for you. I got in too, but I'm not going to go 'cause they don't offer a full ride for cheerleading." I bit my tongue to hold in my thoughts. This lying bitch has got to be kidding me! She went on home study three months ago, which does not get favor from admission boards, and the coursework is a joke. Not to mention she's not even on the cheerleading team; she may have made it in September, but she quit the team after two fucking weeks since it supposedly conflicted with her modeling.

Making every effort to sound sincere, I replied, "Oh that's silly! That's great you got in too. You should still go, take loans or something for the difference, we can have classes together." Silence fell on the line again, allowing me to hear with crystal clarity the sound of a man's voice in the background. "Shhhhh!" Becky quickly hissed, while muffling the phone with her hand. Clearly she did not want me to hear who was in the room, but it was too late—I heard him loud and clear. "Hey girl, I, I—" Becky said nervously.

"All right girl, I know you're busy. I'll catch up with you later," I quickly blurted, cutting her off in midsentence, before pressing the power button and slamming the phone down.

Tears welled in my eyes. This time they were not from sadness or happiness. Running to the bathroom, I turned on the cold water, letting it fill my cupped palms and then splashing it on my face. Trying to convince myself that the unthinkable couldn't be true, I looked in the mirror at the disbelief written all over my face. I tried not to jump to crazy conclusions. "I'll just call," I said out loud, wiping my face with a towel, regaining a cool head. I headed back to my room with four steps, feeling calm and collected, on a mission to find the truth. Stepping over my thirteen-inch television, which rested on the floor right in front of my doorway, I began dialing the numbers on the crumpled napkin. The phone rang, and rang, and rang, and rang. I skillfully pressed the power button on the cordless, which was glued to my ear and shoulder, with my right hand while at the same time putting on my Nike Air Max with my left hand. I knew what I had to do.

Preparing myself at the speed of light to whoop ass was actually quite calming: brush my hair, put it in a bun, apply Vaseline to my entire face, remove my earrings, ensure there are no dangling objects hanging on my clothing that could rip or tear, put rings with sharp edges on as many fingers as possible. "Done," I said, rushing out the door, my heart beginning to race as if it was falling out of my chest. Fight or flight, that's what I learned about animals in school. Why didn't I learn about back stabbers?

My fast-paced walk quickly turned into a cheetah run, and I sprinted all three long blocks to Becky's apartment complex in less then ten minutes. As I contemplated my course of action, I looked into the street and saw clear as day a bright candy-red truck on twenty-twos parked right across the street. Blood boiling, nearing explosion, not thinking, I kicked the glass door of the building. "Ooouch!" I yelled. Apparently the fucking door was made of steel. "Fuck!" I yelled out in frustration, laughing to myself as I paced back and forth. Luckily, my anger seemed to block the pain my big toe.

I ran toward the truck, my keys already in my hand in position to stab. Avoiding oncoming traffic, I made it to the truck, which once held so many warm memories. Enraged from Brandon's betrayal, I quickly made my way all around the car with my house key firmly in my hand as if I was holding a pencil, and I began decorating the candy-red paint with my personal "fuck you" signature. As I admired my artwork, it became clear the tires needed some attention too. I frantically looked for a sharp object to stab the tires.

It was my lucky day. A crowbar and a screwdriver lay in the bed of the truck. I took the screwdriver and carefully wedged it into the edge of his back tire between the rim and the thin rubber surrounding the shining rim. I used my foot as a hammer to drive it in, and air gushed out, flattening the tire instantly. I went around the car, quickly flattening the remaining three tires. Just as I was about to reach for the crowbar to smash the windows, I noticed a red light blinking inside the car. A fucking car alarm! Ha! It clearly doesn't work! Looking up from the blinking light, I saw a black and white police car heading toward me. I quickly ducked down on the side of the truck. Fuck! I hope they didn't see me. Damn, I'm going to jail.

I peeked my head out, trying to control my heart from falling out of my chest. I looked up just in time to watch the police car drive on. They passed right by without apparently noticing the newly-customized lowrider sitting on flats with a zebra-striped design.

When the police were completely out of sight I made my move, dashing across the street. How am I going to get into the building? I thought, pacing back and forth in front of the entrance with the Vaseline now melting into my eyes. I felt like a piece of fried chicken. To my surprise I saw the doors open. Yes! I squeezed past the elderly couple coming out the door fast enough to catch the second inner door before it shut and locked. I stepped into the elevator with revenge on my mind and malice in my heart. I should have brought the damn crowbar with me. Damn. Watching the lights light up announcing the floors I was passing up caused my heart to pound faster and faster as I approached the seventh floor. A loud chime rang from the elevator and the doors opened.

CHAPTER 18
CHENA

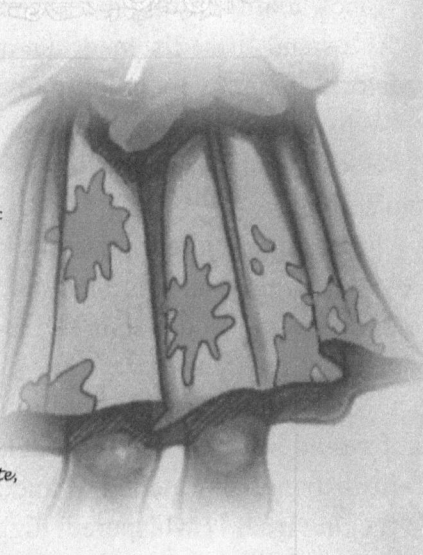

Dear Diary,

My face hasn't changed
I haven't gained weight,
But the unspoken truth is
I'm no longer his cake

He used to adore me
placed me high on the shelf
Every chance he got
he'd indulge himself

In my spirit with a kiss,
kind words, and a touch
Leading to love

What the F
has changed?
Nothing with me,

I'm still that German Chocolate,
carmel sexy sweet.

In the box I'll go back,
no longer to be opened

Picked at and heartbroken

CHENA, THE MAKING OF AN ORPHAN

Walking down the hallway with fists balled and heart racing, I felt like a hunter about to make my first kill. Five feet ahead of me voices came from directly around the edge of the corner before you turned right into the hallway leading to Becky's apartment. I stopped dead in my tracks as I recognized the voices, reality hitting me like a ton of bricks.

At a standstill, I listened like an animal in a forest wary of predators, instinctively holding my breath.

"Why are you leaving like this?"

"Becky, you know why. It's just not cool. I already told you what's up."

"Fine, nigga, then leave! Y'all all the same anyway!" Becky screamed and slammed her front door. I quickly opened the door leading to the stairwell and hid behind it, but cracked it open just enough to see who was walking by without being seen. My heart was racing, and I had to hold my breath for fear that I would be discovered from the noise of my breathing.

In disbelief, I watched Brandon turn the corner. "Noooo! It's fucking true!" I whispered, digging my nails into my palms, making my balled fist as firm as a baseball.

"Crazy bitch," Brandon muttered, shaking his head. Looking down, he was caught completely off guard as I swung the stairwell door open right into his face, knocking him to the ground instantly. Stepping in front of him, I looked around to see if anyone was coming or opening their doors to investigate the loud noise of Brandon's 6'4" frame hitting the ground like the giant who fell from the beanstalk in the sky. There was only silence and no movement from Brandon. I moved in closer to see if he was still breathing.

"Brandon, are you okay?" I whispered, now crouching closer to his face. Even in my rage, looking at him lie there with a fat knot the size of a boulder forming on his forehead, I still could not deny how fine he was. As I hovered over him, watching him lying there in a peaceful coma-like state, all of the memories of us laying together in the Marriott hotel happy and in love filled my thoughts. Holding back tears, I quickly snapped out of my daydream and returned to reality with the abrupt rising of his chest as he inhaled and exhaled unconsciously.

Receiving confirmation that he was still alive somehow angered me. Jumping back up to my feet, I gave him the hardest kick I could to his thigh. He didn't move. Disgusted and enraged, I headed toward Becky's front door like a bull ready to charge. Cleverly standing at an angle to avoid being seen through her peephole, I knocked on the door with three light knocks. To my surprise, she didn't ask who it was, but instead quickly opened the door with a huge smile on her face. I bet she thought I was Brandon.

"Surprise, bitch!" I snapped at her, pushing her through the doorway. Her smile disappeared instantly when my right fist slammed her right in the eye. I said nothing as I delivered punch after punch, forcing her away from the front door into the middle of her living room until she stumbled backwards, falling onto her wooden coffee table.

"What the fuck!" Becky attempted to scream, her voice making a thick gargling sound through the blood in her mouth. Before she could try again, my foot kicked her in the stomach, tumbling her to the floor. Jumping on top of her in a straddling position, I began slapping her upside her head with an open hand like a wild woman.

"You fucking bitch! You fucking backstabbing bitch! I loved you like a sister!" I shouted at the top of my lungs. "Why

did you have to sleep with Brandon? You fucking whore!"
Wrapping my hands around her neck, I began choking her with
all my might. "Ooouch! You fucking bitch!" I screamed as
Becky's nails dug into the flesh of my forearms like a tiger's,
causing me to release her neck.

Without hesitation I grabbed her hair and and knocked her
head against the floor like a rag doll. Completely worn out
and exhausted, I released her head from my grasp and begin to
unstraddle her. I slid off her, pressing my knee into her stomach. Remaining on my knees facing her, I picked up a wooden
coaster off the floor and threw it at her. She made no attempt to
retaliate. She just blocked her face with her hand, attempting to
nurse her bloody nose. "Yeah, just lay there choking and crying
like the bitch you are," I said, spitting the biggest glob of saliva
I could muster right in her face.

"I'm sorry, I'm sorry," she whimpered. Getting up to my
feet, ready to make my exit, I stepped backwards still wondering why I didn't just kill her. My back hit a hard body. Startled,
I quickly turned around and was greeted by the sight of an
angry, confused, bruised Brandon.

"Move out of my fucking way," I muttered, trying to step
around him.

"Are you crazy?" Brandon shouted, grabbing both my
shoulders with his strong hands.

"Let me go!" I struggled to get loose from his grip, but he
just held me tighter and pulled me closer to his body, wrapping his arms around my back in a bear hug. The more I
fought back, the tighter his grip became. "Let me go, you sorry
motherfucker!" I screamed now frustrated and crying. I twisted
against Brandon's arms with all my strength. "Why did you
have to have sex with my friend, why?" I sobbed.

"Chena," Brandon said firmly but soothingly. "I would
never do anything like that, I promise you."

"Liar!" I yelled, stepping on his foot as I attempted to break free again.

"Stop it, Chena!" Brandon yelled, shaking me like a rag doll. "Look Chena, look me in my eye. I'm telling you the truth. Becky, tell Chena!" Brandon demanded with authority.

Becky, who had dragged herself onto the couch, looked up defeated. "He doesn't want me!" she responded, wiping her own tears.

"Then why are you at her fucking house? I'm not stupid! Maybe y'all ain't fucked yet, but something's been going on!" I pulled my arm free and pointed my finger in Brandon's face. "Nigga, you ain't—"

"Brandon doesn't want me! It's me," Becky yelled, interrupting me midsentence. "It's me who came onto him. Chena, you always get everything! My fucking job, perfect grades, perfect man. People hate me but they always love you! You going to the best college!...You! You! You! I just wanted to have something! Just wanted to be loved!" Becky pleaded with bloodshot swollen bruised eyes and snot filling her nose.

Looking at Becky in disgust, I felt angered by her justifications for betrayal. "Becky, I didn't deserve this! Not this! I fucking loved you! I woulda done anything for you! I didn't deserve this...Fuck both of you!" I yelled as I broke free and stormed away, heading towards the door.

"Chena!" Brandon yelled, chasing after me. Running as fast as I could, I made it the elevator just as the doors were about to close. Dashing in frantically, I blindly pressed the inside buttons of the elevator. Looking out, I saw Brandon limping but still in full pursuit, within arm's reach of the elevator. With a panicked glance, I saw that my fucking finger wasn't pressing the lobby button, but instead the open button. I jabbed at the right button, but it was too late.

"Fuck!" I screamed as Brandon charged into the elevator.

"Chena, we need to talk!" Brandon declared, completely out of breath.

"There's nothing to talk about," I said, staring up at the top of the elevator to watch the numbers light up, trying to gauge how long I'd be trapped in the elevator with him.

"Look, just hear my side, and if you never want to talk to me again, I'll leave you be," Brandon pleaded. Taking my eyes away from the lights, I glanced down at my arms, feeling the pain now developing on both my arms from Becky's scratches. When I looked up from surveying the damage, I made eye contact with Brandon. A familiar warm feeling filled my heart, and in that very moment I melted. Deep in my heart I want nothing else but to believe him, but I don't want to be the fool... I've never loved someone this much in my life. What if loving the wrong man permanently blocks love from my life? I thought.

"Fine, let's talk," I said flatly, attempting to conceal every feeling for him that's reviving and growing stronger and stronger by the second.

Brandon stood close to me, respecting my personal space, yet maintaining a closeness that allowed me to feel the body heat radiating off of him. Becoming self-conscious of how I must look, I checked out my reflection in the mirrored elevator doors. What I saw made me pull the bottom half of my blood-stained hot pink T-shirt up toward my face to wipe the remaining Vaseline off my face. Patting my hair down, I slid the extra-small T-shirt over my head, exposing my drenching wet stomach. I used the shirt to pat the sweat from my stomach and damp sports bra. I tugging the waistband of my sweat pants in a down to expose my tight obliques and the bottom half of my six pack. This quickly caught Brandon's attention, and his eyes followed the movements of my hands with precision.

"My truck is right out front," he said, rubbing his forehead with a pain-ridden face.

"Uhmm, we can go to my house. We should probably get you some ice," I said, suddenly nervous as I realized that in about three seconds he would discover the damage I had done to his truck.

"Okay, cool," he replied, laying his hand on my lower back to guide me out the elevator as the doors opened.

His face went blank with shock when we stepped through the doors and he got a glimpse of his truck. "What the fuck happened to my truck?" Brandon gasped, running through traffic towards the scratched-up vehicle sitting on four flat tires. He stopped in front of the truck and slammed his fist on the hood in anger. "Who the fuck would do this?" he yelled as he walked around the perimeter of his truck, the dramatic distraught open-jawed look on his face making it seem as if the world had ended. He looked at me in total shock and disbelief as if expecting some sort of explanation. Without a care in the world, I shrugged my shoulders and remained silent, staring at the hood of his truck with no reaction or emotion for him to feed on. A smile began to creep along the edge of my face, but quickly catching myself, with my eyes still on the hood, I bit my bottom lip. Attempting to mask my satisfaction from Brandon's rage, I instinctively shook my head from side to side, illustrating disbelief and disapproval.

"Fuck, I'll just deal with this later. Let's walk to your house," Brandon said, throwing his arms in the air in a defeated motion. He set the pace briskly, walking in the direction of my home. The walk was silent and awkward. I don't feel bad for destroying his truck, I told myself. He shouldna had his ass at her house in the first place... I'll never admit doing it either. Hope he got full coverage...Hahahahaha!

CHAPTER 19
LIL CHENA

Dear Diary,
Love, does it truly exist?
Is it locked in a cloud of mist?
Crossing a mountain?
Under a river?
Up high in a tree?

Love Love Love, where can I find thee?

Is it only a myth?
Is it a bedtime story?
Is it a fairytale untold?

Love Love, where can I find thee?

Is it in the arms of a new mother?
Is it wrapped in a hug?
Is it locked without a key?

Love, where can I find thee?

CHENA, THE MAKING OF AN ORPHAN

Miss Shelly continued to reassure us in a motherly tone, "You guys are going to love your new home." She looked back at us in her rearview mirror with a smile, waiting for a response, but both Dominick and I remained silent as we looked out the back passenger windows of her Nissan Sunny. This would be the fourth home that we'd had to move to within the last two months, and all of them were horrific experiences. I thought we were going to go to a warm loving home with a mommy who would read to us, cook for us, and give us ice cream. But no mommy was ever waiting for us.

When we pulled up to the guarded electric gates of our first home, it looked like a hospital. Miss Shelly called it an orphanage. Miss Shelly explained, "We couldn't get you a foster home because of overcrowding, so you two will be safe here until we get things sorted out." The place housed about one hundred kids. The girls were sectioned off to one side of the building and the boys to the other. There were two people to a room. All of the rooms were the size of a walk-in closet, painted white with cement floors. There were no My Little Pony–decorated bunk beds or Cinderella canopy beds or big treasure boxes full of toys like I'd imagined on the drive there; only two rollaway beds and a dresser. The doors were solid steel with a small window in the middle and were kept locked at night. The kids all wore the same clothes: tan slacks, a white t-shirt, and a navy blue long-sleeved sweater. When we arrived Dominick and I had to change into these same clothes and then they took all of our old clothes and everything else, including my Mr. Bear.

I was immediately taken to the nurse's office, where my burns were cleaned and bandaged. Then I was taken to my room. On the way I passed kids with mops and brooms in their hands. I waved to them, but they just looked up at me and licked their tongues or rolled their eyes. "This place is for bad kids," I mumbled to the female officer who was carrying me on her shoulders. "If I hadn't open the 'frigerator me and my brother wouldn't be here," I sobbed, but the female guard didn't stop to listen. She just patted my back and continued walking.

"Okay Chena, here we are! This is your roommate Roshell. You girls play nice," the female guard said in a warm voice before she placed me on my bed and left the room.

They had put me in a room with a seven-year-old monster who thought it would be a fun idea to use my body as a punching bag while I slept. Roshell waited till the lights went out and I was fast asleep, before she climbed on top of me and woke me up with slaps and punches to my face. But Roshell didn't realize that I had all my teeth, and razor-sharp nails, and would use them.

"No! No, Mr. Bob!" I screamed as I scratched her face and eyes and bit down hard into her neck. No matter how much blood got in my mouth or how much she screamed and cried, I bit down harder and chewed her on her flesh. I didn't release my bite until the guards rushed in and pulled her off of me. For the rest of the night I was put in a room by myself, and the following morning Dominick and I were picked up by Miss Shelly.

We then got moved to two of what Miss Shelly referred to as "temporary foster homes," where we were bullied, beat up by the older foster kids, and ignored by the foster parents. Finally we had arrived at another new home.

"When I'ma gon' have my Mr. Bear?" I whined as Miss Shelly pulled into a small parking lot facing a large apartment complex that took up the entire block.

"Soon, sweetie," she sung out in a warm tone. All of the tan and brown apartments looked exactly the same and were connected in rows. There was a big brown wooden sign with yellow writing right in front of Miss Shelly's parking spot.

"What's that say?" I asked Miss Shelly, pointing with my arm in between the front seats to the sign, hoping it was not another orphanage.

"Acorn Housing Projects of Oaktown," she replied, putting the car into park. "Okay kids, time to meet your new foster mother." Miss Shelly said as she turns to look back at us.

"I want my mommie!" Dominick screamed as he started throwing one of his fits.

"Dominick, don't cry, you'll see your mother very soon," Miss Shelly said. She hurried to open the back door of her Nissan Sunny.

"Wheeeeeen?" Dominick yelled, kicking the front seat over and over with all his might like a propeller in the water. Miss Shelly bent down and grabbed ahold of Dominick's legs to stop them.

"She's sick right now...as soon as she gets better." Dominick, in full streaming tears, reached his hands out for Miss Shelly to hug him. "Shhh, shhh. It's going to be okay," Miss Shelly whispered in Dominick's ear as she lifted him out of the car and held him.

"I want Mr. Bear now!" I screamed, folding my arms.

"You can't have him now. I have to go and pick him up," Miss Shelly replied, rocking Dominick over her shoulder.

"I don't wanna live here! I don't wanna! Stupid bitch whore! I wanna live with Miss Lucy! I wanna live with Miss Lucy!" I screamed, crawling out of the back seat on my brother's side.

"Chena, that's not good behavior!" Miss Shelly snapped.

"I don't waaaaannnnnnna! I hate you!" I screamed, right before kicking Miss Shelly's lower leg as hard as I could.

"Awwww...Chena!" Miss Shelly yelled. Before she could grab ahold of my arm, I took off running as fast as I could, away from Miss Shelly and this new foster home that promised nothing but terror.

Three hours later, holding the hand of Mr. Police Officer Ben, who was dressed in a black police uniform and wearing a black hat and a badge, I walked with him up to a big brown door. I kept licking the tasty vanilla ice cream firmly held in my left hand, while Police Officer Ben rang the doorbell. After three licks of my vanilla ice cream, the door opened, and a young teenage girl with her hair neatly braided in cornrows with clear, red, and blue beads on the ends moved to the left of the doorway and waved us in.

We walked through the short hallway and passed the kitchen to my left and a staircase to my right, before we entered the living room. I saw Miss Shelly sitting on a lime green floral couch covered in a yellow plastic covering. She was talking to an older lady who looked like my Grannie, but about ten years younger. She stopped and gasped with a smile when she saw me.

"Chena, thank goodness you're okay," Miss Shelly said, before turning her attention to Mr. Police Officer Ben. "Thank you, officer, for bringing her back to us so quickly." Miss Shelly then looked him up and down and smiles. "Look how good Chena's behavior is in your charge. I bet you're a great father and husband," she remarked in a high-pitched yet soft tone.

"You're welcome, ma'am. I'm happy I could oblige... and I hope to one day make a great father and husband," Mr. Police Officer Ben said, releasing my right hand so he can show his bare left hand to Miss Shelly.

Dominick was on the floor in front of the big brown TV, playing with some yellow Tonka trucks. "Sister!" he yelled, jumping up to give me a hug. "Wanna play?" He gleefully pulled my right arm, tugging me down to play on the floor with him.

"She's a feisty one. I hope she didn't give you any trouble," Miss Shelly whispered, smiling ear to ear at Mr. Police Officer Ben.

"No ma'am. She's the sweetest, cutest perpetrator I've ever picked up. I found her about ten blocks east of here, standing in front of an ice cream truck," Mr. Police Officer Ben said with a chuckle.

"Well, even so, thank you officer, for taking the time to find Chena and bring her back safely before anything bad coulda happened to her," the old lady said as she leaned forward on the sofa to take a good look at me. "Would you care for something to eat or drink?" she added, with a sweet warm smile.

"No, thank you ma'am. I'm still on duty and have to get back to my beat. But I sure appreciate the offer."

"You're welcome, and you're welcome to come back if you get hungry from all that protecting you doing, you hear me now?" the old lady replied as she reached up to shake Mr. Police Officer Ben's hand.

"Let me walk you out, officer," Miss Shelly said as she got up from the couch, the plastic making a rustling sound as she rose.

"You can just call me Ben," Mr. Police Officer Ben said with a smile, extending his hand to Miss Shelly to assist her off the couch. She stepped over Dominick's legs, which are sprawled out on the carpet as he lay on his stomach playing with his trucks. The two grownups disappeared down the hall speaking in low voices, laughing and smiling.

"Chena, come on now so I can wash that mess you made off your face and hands," the old lady said with a smile as she got to her feet. She wore a green turban, beige blouse, brown polyester pants, and black orthopedic shoes. She grabbed my hand with her left hand and gripped the bannister with her right hand to lead me up two flights of stairs. At the top of the staircase she directed me left. Walking down the small hallway, I stopped in front of one of the open doorways we passed with my mouth wide open.

"Wow!" I exclaimed. This bedroom was filled with beautiful furniture. A white wooden dresser sat catty-corner to a set of bunk beds positioned to the left of the door. A small white wooden desk with a matching white wooden wicker-bottomed chair sat under the window, tightly tucked between a white iron day bed and the dark brown wooden-framed bunk beds. The bunk beds had solid navy blue matching bedding, but the bedding on the day bed displayed a red-and-white Strawberry Shortcake print. Sitting on top of the day bed were three big pink pillows with three fully clothed Cabbage Patch dolls lying on them. One was a white girl doll with a head full of stringy brown yarn hair, wearing a green dress with white socks and brown shoes. Next to her were two bald black infant dolls with their two front teeth showing. One wore a pink nightgown and the other had a blue one, and they both had matching bibs. "Oooh, Cabbage Patch babies!" I yelled out with glee as my eyes lit up.

"Come on now, we get you all cleaned up first, then I'ma show you to your room, okay?" the old lady said, tugging my hand and leading me towards the bathroom.

Looking up at the brown-skinned, brown-eyed lady smiling at me, I asked, "You trying to take my youth?"

The old lady's face screwed up in a confused expression, then she smiled and started laughing. "Ha! Take your youth? Ha ha, child who taught you dat?"

"My Grannie say old people wish they have my youth," I said, smiling back as she took a yellow washcloth from the cabinet under the sink. I leaned closer, watching as she turned the knobs and put the yellow washcloth under the running water in the sink.

"Baby, can't nobody take your youth away from you but God," the old lady said, patting my head and smiling. She began to hum in a sweet melody as used the washcloth to wipe my mouth, neck, arms, and hands completely clean. "Well, look at you! Ain't you just the prettiest little girl?"

Looking in the mirror, I started smiling. "Me pretty," I said with a giggle as I covered my face with my hands. Peeking through my fingers, I mumbled, "Can I play wit' Cabbage Patch babies?"

"What Cabbage Patch babies you talking 'bout?"

I hopped down from the toilet seat, eager to walk back to the bedroom and hoping it was mine. I grabbed the old lady's hand and led her into the room. Stepping into the room, I released the old lady's hand and jumped up on the bed, but slid back down. Giggling, I tried again. "This bed big!" I yelped, in between giggles and falls to the floor. The old lady just stood with her legs crossed over each other, arms folded as she leaned against the bunk beds; smiling with light laughter in her eyes.

"Child, you need some help."

"I can do!" I said, blowing air out of my mouth. I wanted to prove that I was a big girl. After three failed attempts to climb onto the day bed, I walked over to the desk and pushed the white wooden chair close to the bed. I climbed on the chair and then leapt onto the bed, yelling, "Wheee!" I immediately grabbed the Cabbage Patch baby in the pink nightgown. Dropping from my knees onto my butt and sitting up tall, I pulled the baby doll close to my chest and began rocking her. "Hush 'ittle ba—bby, don't 'ou cry, mamma's gonna sing you a lots of buy..." I mumbled, kissing the baby doll on her cheeks.

"Mine?" I asked after a minute, still holding the baby doll close to my face.

"She sure is! What's your new baby's name?"

"Her name Baby Girl," I said, looking up at the old lady as she walked over and sat down next to me smiling. "What's yo' name?"

"You can call me Nanna," the old lady replied, a sweet smile still plastered on her face.

"Nanna, t'is my room?"

"Yes baby, you and your brother's room." As I looked around the room, a big smile grew across my face as I started taking in all the toys in the toy box near the closet and the Dr. Suess books on the desk. Carefully laying Baby Girl down onto the pillow, I flattened the palm of my hand out and fanned it across the bed, feeling the softness of the cotton Strawberry Shortcake comforter and the pink lace on the edge of each pillow.

"T'is my bed!" I screamed. Filled with joy, I looked up at Nanna, who smiled and nodded her head. "You my Nanna!" I said, jumping up to wrap my arms around Nanna's neck.

Nanna hugged me back and held me tight. "Yes baby," she whispered in my ear, as I rested my head on her soft pudgy shoulder and nuzzled my head into her neck, taking in her fruity smell. She smelled just like sweet apple pie, and her soft pudgy body felt like I could finally be home.

CHAPTER 20
CHENA

Dear Diary,

I don't know why
this want for him
is so strong

when he's made
me sad, though

my mind and heart
are twisted in a circle ...

why can't these feelings

be tangible?

"Have a seat in the living room, I'll get you some ice," I said, turning my back to lock the front door. Brandon didn't head to the living room as instructed, but instead followed me into the kitchen and leaned against the counter, watching my every move as I prepared in ice pack for him. "Would you like something to drink?" I asked, bending down to reach the bottom shelf of the empty refrigerator, which only contained yogurt, fruit, and a half dozen eggs. I could feel Brandon's body heat directly behind me while the cold refrigerator air poured into my face. Ignoring the warmness forming between my legs, I grabbed the pitcher of Kool-Aid with my right hand while I grabbed the refrigerator door for balance with my left.

Brandon pulled two cups out of the cabinet and took the pitcher from me. As I stood up and shut the refrigerator, he began filling the two cups.

"Chena, it really wasn't what it looked like," Brandon said, passing me a half-filled cup. Putting the cup to my lips I drank the entire thing, enjoying the sweet grape and lemon flavor as it attacked my taste buds. The cold liquid cooled my body instantly. Then I set the cup down firmly.

"Then why were you there, Brandon?"

"I was there because I thought Becky needed a friend."

"Really?" I said sarcastically, sucking my teeth.

"We got cool when I joined her independent studies section, and I had that class twice for an hour." Brandon searched my face unsuccessfully for a clue that would let him know whether or not I believed him. "I hadn't heard from you, and didn't know how to call you, after all that time...so I was hoping that Becky could put in a good word for me. But she said you guys weren't friends anymore and that you were dating someone else."

"Fucking bitch!" I yelled, rolling my eyes.

Encouraged by my emotional outburst, Brandon continued with enthusiasm, "She confided in me that she had been molested as a little girl." Brandon paused in midsentence as he registered the shock on my face.

"What? She never told me that," I sighed.

"Yeah, and she'd gotten pregnant by Ibrahima a few weeks ago and was worried she'd gotten a STD from him or given him one, I don't know..." Brandon inched closer to me as we locked eyes. "The girl had no one to turn to, so my heart went out to her. I went with her to the doctor to get her abortion."

"Why didn't Ibrahima go?" I snapped.

"Ibrahima wouldn't have anything to do with her. And so like I said, we just became cool..."

Brandon grew quiet and walked towards me, looking for me to say something, but I shut down and went blank as I headed into deep thought. Oh my God! Was Becky one of the little girls in her uncle's videos? She coulda talked to me, I woulda been there for her. We have more in common then she thinks...Adjusting my footing to lean on the counter, I listened like a hawk in utter shock and disbelief, waiting for Brandon to say that the words that had come out of his mouth were not true. But instead there was only an awkward silence growing deeper and deeper. [QA: I did mark the spot in chapter 4 where the videotape was described, if you also want to change that description.]

Brandon worried eyes looked as if he was searching for the right words to say. "Uhmmmm...uhh, and my mom is going through it with her chemo treatments. I needed someone to talk to, so I talked with her about it, and we just got cool, like brother and sister. That's it."

"That's it, huh?" I asked, pouring myself another glass of Kool-Aid.

"Yeah, until today!" Facing the refrigerator, I raised my eyebrows and focused my attention, bracing myself for the truth. I held my breath, anticipating the devastating news. "I gave her a ride home from our study group."

"Oh, and that's why you were all up in her house?" I pointed my finger at his chest, ready to tell this lying nigga to get the hell out of my house before he broke my heart again.

"She asked me to come up to get this book I loaned her for our test, and plus I had to use the bathroom. When I came out the bathroom she was on the phone. I was trying to say bye and bounce, but she hushed me up and said wait. Then when she got off the phone, she started crying. I was trying to console her, then she tried to kiss me, then all this happened," Brandon said, reaching for my hand.

Feeling his hand brought back memories of our love, and the tears of pain that I had desperately tried to hold in for months returned. Brandon pulled me close to him, wrapping his arms around me and holding me tight. "Chena, I never meant to hurt you. I'm so sorry things came to this, I just didn't know how to handle all the shit that was going on." Crying uncontrollably now, and embarrassed by the snot dripping from my nose, I pulled back. But Brandon pulled me in tighter while he reached over to grab a paper towel with his left hand, maintaining his hold on me with his right arm. He began wiping my eyes, then my nose. Taking the paper towel from him, I blew into it like my nose was a horn.

Brandon's eyes never left mine, and a smile appeared on his face. "Did you blow your brains out, too?" he said, pulling me close to him. He kissed my eyes, then my forehead, and then looked at me as if waiting for approval to continue. Looking at him with my deep dark piercing brown eyes, I nuzzled my head into his strong neck, inhaling the scent of his cologne. Rubbing my back with his left hand, he gently took the chopstick out of my pinned-up hair with his right hand. My hair immediately unwound, spiraling into a downward fall to my shoulders. With both palms softly cupping my jawline he pulled my face toward his and kissed me passionately. I released all the tension in my body and succumbed to my need for affection, security, and love.

My tongue danced with his tongue in a circular motion, taking charge with full force in his mouth. My hands began to explore his body. "Uhmmm," Brandon moaned as my hands moved across the hard firm surface of his chest. I made my way down to feel his rock-hard strong manhood bulging out of his CK dark denim jeans. Taking his hands from my face, he placed them on my round soft butt, and immediately I wrapped my hands around his neck. Sensing my yearning to be taken, he pulled me into his pelvis with one quick thrust, causing my pussy to release a warm liquid that began moisturizing the lips of my vagina.

My mind, body, and soul without a doubt desired Brandon's manhood, his essence, and his soul. His every touch was heavenly, making me to moan with each caress that sent euphoric sensations up and down my spine. Brandon's lips softly kissed my ear and made their way down my neck. His hands explored my erect nipples as he carefully pulled my Nike sports bra over my head. Cupping my butt cheeks with a firm grip he picked me up, and I instinctively wrapped my legs around him. Holding onto me with one hand, he used his left arm to clear off the kitchen table with one powerful swipe.

The noise of the salt and pepper shakers and the napkin holder hitting the wall turned me on even more. Laying me down on the firm strong cold wooden table, Brandon stepped out of his black and white Air Jordans and stripped off his white

V-neck T-shirt, exposing his smooth strong carmel-colored chest and rippling abs. He looked down at me, then leaned down and kissed my neck firmly like a snake striking to bite, sliding his body down mine in a slithering motion. The weight of his body pinned my body down as his tongue traveled from my neck to my stomach.

Teasing my stomach with sucks, licks, and kisses, he skillfully began removing my gray Bebe sweatpants, pink Victoria's Secret underwear, and my black Nike Air Maxes, which were already dangling half off my feet. Filled with excitement and anticipation as Brandon stood before me at the edge of the table unbuckling his belt, I watched him stop halfway to remove the contents of pockets. Carefully he laid his wallet and keys on the kitchen counter near the dish rack, never taking his eyes off my body. Butterflies and chill bumps raced from my head to my toes as Brandon continued to unbuckle his belt, allowing his jeans to fall off his waist, stopping at his thighs.

He peeled his boxers downward with his right hand, bending forward just a slight bit to successfully slide them completely off. I greedily stared at his strong butt cheeks that I can't wait to grab. Blushing from cheek to cheek, I admired Brandon's fully erect penis standing at attention. Brandon gave himself two strokes before he placed both his hands on my legs and pulled me forward towards him, leaving a trail of the moisture pouring out of my hot wet pussy. He continued to pull me forward until my butt cheeks were at the edge of the table.

"Oooooh! Uhmmmmm...," I cried as Brandon slipped the tip of his finger into the waterfall between my legs. Moaning from the instant pleasure, trying to anticipate Brandon's next move, I lay there vulnerable, ready to be taken.

Brandon quickly dropped to his knees, spread my legs over his shoulders, and buried his face into my welcoming vagina.

Slurping and sucking began, immediately making my body flap up and down like a fish out of water. I desperately tried to control my convulsions, but my body continued to jerk up and down. "Uhhhmmmmm, yes!" I covered my mouth to hold back the screams. "Ooooh, oooh!" I cried through the fingers covering my mouth. Taking my hand off my mouth, I reached for the top of Brandon's head, attempting to push him out of my cookie box. "Yes! Yes! OOOOH my God!" I yelled, climaxing again and again and again...

Gripping my hands on the surface of the table, I attempted with no avail to push my body backwards away from Brandon's pleasure-giving tongue, but the more I pushed, the harder Brandon's grip became on my legs, pinning me down, forcing me to enjoy every moment of his tongue stroking my clitoris. He continued with no mercy, making me beg, "Please no more, please no more, oooooh, I can't take any more...ahhhh...I want you!"

Brandon rose, wiped his month, and placed himself on top of me. "Baby, I want you so bad! Can I have you?"

"Yes," I mumbled, in between his firm kisses. Sliding back down my body and standing to his feet, he reached for his wallet and pulled out a gold foil square. He ripped the wrapper with his teeth and pulled out a beige colored Latex condom. Letting the wrapper fall to the ground, Brandon focused all his attention on sliding the condom over his massive manhood, which looked ready to explode as it thumped up and down on its own.

Climbing back on the table with a look of desire in his eyes, he hesitated, then immediately jumped off and stood up. "No baby, not here," Brandon whispered in a soothing tone as he picked me up off the table and cradled me in his arms, carrying me into my bedroom. "Baby, what happened in here?" he asked, stepping over the television to lay me on my day bed.

Ignoring his question, I pulled his face close to mine and kissed him passionately. Without words, he entered my body with one slow yet powerful stroke. Oh my goodness, this hurts so bad! I thought as I held my breath.

"Are you okay baby? You want me to stop?" Brandon asked noticing my sharp inhalation.

"No, I'm okay," I reassured him in a seductive tone. I can't believe it, I'm losing my virginity! I never took my eyes off Brandon, wanting to soak up every facial expression of gratification, hoping this moment would last forever.

"Ummmmmm...baby, you're so tight, you feel so good." Brandon continued to moan in my ear as he delivered soft gentle strokes of passion. We were truly connected mind, body, and soul, and between each and every stroke the feeling got more and more pleasurable and the pain faded and finally disappeared, causing me to reach the height of pure joy. Wrapped securely in Brandon's arms afterward, I slipped away into a deep slumber of ecstasy, and a whisper of "I love you" was the last thing I heard as I closed my eyes.

CHAPTER 21
LIL CHENA

Dear Diary,
I am sad
and I cannot cry
My being
Means nothing,
Built only
For entertainment
A chessboard
Mind game
Played by the pessimistic
One I wish was never played!
Family is a losing game...

CHENA, THE MAKING OF AN ORPHAN

Running down the stairs, giggling and smiling, I tried to keep quiet as I searched for a hiding place. My heart was racing. I held my breath and dashed under the dining room table. My brother and I used to play hide and seek all the time with Daisy, Nanna's other foster daughter. She would always find my brother under the table, but she couldn't find me hidden right in the kitchen under the sink, or in the closet, or tangled up in the living room curtains. Daisy said, "You the best at playing, '.cause in a year's time you know the house like the back of my hand and every hidden spot in it" Tears started to fill my eyes as I remember when Daisy and Dominick used to be here. Daisy went away to college last month, and father got custody of Dominick three months ago. I didn't go 'cause father said he didn't want me, I wasn't his daughter. So now it's just me and Nanna playing.

"Chena! Where are you?" Nanna called out in a playful tone, but I stayed hidden under the dining room table's long tablecloth, sniffling. Footsteps came down the stairs, headed into the living room, stopped, then moved again towards the kitchen, where they came to a final stop. "Chena, come on out, we gotta go visit Dominick! We gon' be late...come on now, child, stop playing," Nanna yelled out in frustration. "If you keep hiding we not gon' have time to get you ice cream."

"Ice cream...ice cream, ice cream!" I yelled, forgetting why I was sad. I quickly crawled from under the table and ran into the kitchen to meet Nanna's smiling eyes.

"There's the prettiest girl!" she said, while I wrapped my arms around her soft leg and gave it a tight hug.

We headed out the door, and I held Nanna's hand and watched her lock both the top and bottom locks of the door, and then the iron screen door, which had the same curvy design as the iron bars on all the windows. Nanna fumbled with her key ring trying to locate the car key while we walked towards her green Ford Granada. She opened the back door, and I crawled onto the green leather back seat.

As she closed the door, she abruptly turned around at the sound of a strange voice. "Hey, can you help a brotha get something to eat?" A tall skinny brown-skinned man with barely any teeth in his mouth walked up to Nanna with his hand out. He wore dirty white sneakers covered with mustard-yellow and brown stains, worn-down dirty denim jeans, and a brown V-neck sweater with moth-eaten holes.

"Baby, I ain't got no money to give you for them drugs. Now I already told you if you's hungry the community center's serving lunch, just two buildings down that way," Nana said, taking a step back and pointing behind him and to the left.

"You think you better then me, huh?" the skinny man snapped, looking Nanna up and down before his gaze fixated on her purse. His head twitched to the right, and he kept scratching his neck and arms vigorously. The skinny man turned his head away from Nanna and looked at me looking at him. I quickly put up my middle finger and stuck my tongue out, but snatched it down before Nanna could catch me. He wrinkled up his face and narrowed his eyes at me. Turning back to Nanna and scratching under his chin, he said, "You always say you ain't got no money, and be leaving in yo' fancy car, and coming back with bags in yo' hands." The skinny man sucked the three teeth left in the front of his mouth and rolled his eyes.

The skinny man stared Nanna down, but Nanna didn't flinch a bit. She stood her ground and looked him up and down with a displeased expression. The skinny man looked to his left, then to his right, then turned his head toward Nanna with a devious grin on his face. Licking his lips, and shuffling his jaw around, he took a step forward, almost touching Nanna with his arm.

"Get back out my face!" Nanna yelled out at the top of her lungs, catching the attention of some young boys walking by.

"Yo, crackhead, get the fuck away from the old lady, before I fuck you up," growled a tall muscular light-skinned boy, who brandished a forty-ounce beer bottle in the air. He wore a red Adidas tracksuit, a black Kano hat, and three big gold chains wrapped around his neck. With a defeated look, the skinny man turned around and briskly headed in the direction that Nanna's had pointed, mumbling to himself and rolling his eyes.

Nanna grabbed her chest, her keys still in her hand, and leaned against the car, exhaling. "Nanna!" I yelled through the window. She didn't respond. She just leaned on the car, with her eyes closed, holding her right hand over her left breast. Worried and scared, I screamed, "Nanna... Nannnnnaa! Nanna!" with tears jumping out of my eyes. I started hitting the windows with my hands as hard as I could, slapping my open palms onto the window and pushing, trying unsuccessfully to open it while crying and screaming at the top of my lungs.

"Hush now child, I'm all right," Nanna yelled into the car, as she slowly pushed her weight off the car and reached for the door handle. Nanna slid herself into the front seat, moaning and grunting. Ensuring that all of her wide soft body was completely inside of the car, she leaned to the left, reached out to grab the door handle on the armrest of the heavy door, and pulled, slamming the door shut. She then pressed the lock bottom down with her index finger.

Sitting behind Nanny sniffling, I looked out the window to see if the skinny man was gone. Nanna looked back at me with worried eyes. "Hush now baby, everything gonna be all right."

"That bad man hurt you?" I asked in a timid voice.

"Naw, child, he just gave me a bit of a scare is all. Yo' Nanna got a bad heart," she replied, tapping her chest and smiling, as she turned around to twist the key and start the car. Putting the car in reverse, she turned to look out the back window, and then looked down at me. "We going to see your brother and get some ice cream!" Nanna said, smiling.

"Yaaay...ice cream!" I yelled out, throwing my hands in the air with excitement.

When we arrived at the building and walked out the elevator on the third floor, the sound of crying babies and kids playing could be heard from every direction. "Chena, this way," Nanna snapped. Turning around full circle, I ran at full speed down the hallway lined with offices. Speeding past open doors, I made funny faces and stuck my tongue out at the people sitting at their desks, talking on the phone, and reading files. I reached the end of the hallway, catching up to Nanna, who was standing in front of a middle-aged Mexican lady sitting behind a light brown wooden desk.

"Where's brother?" I asked in a giggle, after bumping into Nanna's thigh.

"Chena, go and be a good girl and sit down," Nanna replied in a warm yet firm voice.

"Good afternoon, I have Chena Johnson here to visit with her brother Dominick Johnson," the Mexican woman said into her phone, as Nanny walked away, heading towards me. Nanna sat next to me and scooted her chair closer to mine to place her arm around me. The doors behind the Mexican lady's desk opened, and Miss Shelly walked out. She looked into the waiting room and locked eyes with me and Nanna. We smiled back at her.

"Miss Shelly!" I yelled out, hopping down from my chair and waving my hand from side to side.

"Hi Chena, how are you?" Miss Shelly said as she came over and bent down to her knees to give me a hug. "Hi Miss Thompson, good to see you."

"Sorry we late, got here as fast as I could," Nanny replied.

"Don't worry. The visit start time isn't for another ten minutes anyway," Miss Shelly replied.

"Sister!" Dominick yelled, running up from behind me and wrapping his arms around me.

"Dominick! I can tie my shoooie!" I yelled. Releasing his embrace, I dropped down to my knee and began undoing my laces so I could show him how to do it.

"Me do it too!" Dominick announced, grabbing the shoe-strings out my hand.

"Okay children, let's go into my office and play with some toys."

Dominick's eyes lit up, and he jumped to his feet to follow Miss Shelly. I finished tying my shoelace into a pretty bow first. "Toys!" I yelled jumping up to my feet. As I turned around, searching for Dominick and Miss Shelly, I saw father looking down at me, from across the room. He gave me a smile and waved. My head started boiling with hate and I twisted my face up at him, squinted my eyes and put up my middle finger. He took my brother away! The last time I saw him, he told the judge, "I don't want her. I can't afford to take care of her and my son, and I'm not even sure she's mine."

"Chena, don't act that way!" Nanna snapped from behind me, but ignoring her I walked toward him, sucking up all the liquid in my mouth, and I spit it on him. I smiled from ear to ear as I watched it land on his shiny black penny loafers. Before father could say anything, I ran to catch up with Miss Shelly and Dominick, who were walking hand and hand through the open doors behind the Mexican lady's desk. "Wait for me!" I yelled out as Miss Shelly and Dominick turned right down a hallway and entered an office.

"Chena we're right here!" Miss Shelly yelled out with a smile as she stood at the door and ushered me inside. My attention was instantly captured by the six-shelf bookcase filled with action figure toys, a small sandbox the size of a coffee table filled with more toys, and a chest filled with board games, dolls, and Tonka trucks.

"OOOH, toys!" Dominick yelled out. He ran to the chest on the floor and pulled out a big yellow construction truck.

"Mr. Police Officer Ben!" I screamed, pointing to a framed photograph of Police Officer Ben and Miss Shelly kissing. Miss Shelly started blushing as she picked up the silver framed photo off her desk and held it to her chest, before bending down with the frame to hand to me.

"Police Officer Ben is my husband now!" Miss Shelly said with a smile on her face.

"Oooh, you kissing," Dominick yelled out, as he breaks into a giggle on the floor.

"Hahaha...you and Mr. Police Officer Ben have cooties!" I announced with a smile, handing Miss Shelly back the picture frame.

"Yes, we...um...LOVE each other very much," Miss Shelly said. Before she could finish, I was already on the floor having fun with Dominick, getting ready to open up the game Candyland.

The visit with my brother was over before I knew it. We were both sad and crying, holding onto to each other for dear life, until I was ripped away and led by Nana's soft pudgy hand down the hall. Nanna quickly bought me my promised ice cream at the corner store next to the parking lot, bringing my tears to an immediate stop.

Standing up on the seat of the car, I gazed out the back window at the orange and blue and said, "The sun go nite nite." Sitting back down in my seat, I finished the last bite of my ice cream cone and licked my hands as Nanna pulled into the parking lot.

"Don't you go wiping your hands on your dress," Nanna said, looking through the review mirror at me wiping my hands on my dress.

"Oopsie," I replied with a smile. Nanna shook her head and sucked her teeth, before revealing a slight smile. After parking the car, Nanna opened her car door and slid her pudgy body out. First she put her left leg out, then she put her left hand on the open door's armrest and leaned her weight onto the door, while pulling the rest of her body out of the car. Once out the car, she reached down and grabbed her purse sitting on the seat, closed the door and opened the passenger door for me.

"Oooh, hold on baby, I forgot my reading glasses." Nanna said as I crawled out of the back seat. She then turned around and opened the driver's side door again.

When Nanna bent in to grab the glasses lying on the passenger seat, I dashed around the long green back side of the car and ducked down next to the back tire. "Chena! Child, stop playing, and come on back here," Nanna demanded in an irritated voice.

"Surprise!" I shouted, jumping up from my crouched position. Nanna turned around and spotted me.

"Child, come on over here," Nanna said with relief, reaching out for my hand, but before I could run into Nanna's arms a man's voice sounded from a few feet away.

"Give me your fucking purse, bitch." A tall slim figure appeared out of the shadows cast by the tall trees surrounding the parking lot. The light from the street lamp illuminated the moving shadow as he came closer, revealing the snaggle-toothed crackhead from this afternoon.

He walked briskly toward Nanna, shouting, "Bitch, I mean now!" Scared and afraid, I ducked back down and crawled under the car. All I could see was Nanna's feet and her big soft ankles.

"Help! Help! Help!" Nanna yelled out in panic as the man's shadow came closer to her feet.

Laughter poured out of the man's throat. "Ain't nobody here to help you, now what you gon' do?"

"Get back, you devil!" Nanna yelled. The man's feet quickly moved forward until his dirty shoes were touching Nanna's feet. Scuffles came from the two sets of feet.

"Let go bitch, or I'll kill you!" The man's voice demanded in a vicious tone. All movement stopped when I heard the sound of a slap. Did he hit Nanna? The skinny man's dirty yellowish-brown sneakers with the missing shoelaces started to quickly run away.

"Nanna? Nanna?" I whispered, as I watch Nanna's body slowly slump down to the ground with her back now laying against the fender of the car, slightly tilted to the left. I crawled out from under the car and ran into Nanna's arms, but she didn't hug me back. She sat there holding her left breast with her right hand. Her eyes were rolling in her head; she was trying to say something. "Bab...hel'..." but the words weren't coming out.

"Nanna! Nannna, me save you," I cried through my tears. Nanna started breathing heavily and closed her eyes. I grabbed Nanna's arm, trying with all my might to pull her up, but she fell over to her left side.

"Nanna...pweese, get up, get up!...I pwomise to be good!" I cried, crouched on my hands and knees on the ground next to Nanna. Nanna's eyes opened real wide, then her heavy breathing stopped and she stopped moving. "Nanna, wake up...wake up!" I mumbled, trembling in fear, as Nanna's remained still.

I touched Nanna's soft wrinkled face, hoping she'd open her eyes, but she didn't move. "You hurt 'cause me was a bad girl," I cried out, burying my face into her chest. Then I screamed my lungs out until finally, bright red and blue lights came, and my numb frightened little form was pulled off of Nanna's motionless body.

CHAPTER 22
CHENA

Dear Diary,

I am going
to hold on
to the times
we had

Instead of
holding on
to a bitter
memory

I
will hold on
to
what
friendship
means.

CHENA, THE MAKING OF AN ORPHAN

I woke up to the sun hitting my eyelids, smiling as the memories of lovemaking danced across my thoughts. Scooting backwards, yearning to feel Brandon's warm touch, all I felt was the pain between my legs and the cold sheet instead. Scooting backwards even further, I still didn't feel him, just the cold air behind me as my exposed back slipped out of the sheet. Listening like a lion in the jungle for Brandon's presence, I realized he wasn't there. I rolled over, still in disbelief, to discover that not only was he gone, but he left a note on the pillow.

"A fucking note?" I wailed. Sitting up shivering, I grabbed the pink and teal-green sheet to cover my nude body. Carefully I picked up the note, which he had written on a yellow notepad page. After examining the paper, I turn my head to look at my desk and saw a yellow notebook hanging off the edge. He must have grabbed it off my desk. Noticing how he laid the note out on the pillow, not even bothering to fold it, I guessed that he must have been in a hurry. But why?

"Dear Chena, Good Morning, I didn't want to wake you as you were sleeping so peacefully, I had to leave to go take care of my truck. xoxo Brandon," the note read. Irritated by Brandon's note, I looked around at the aftermath of my meltdown and rolled my eyes, throwing my pillow against the wall.

"Psshh! He could have at least kissed me good-bye!" I shouted as I jumped out of bed, determined to clean up this mess of a room before Dena came back home.

Ring! Ring!

"Oh shit, the phone!" I clicked the vacuum's power switch off and pressed the power button on the TV blasting music videos. Running to the kitchen to grab the cordless off the charger, I stumbled over my Nikes. "Ooh, shoot! Hello?" I gasped.

"Hey," Dena replied, then paused, trying to analyze my voice. "You alright?" she asked with worry.

"Yes, ahhh...I'm fine. Why, what's up?" My heart started skipping a beat, wondering if Dena knew any information on yesterday's events.

"Why did you take so long to answer the phone? This is my third time calling."

"Oh, 'cause I'm vacuuming, and I just tripped over my stupid Nikes," I pleaded.

"Oh, okay. Well, I'm about to go for my facial. I was just checking on you; there's some money in my top drawer if you need anything, and I got my mobile phone on," Dena said with relief before abruptly hanging up the phone.

Still holding the phone in my hand, I looked at the clock above the kitchen table to check the time. It's almost ten a.m.— Bee and Tanisha should be up. I leaned my elbows on the counter as I dialed.

"Hello?" Bee answered in a groggy voice.

"Hey girl, you asleep?"

"Naw, not anymore!" Bee snapped sarcastically into the phone.

"Okay good, 'cause I got some news to tell you! But let me three-way Nisha too so I can tell y'all at the same time." I clicked over to dial Tanisha's number, but there wasn't a dial tone. Ooh shit is Dena still on the phone? I thought.

"Ahh, hello? Hello?"

"Hello, Chena?" I immediately recognized the shaky voice as Becky's grandmother's.

"Ummm...Hi," I replied, unsure as to what to say. I just kicked her granddaughter's ass! I hope I'm not in trouble, fuck, what if she's going press charges...Damn!

"Chena, I hope I haven't caught you at a bad time. I really need to talk to you."

"Okay, can you hold for a second?" Remembering Bee was on the other line, I quickly clicked over. "Hey girl, you still there?"

"Yeah I'm here! What, you forgot how to connect the calls again?" Bee said, sucking her teeth, now fully awake.

"Naw! Girl, when I clicked over Becky's grandma was on the other line, so I—"

"What she want?" Bee said, cutting me off midsentence.

"I don't know what she wants, yet, but I was going tell you, that I kicked Becky's ass yesterday in her house for trying to sleep with Brandon, I fucked up Brandon's truck, and me and Brandon did it! But I'll call you right back, okay?"

"What?...Damn! Okay, hurry up and call me back! Bye."

I clicked back over to Becky's grandmother with a big grin on my face, blushing from revealing to Bee that I'd been "doing the grownup." "Hi, sorry about that, I was in a middle of a long distance call when you called," I lied, embarrassed for keeping her on hold for so long.

"Chena, something bad has happened, and...I...," Becky's grandmother mumbled, then stopped midsentence. I could hear her fighting back tears. She cleared her throat, attempting to compose herself, and continued, "Becky is..." She stopped again and started crying. Oh my God, is she dead? What's going on? I thought, the smirk dropping off my face. But I didn't have the heart to push the words out of my mouth into the receiver. There was a long silence. She cleared her throat again and finally continued. "Becky attempted suicide last night, and she left a note. The note mentioned her uncle and you."

"Is she okay?" I asked nervously.

"No, baby. She's in intensive care now, fighting for her life," Becky's grandmother managed to say before she fell into a complete breakdown. Not sure of what to say, I just held onto the phone, listening to Becky's grandmother sobbing for her grandchild. In between the sobs, she choked out more of the details, and I gathered that Becky had swallowed pills and cut her wrist. Luckily, her mother found her unconscious but breathing and quickly called the paramedics before it was too late.

As soon as I could decently get off the phone with Becky's grandma, I called Bee, panicking. Bee agreed to drive me and Tanisha up to Saint John's Hospital. Bee swooped Tanisha up first and they were out to my house within the hour. I paced nervously the entire time I waited.

Ring! Ring!

"Hello?"

"Hey girl, we here," Tanisha screamed into the intercom.

"Okay, here I come!" I slammed the phone down. Dressed and ready to go in my black Bebe sweat pants and white Old Navy tank top, I grabbed my black Bebe hoodie and ran out the door. Ensuring the bottom lock was locked, I slammed the door and gave the knob a twist to check before running down all four flights of stairs.

Tanisha greeted me with a soft smile, hopping out of Becky's purple Camaro, sliding the front seat up and jumping into the back. That was odd, as she usually rode in the front, especially if she got picked up first.

"Hey." Bee nodded and smiled. Bee and Tanisha listened intently as I told them what had taken place yesterday, leaving out the Brandon story, as this moment's focus was on Becky. The memories of our friendship flashed before our eyes, as we shared stories of how we all met, laughing to fight back tears. Trying unsuccessfully to hold back tears, I sat back silently, pulling my shirt up with my right hand to cover my eyes. I quietly listened to Bee and Nisha talk about the factors that had brought Becky to this. They told me not to blame myself, but I couldn't help but think that it was all my fault. Before Becky's grandmother's call, I hated her guts so much! I wished she was dead, and now all I feel is regret. I wish I could take everything back...God please, please, let her be okay.

"Chena, you all right?" Bee asked, snapping her fingers to get my attention.

"Oh, yeah, sorry. Just thinking about how fucked up this situation is."

"Yeah, I know, but we here now," Bee said as she pulled into the Saint John's parking lot. After we checked in with the nurse at the front desk, she directed us to the intensive care waiting room on the third floor. Everyone was silent, as if time had frozen, and we stood still as the elevator took centuries to stop on the third floor. We could sense the spine-chilling feel of death dancing around the room as we exited the elevator, walking past grieving people who were either in prayer or holding each other for support.

"Hi babies." Becky's grandmother rose from her chair to give each of us a hug. Becky's mother sat with Becky's uncle in a corner on the floor. She didn't move or even look up at us. This was the first time I had seen Becky's mother without makeup on, and she looked a hot mess. Her hair was wild all over her head, and her black leggings and green-and-black blouse were all covered in blood. "Thank you girls for coming so quickly," Becky's grandmother said, right before breaking down into tears again. We all instinctively crowded around her, each of us hugging a piece of her soft warm body. Clasping her shoulder, arm, and back, we each held on quietly and cried.

"Come on now and join hands," Becky's mother called out from behind us, where she and Becky's uncle formed the start of a semi-circle. His eyes were so filled with guilt he couldn't lift them off the ground. Not wanting to touch

Becky's perverted uncle's hand, I stood in between Becky's grandmother and Bee, causing her uncle to be sandwiched in between his mother and sister-in-law.

Becky's grandmother cleared her throat and provided the prayer. "Oh, heavenly father we come before you now and ask that you provide a miracle and bless Becky with a healing. Bless her Lord, and let her live a healthy full life. Forgive her, Lord, for what she has done, and give her a second chance, God. Please cover her with the blood of Jesus and bring her back to us."

"Amen," we declared in unison.

After Becky's grandmother's prayer, we remained standing in silence, still holding hands, until a tall doctor in a full smoky-blue smock wearing a green paper shower cap on his head and green paper booties on both of his feet interrupted us. He beckoned Becky's mother toward him, and they stood off to the side as he whispered something to her. Becky's mother looked at him with appalled eyes, shaking her head and screaming, "No! No!..." She collapsed to the floor weeping. We all looked at one another knowing at that moment that Becky had died.

"I need to breathe...I can't breathe! I need some air," I mumbled as I walked backwards, moving away from the heart-wrenching scene. This is just overwhelming. I haven't lost many people close to me since I was a child....It just always seems to be my fault, am I the bringer of death? I thought as my body and heart grew numb. Shaking tears from my eyes, looking straight ahead of me, I made eye contact with Becky's uncle, and I instantly realized who the true culprit was.

Halting my backwards steps, I moved forward, walking past Bee and Tanisha and heading straight toward Becky's uncle. He was a pathetic, weak looking man, standing just 5'7", pudgy, and going bald. He was about thirty-five, and he had acne and still wore braces. I bent down to sit next to him, looking at him with a deadly piercing look. His eyes slowly looked up to meet mine. Leaning in real close to his right ear I whispered, "I know what you did, you sick fucking freak!" His jaw dropped, practically hitting the ground. I kept my eyes fixed on the black center of his evil pupils, and his brow immediately wrinkled with worry. I rose up from my seat, squinting my eyes with a downward tilt of my head while my lips turned up into a piercing smirk. My face sent him the clear message, That's right motherfucker; I know what you did, and I'm going to tell.

Walking toward the elevator, I could feel Becky's uncle's eyes digging a hole into my back. Before my finger could reach out to press the down button for the elevator, Becky's grand-mother stopped me with a touch on my shoulder. "Baby, now don't go on and beat yourself up about this. Everyone has their time to go. You were like a sister to Becky, and I know you meant a lot to her," she said, hugging me and placing a folded envelope in my hand. My throat was so full of the emotion I was trying desperately to suppress that I could not respond. I could only nod, acknowledging her gesture of comfort, before I turned around to face the elevator.

The car ride back home was silent. There didn't seem to be anything to say; everyone just wanted to go home and cry. "I'll hit y'all tomorrow," I said, crawling out of Bee's Camaro and lifting the back seat for Tanisha to jump into the front seat. Walking up to the glass door of my building, I looked back to give one last wave, but Bee's wheels had already pulled away, moving out of the sight. Choosing the four flights of stairs over the elevator brought back memories of the many times Becky and I had taken those steps together sneaking out, or just coming up after work and school to hang out.

Tears took ahold of me, filling my eyes to the point of temporarily blindness. I couldn't see the key to unlock the bottom lock. Flipping through my keys over and over again, unable to find the right one, I muttered, "Fuck!" I wiped my eyes with my forearm and shuffled through the keys once more, desperately trying to find the right key. "Got it!" I sighed, turning the key to the right and pushing the door open. Once inside, I exhaled fully. Double checking that the door was closed and securely locked behind me, I walked towards the green leather sofa, fell down onto it, and kicked off my shoes.

After I lay in stillness on the couch, thinking about nothing for a while, it dawned on me that I hadn't talked to Brandon all day. Checking in my purse for my red Beeper City Motorola pager, I noticed it sitting on the coffee table in front of me, blinking red. "Ooh, I musta left it, running out the house," I mumbled with my hand still in my purse. I felt an unfamiliar piece of paper under my fingers, and realized it had to be the folded envelope that Becky's grandmother had placed in my hand. Carefully pulling the envelope out of my purse, I unfolded it, reading Becky's grandmother's name on the front of the envelope, written inside of a heart: "Gwene, my loving Grandmother." Turning the envelope over, I pulled the letter out through the tattered ripped edges of the opened envelope.

"Dearest Grandmother," the letter read. "I love you, and I am sorry I did not get to say good-bye. I am doing what I am doing because I can no longer go on living with the pain of loneliness and rejection. I am sorry that I could not be the daughter my mother always wanted, the granddaughter you deserved, or a true friend and sister to Chena. Please tell Chena I am sorry and I love her, and that it is time to free Uncle Leroy. Love always and forever, Becky Washington."

"It is time to free Uncle Leroy? What the hell is she talking about, free Uncle Leroy?" Like a boulder falling off a cliff it hits me, remembering what Brandon had said, Becky was molested by her uncle. "Becky wants her uncle to suffer for stealing her innocence," I said, tightening my fist. Clarity filled my brain, and I instantly decided. I had to grant Becky her last wish. "He will never be able to hurt another innocent child!" I mumbled to myself, putting the letter back into the envelope. Jumping to my feet and heading into the kitchen, I grabbed the phone off the cordless charger. Dialing Bee's number, I quickly thought twice and hung up. I can't tell the girls. Becky didn't want anybody to know...but I can't do this alone. I'm going to need some help!

Dialing Brandon's number, secretly hoping he wouldn't answer so I wouldn't have to tell him the bad news. Ring!... Ring!...Ring!...Ring!

"Hello?"

"Hello!"

"Hello, who is this?" Brandon snapped into the phone.

"Hey, it's me," I announced.

"Chena?"

"Yeah, I got some bad news."

"Are you okay?" Brandon asked in panic.

"Yeah, I'm all right. It's...Becky. She—" I couldn't go on, and silence filled the phone. The emotion that choked my throat traveled up into my eyes and forced tears from them. "She's dead!" I cried out.

"What?...Aww man, are you serious?"

"I wish I wasn't," I said, sniffling.

"Damn!...I had a bad feeling all day that something happened! What happened?"

"Umm...she, she committed suicide."

"Word!...Damn!...How?"

"Pills, and her wrists were cut."

"Wow!...Dang, I mean she had some issues, but she didn't have to go out like that." There was a long pause, with sniffling coming from both ends of the phone, until Brandon cleared his throat and continued, "She left me a fucked up voicemail, late last night. I shoulda checked it when I woke up in the middle of the night, but I waited too late."

I broke in before Brandon could continue. "What did she say?"

"Man, just crazy talk. She was crying and rambling...saying she was sorry for the pain she caused, and she won't be causing no more pain. I didn't know this would happen! Man...I didn't know."

"Well, did you call her back?" I asked with urgency.

"Yeah, but when I tried to hit her up in the morning she didn't answer. So I figured I'd stop by her house while I was picking up my truck, to check on her."

"Was she alive when you got there?"

"She didn't answer the intercom, and when I knocked on her door, she didn't answer, so I just left," Brandon said, sounding distraught.

"Look, the reason's Becky did what she did was deeper then you and me. I think it goes back to her uncle!"

"The motherfucker who molested her?" Brandon asked in a cold tone.

"Yes! His name is Leroy Washington, it's her grandmother's son. I have a plan for his ass, but I'ma need some help."

"Baby, you know I'm there. What you wanna do?"

Sounding more calm and collected in my reply than I felt, I said, "I wanna make him pay first, then I want his ass to rot in jail!"

"Whatever you need me to do, it's done," Brandon shouted with enthusiasm.

"I don't know just yet, but I'll fill you in tomorrow. I need a ride tomorrow, can you take me?"

"My truck is in the shop, but I'll ask my dad if I can use his car...Hello?" Brandon asked as I fell silent, searching for my response.

"Yeah, sorry, I'm just out of it. Got a lot on my mind."

"You want me to come over? We can just talk," Brandon suggested in a soft comforting voice.

"Aww, thanks sweetie, but I need to be alone. I need to think of a plan for Leroy and clear my head. I'll talk to you tomorrow morning, okay?"

"All'ite then, I holla at you in the morning. I love you, baby."

"Me too," I whispered, caught off guard by Brandon's words, too hesitant to respond in kind. Hanging up the phone in a frustrated, emotional daze, I wondered if my need for Brandon's love had caused Becky's death. Maybe if I had been more of a loving friend, she would still be here...

CHAPTER 23
CHENA

Dear Diary,

Fuck the injustice, I'm mad,
Angry as hell,

Fuck it if my words sound twisted,
Distorted and frail,
Fuck it if I sound violent and
unkind,

Fuck those motherfuckers who
spread the hurt of hurting,

Fuck those angelic impostors who
talk about God,
while they rob the innocent

Fuck those demonic
weak-minded who prey
And condemn the helpless naive
as victims.
Fuck those that look the other way
as the predators play

The time for action is NOW! TODAY!

CHENA, THE MAKING OF AN ORPHAN

"Good morning, baby. Y'all come on in," Gwene, Becky's grandmother invited us in a welcoming voice, skillfully masking her sadness.

"Good morning, ma'am. I'm Brandon," Brandon introduced himself, shaking Gwene's soft little pudgy wrinkled hand. He sat on the brown and beige sofa and scooted to the right, making room for me to join him.

"I just finished making some lunch for Leroy and I. Would you two care for a something to eat?"

"Ooh, you know how I love your cooking. I'd love some," I replied with a warm smile, elbowing Brandon's arm.

"Yes ma'am, I could never turn down some home cooking," Brandon added.

"Okay, I'ma set the table," Gwene announced as she exits the living room.

"Brandon, I'ma run to Becky's room. Cover me. If anyone asks, I needed to go to the bathroom," I whispered and crept upstairs. Walking up the staircase, I heard jazz music coming from the guest bedroom. Shit, Leroy must be in there. Passing his door and turning left toward Becky's room, I held my breath, not wanting to make a sound. I reached for Becky's door, quietly nudging it open while slowly turning the door handle. The sound of the guest room door opening hit my ears and sent chills running down my spine. I quickly dashed inside of Becky's room, and lightly closed the door behind me, keeping the knob twisted counterclockwise to avoid the telltale click of the lock. To ensure that I was not discovered, I released my hold slowly, allowing the doorknob to turn itself clockwise noiselessly, and the door latched.

Listening at the door as Leroy's footsteps moved closer, then stopped and turned into the bathroom, I exhaled and composed myself, scanning the contents of Becky's room. "The VCR," I whispered, walking to Becky's dresser. I pressed the eject button on her VCR, but it was empty. "Fuck, where is it?" I opened the top dresser drawer, quickly pushing through her garments in frustration, then pulled open the second drawer, and the third, and the fourth, finding only clothes. "Where did you put it Becky?" I mumbled as I zeroed in on her bed. Running to her bed, I swiftly fell to my knees and peeked under it, lifting the pink lace bedskirt over my head.

Underneath was a flat brown box. I carefully pulled the medium-sized rectangular box out from under the bed, along with a huge amount of dust. Inspecting the box, I cautiously slid off the lid. Rapidly lifting homemade cards, letter, and child-hood photos of Becky out of the box onto the floor, I revealed a black videotape. "Bingo! I found you," I whispered. I quickly stuffed the papers and folders back into the box and pushed it back under the bed. Then I grabbed the videotape and jumped to my feet. My heart was racing out of my chest; it beat a mile a minute in my eardrums as I turned the doorknob just as I heard the toilet flushing. Panicking, my heart began pounding harder, the large thumps echoing inside of my chest. My hands trem-bled as I lifted the edge of my ocean-blue hoodie and quickly shoved the cold VHS tape into the waistband of my jeans, wedging it against my stomach between my pelvic bones.

After ensuring that the tape was well hidden under my hoodie, I begin walking briskly toward the staircase. When I had nearly reached the staircase, the bathroom door suddenly opened, and Leroy stepped out in front of me. He gasped at the sight of me, as if he had seen a ghost. I jumped back and covered my mouth to avoid releasing the terrified scream trapped in my throat.

Leroy grabbed my wrist. "What were you doing in there?" he hissed, tightening his grip.

"What are you talking about? I was waiting to use the bathroom!" I snapped back, attempting to pull my wrist out of his grasp.

"No you weren't! You were in Becky's room—probably stealing, you thieving orphan." His grip was so tight that he was cutting off the blood circulation in my hand, which began to go numb.

"Let go of me, you fucking pervert, I'm not a thief!"

"What did you just call me?" Leroy barked, instantly releasing my hand. Cradling my wrist to my chest and holding back tears of anger, I stood helplessly looking into Leroy's evil eyes, which were carving up me like a knife.

"You heard me!" I shot back in a whisper.

"Look, little girl—you better be careful what you say, or you might end up like Becky," Leroy whispered as he leaned in closer, now standing so close I can feel the hard hatred stabbing from his piercing eyes.

"Move out of my way!" I demanded. I moved my arms down, cradling my left wrist in my right hand, to unobtrusively press my right arm into my stomach. Skillfully holding the VHS tape in place, I pushed pass Leroy and headed down the stairs.

"Hey, there you are! We were just wondering if you had fallen in the toilet or something," Gwene said with a chuckle as I came into the kitchen.

"Ha ha...sorry about that, I'm so embarrassed," I said, trying to mask my confusion with a smile. The confrontation with Leroy still had me off guard, and I had forgotten my alibi was the bathroom. I sat next to Brandon, giving him a direct stare to make eye contact. I wished I could telepathically communicate that somehow we needed to leave right away without raising suspicion. Gwene turned around from the stove and brought a plate of chicken breasts over to the table and set it down next to the mashed potatoes, green beans, and corn already laid out in the center of the square glass table. The mouth-watering aromas of the food mingled in the air. She headed towards the staircase, calling, "Leroy!...Lunch is ready! Come on to the table now."

Before Gwene could make it back to the table, Brandon leaned close to my ear and whispered, "You okay?"

My heart still racing out of my chest, I couldn't speak, so I responded with a fake smile and nod. Gwene was only four feet away from us. I nonchalantly pulled Brandon's arm to make him lean toward me. Pretending to give him a kiss on the cheek, I hissed in his ear, "I got it!" Brandon gave me a nod to show he got it, just as Gwene reached the table. Leroy's footsteps pounded out as he galloped down the stairs, through the living room, and into the kitchen.

"Leroy, this is Brandon, one of Becky's school friends, and you know Chena," Gwene said, ushering Leroy to sit down directly across from me.

"Hi, nice to meet you," Leroy quickly spit out without making eye contact. "Mother, this looks delicious," he said as he put a serving of mashed potatoes on his plate.

"It sure does, Grandmother. Becky always praised your cooking," I said, looking at Gwene. I turned my eyes slightly to meet Leroy's, and we exchanged phony smiles.

"Grandmother?" I say, still watching Leroy fill his plate with mashed potatoes.

"Yes, dear?"

I turned my head toward Gwene. "I think my roller blades are here. I loaned them to Becky, and every time I asked her about them, she'd say 'they're at Grandmother's,' but every time we'd be here, I'd forget about them. Do you mind if I could check in the garage to see if they're there?"

"Of course not, baby. Go on."

Leroy suddenly started choking and coughing. Taking his glass from his lips and covering his mouth with his dinner napkin, between coughs he sputtered, "I'll go check for you, so you can finish eating."

"No, you go on and eat sweetie. I remember seeing them skates, I'll point them out to you, baby," Gwen announced as she got up from the table and headed toward the patio door. I jumped up quickly and followed behind her.

"It's dusty in here, so you watch out for those spider webs. They get everywhere," Gwene said as she pressed the button for the garage door, causing it to slowly open. "I remember seeing them on the left side next to that big brown chest," she said in a motherly tone. The brown chest! that's the chest with the videotapes in it, I thought. "Baby, you go on and look over there in that corner. My eyes too bad to see in this dim light, and I can't be bending over no way, 'cause my back." Dutifully heading over to the corner, where a yellow ladder leaned propped against the wall next to an open black toolbox, I stepped over the brown chest, and grabbed the skates, which lay against the wall.

"Yep, here they are!" I yelled with a smile, picking up the skates and narrowing my gaze on the big brown chest.

"She woulda wanted you to have 'em back," Gwene said as her smile faded and her eyes begin to fill with tears. Walking closer to Gwene, I could see that she was about to have a breakdown at any moment.

"Yes, and she woulda wanted you to keep this," I said softly, reaching in my hoodie's front pocket to retrieve Becky's suicide note. Gwene looked down at the note in my hand and with out a word, carefully took the envelope and folded it in half. She lifted the neckline of her peach-colored T-shirt and placed the envelope into her bra. Walking in silence, we returned to the kitchen, where Brandon and Leroy sat in an awkward silence broken only by the sound of their forks scraping their nearly empty plates.

"Oh good, I see you found what you were looking for," Leroy declared with relief, as he got up from the table with his plate in hand and headed towards the sink.

"Yes, Grandmother knew exactly where they were," I said with a contrite smile.

Leroy ignored my comment and kissed his mother on the forehead. He locked eyes with me as he said, "Thank you, Mother, for lunch. I'm going upstairs to make some phone calls."

"Okay baby. Don't forget to call Reverend John." Gwene tapped Leroy's hand, which rested on her right shoulder, with her right hand.

Leroy flicked his gaze to Brandon. "Good afternoon, Chena...and nice to have met you, Brandon," he said smoothly. Then like the deceitful snake he was, he slithered back upstairs.

Waving good-bye to Gwene, Brandon and I hurried walked to his Dad's car, parked just down the hill from Gwene's two-story house. "Can you believe it? That motherfucker grabbed my arm and threatened me!" I screamed once Brandon and I were inside the safety of his dad's 1993 turquoise-colored Toyota Tercel.

"What?! That little motherfucker! I'ma go back and fuck him up!" Brandon yelled, slamming his fist down hard on the cracked gray plastic dashboard.

"Don't worry, we gonna fuck him up in more ways than one," I said as I pulled the videotape out from under my hoodie and buckled my seatbelt.

"Yeah, we gonna stick to the plan and get his ass," Brandon said, looking at the VHS tape. "I know Ibrahima and Michael will help us. And all I gotta tell my crazy uncle Jeffery, the veterinarian, is that this motherfucker is a child molester, and he'll be on board," Brandon added as he turned on the engine.

"Are you sure you can get your dad's cargo van?" I asked, mapping out Operation "Set Uncle Leroy Free" in my head.

"Yeah, after I drop you off I'ma go up to the gym and holla at Michael and Ibrahima. Then tonight I'll talk to my dad and uncle Jeffery," Brandon said in a reassuring manner.

"Good," I said, absent-mindedly looking out the window and thinking about which knife would be suitable for this special occasion.

CHAPTER 24
LIL CHENA

Dear Diary,
I inhale, pause froze in a daze
hoping to be picked up
flown away

saved!

Superman in disguise, I can't
Believe my eyes
Am I seeing Lies?

The righteous does the
unspeakable,
An eye for an eye
I exhale, Breath and open my eyes
Saved!

CHENA, THE MAKING OF AN ORPHAN

"Chena, you wait right here, and I'll be back with some hot cocoa, okay sweetheart?" Miss Shelly crooned in a soft voice. Ignoring Miss Shelly, I remained sitting indian-style with the palms of my hands covering my eyes, facing the wall. As soon as the door closed, I quickly clutched Mr. Bear tight to my chest and crawled under Miss Shelly's desk.

"Mr. Bear, I missed you! Mr. Bear, what you say? Why'm I sad? 'Cause...Mr. Bear...I t'ink Nanna die....What you say, Mr. Bear?...What happen? The ambulance people come an' try and help Nanna, but she wouldn' wake up. They put her on a white bed with wheels, then they put her in their big ole truck. I wanted be next to Nanna, so she'd see I's a good girl when she wake up, but they say they's no room with Nanna. But they say I can sit up front, and turn on the red and white lights and the noisemaker. Then I say okay...we got to the hospital, they put Nanna inside first, then the nurse lady came and got me. She take me to the nurse's room. She was nice, she give me a Sesame Street coloring book. I didn't color, though. I just lay on the floor and waited and waited and waited, then Miss Shelly came with you...I missed you...I'ma keep you safe...I promise."

My heart skipped a beat when I heard footsteps approach the door. Scared that the skinny man might come back to hurt me, I sat quietly and held my breath. The footsteps stopped, and the door opened. "Ooh, my goodness! Chena? Miss Shelly called out, panic in her voice. "Where is she?"

"I think I see her foot under the desk," A second voice whispered. Instantly recognizing the voice, I began to crawl out from under the desk.

"Miss Lucy?" I asked in a timid voice, before completely revealing myself.

"Yes sweetheart, it's me." Hopping up from my knees, I ran right into Miss Lucy's open arms. "I'm going to take you home with me. Would you like to live me?" Miss Lucy asked as she picked me up.

"Yes," I whispered, holding Miss Lucy's neck as tight as I can, hoping she would never let me go.

*****

I looked down at my birthday cake with a big smile, 'cause I know its just for me. I counted the candles and I remembered my fourth birthday cake. I helped Miss Lucy mix it up in a bowl, then she let me lick the big silver spoon. This year she got me one from the big store. I never got a cake before Miss Lucy, she makes me feel special. "I'm a big girl now!" I yelled with excitement after I blew out my five candles.

"Did you make a wish?" Miss Lucy asked as she removed the cake from in front of my face and placed it on the kitchenette counter.

"Yes...I wished for you to be my real mommy."

"You did!...Well, I'd love to become your new mom." Miss Lucy said with a smile. Then she turned to cut a piece of cake. Miss Lucy carefully sliced the strawberry shortcake with white cream filling, making sure to cut me the piece with my name on it, then she wrapped aluminum foil over the remaining cake and placed it in the tiny fridge.

"Miss Lucy, uhmm...can I call you mommy?"

"You sure can," she said, placing the piece of cake in front of me and pinching my cheek.

"Mommy, Mommy, Mommy!" I sang out with pride.

"Yes dear?"

"I love you, Mommy!" I said as my eyes opened wide and I picked up my fork and tore into my cake. Miss Lucy was the best mommy. She made my lunch every day for school. When

I didn't have school, we went camping and fishing, and sometimes she let me go to work with her. On her lunch breaks she let me sit in the big ole driver seat. I turned the wheel and pretended to be a bus driver.

"Chena, hurry up now and finish your cake. We have to get ready to go visit Charlie," Mommy replied as she headed into the bathroom. Scarfing down the last three bites of my birthday cake, I wiped my mouth and fingers with my paper towel and slid off the chair. I walked over to the large queen bed in the middle of the room and jumped up on it, laying my head on Mr. Bear's chest and staring at the Scooby Doo cartoons on the thirteen-inch black-and-white TV. "Okay Chena, let's go," Mommy said as she grabbed her purse and the motel room key.

"We forgot to bring Charlie some birthday cake!" I said, suddenly remembering as I watched Mommy lock the bottom lock of our hotel room.

"It's okay, we'll eat it for him on our drive home. Now let's hurry, or we'll miss visiting hours."

As we pull up to the massive steel gates of Charlie's castle, Mommy rolled the window of her yellow Ford station wagon down, stopping with her bumper in front of a wooden barrier pole painted red and white. "Name and driver's license please," the police lady sitting on a stool asked in a tired voice, as she leaned her body halfway out of her little wooden checkpoint box. She wore a tan shirt, a gold badge, brown slacks with black fireman boots, and a gun on her belt.

"Lucy Cooperton," Mommy replies as she reached in her large black leather purse and pulled out a card with her picture on it.

"I don't see your name, ma'am. Who are you here to visit?"

"Oooh, I may be listed under my maiden name, Lucy Anderson."

"Yes, here you are...visiting Charlie Cooperton?" The police lady remarks as she leaned into the car and looks at me with a smile. Mommy nods. "Okay, please step out of the vehicle and open up the trunk," the police lady directed as she walked toward the back of the car. Mommy left the engine running, stepped out of the car, and headed toward the trunk. Mommy opened it up, and I could hear the police officer lifts my Care Bear blanket and shuffling my panda bear duffle bag around before she shuts the trunk lid again.

While the police lady did that, another policeman walked over with a German Shepherd. He walked around the car and stops in front of my door. "Hi doggie!" I yelled, waving through my closed window, but the German Shepherd ignored me and started to sniff the car tire.

Inside, we had to wait for a long time. Finally Mommy's name was called, but my butt still hurt from sitting on the cement benches for two hours, just so we can go through the metal detectors, get patted down, and go in the visitor's room. Walking out of the metal detector, Mommy waited for an officer to go through her purse, then we were allowed to walk through the brown-painted steel doors into the visitor's room.

The room was as large as my school's cafeteria. It was filled with round tables, little benches, vending machines, and a kids' area full of books, large building blocks, two rocking ponies that were bolted down to the floor, and a big old color TV showing cartoons.

Looking around the room for Charlie, I saw all of the men wore identical blue jeans, with a light blue long-sleeve button-down shirt, and numbers on the front pocket of each shirt. Each new place Charlie moves to, they wear different clothes. The last place he had on an orange one-piece jumpsuit, but in that place we could only talk to Charlie behind glass. The place before that he had a grey one, and the place before that, a yellow one.

"Oooh, Sesame Street is on!" I yelled, looking up at Mommy for permission to go and join the other kids surrounding the television in the play area.

"Go ahead, I'll be sitting right there with Charlie," Mommy said as she bent down to tuck my lavender polo shirt into my white shorts. She then pointed over to the left, where Charlie sat at the fourth round table from the back. I waved to Charlie as I ran as fast as I could past his table in a desperate attempt to secure a place on the empty green beanbag.

After positioning the beanbag directly in front of the TV, I walked over to the box of books against the wall to the left of the television and reached in and grabbed three Dr. Seuss books. Turning around to head back to my beanbag, I saw a blonde boy who was just a little taller than me looking right at me as he flopped right down on top of it.

"Hey! That's my seat!" I screamed as I dropped the books and ran across the floor, stopping right in front of the boy.

"No, it's not!" he yelled back.

"I was here first, gimme my seat back!" I yelled, trying to pull him up by his arm, but he didn't move. He snatched his arm out of my grip.

"Move your meat, lose your seat!" he said. Then he started laughing and put his thumbs in his ears, crossed his eyes and stuck his tongue out at me.

"That's not fair! I was getting a book," I whined, trying to reason with him.

"You heard my brother, nigger! Now move it!" Startled, I quickly turned around to see who just screamed at the back of my head. I stood with a look of confusion on my face. This was the first time I'd ever seen doubles. The boy looked just like his brother, and they were wearing the same blue denim shorts with a red and white and blue striped t-shirt and blue open-toe sandals. Before I could respond, the first brother jumped off the green beanbag and he gave me a hard shove, making me to stumble and fall onto the ground. Looking at them both laughing at me made me so angry that tears sprang to my eyes.

"Ooh, the nigger's crying...ha ha!" the boys giggled and pointed at me. Unsure of what to do, I slowly stood up and walked towards them. As I reached them, they both folded their arms, guarding the beanbag. Slowly stepping close enough to touch them, I quickly extended my arms and put one hand on each of their heads as if I am about to make a really big clap. Slamming my arms together as hard as I could, I made both of their heads smack together with a loud thump. I felt proud of myself, thinking that I did it just like I saw Bruce Lee do it in one of his movies. Except when he did it, then he spun around and kicked both men. But I didn't need to kick them. Both of the boys immediately fell to the floor holding their heads and crying. As they got up to run over to their mom, I sat down on the beanbag and started watching TV.

A minute later, a tall skinny blonde woman with shaggy hair wearing an oversized pink dress that hung off her bony shoulders and a pair of white flip flops stood over me, blocking the TV. "Move," I whined and sucked my teeth.

She grabbed my arm, pulled me up off the beanbag, and started shaking me. "You apologize right now!" she demands. I instantly started crying and screaming, catching my mommy's attention. Looking toward the table where Charlie sat, I saw Mommy rushing full speed toward me.

"Get your fucking hands off my daughter!" Mommy said, grabbing me from the lady's grip and pushing me behind her back.

"That nigger child of yours attacked my boys! This ain't no daycare—you need to be watching your kids, lady."

Mommy leaned in real close to the lady, making her jump back. Mommy looked around to make sure no one could hear her, then she whispered in a stern voice, "Look here, bitch. You keep your white trash, honky ass away from us, or I will have you and your brats taken care of outside of the walls of this prison. Don't fuck with me, bitch. You have no idea who we are!"

The lady stood there with her mouth open and her arms folded, staring at us with an evil look as we walked away. Twisting around to look back as we walked away, I could still see the lady staring at us, so I discreetly stuck my tongue out at her and put my right middle finger up, snatching it down quickly and turning back around so Mommy wouldn't see. Letting go of Mommy's hand, I ran full speed to Charlie's table.

"Hi Chena!" Charlie said as he put out his hand to shake mine.

"Hi...guess what?" I said with a big smile, my hand still in his.

"What?" Charlie said in a playful voice.

"It's my birthday!" I screamed with excitement. "Mommy said we can eat your piece of cake on the drive home."

"She did, did she?" Charlie said, directing a big smile at Mommy.

"Umm hmm! Yep, it's a big ole strawberry cake, with whipped cream an' strawberries, and it has my name on it. Oh, but I ate that piece already," I said and broke into a giggle.

"Happy birthday, sweetheart. Mommy's going to take you to pick up your gift from me at Toys 'R' Us when you get home," Charlie said with a grin.

"Oooh-wee! Is it a Cabbage Patch baby?" I asked, eagerly waiting for a response. But Charlie ignored me. He leaned close to Mommy and kissed her neck. Mommy blushed, then reached into her purse and pulled out my My Little Pony coloring book and Crayola crayons.

"Baby, I need you to get that thing we talked about," Charlie said, grabbing Mommy's hand.

"You said last time would be the last time," Mommy said and twisted up her face.

"I know, but I'm trying to set things up for us when I get out, so I need it done," Charlie said in a firm voice.

"I can get it for you, so Mommy doesn't have to get it," I said without looking up from my coloring book. I didn't want to mess up my focus on staying in between the lines with my blue crayon.

"What did I tell you about listening to grown folks' conversations, Chena?" Mommy snapped at me. Looking up at her near tears with my big brown eyes open wide, I put hands over my eyes, confused as to why she was mad at me.

"Chena, I always knew you were a little businesswoman. I could tell by your handshake," Charlie said and started laughing as he reached over and pulled my hands away from my face.

"Charlie, it's not funny!" Mommy snapped, then looked back at me. "Chena, I'm not mad at you, okay? But Charlie and I have to talk grown folk talk, so go take a break from coloring and go to the bathroom like a big girl, and when you come back, we'll get you a surprise from the vending machine, okay?" Mommy smiled at me and rubbed my back.

"Okay, Mommy. I'm a big girl now, I can go to the bathroom by myself."

"Yes, you are a big girl. No playing in the sink—you wash your hands and come on right back," Mommy said as I put my blue crayon down, slid off the bench, and headed to the bathroom.

Squeezing through all of the tables closely placed together, I finally reached the entrance to the bathroom hallway. I stopped and looked up at the policeman standing against the wall, smiling at him, showing off my two missing front teeth. He looked down at me, smiled, and tipped his big straw cowboy hat as I walked past him. The sun hit me immediately as I walked into the hallway. I squinted my eyes as the sun from the outdoor patio rushed in and slapped me in the face. Using my arm as a shield over my forehead, I walked to the patio doorway and looked out at the few families sitting outside playing cards on the umbrella-covered tables. Mommy and Charlie always said it was too hot to sit outside, so we sat inside, and Charlie always sat at the same table.

"Hey little girl, you lost?" The unfamiliar voice instantly gave me chills. Slowly turning around, I met the blue eyes of a short stocky white man who was wearing the same clothes as Charlie. He was bald and had a long grey beard and mustache with a big skull tattoo on his neck.

Flinching backwards as the man took a step towards me, I yelled, "My mommy told me not to talk to strangers!" and ran past him a few feet, turning left into the women's bathroom.

Running into the bathroom, I slowed down and walked past the puddles of water on the ground near the sinks. I looked at the two stalls facing me. They looked like they were made for little people, just like the ones at my school. The walls were low enough that a grown up person could peek over into the next stall. The doors didn't go all the way down to the floor either. I could see fat pink calves and ankles attached to a pair of fat feet with red toenail polish stuffed into flat white leather sandals below the door of one stall. Reaching for the handle of the second stall, I opened the door, closed it behind me, and turned the lock. Reaching for the toilet paper, I carefully laid strips of paper down all over the toilet seat, making sure to cover the entire thing. The toilet flushed next to me as I unbuttoning my white shorts and sat down on the toilet. Heavy footsteps quickly ran into the stall next to me while I was peeing, then I heard the sound of someone breathing heavy. Then I heard the sound of something slapping against skin in a fast rhythm. I looked up, and I saw the man with the skull tattoo on his neck looking down at me.

"Ahhhh! Ahhhh!" I screamed at the top of my lungs. He didn't move, he just kept looking at me.

"You sure are pretty," he said, licking his lips, and the sound of the slapping noise sped up. I screamed again and jumped off the toilet, pulling my underwear and white shorts up at the same time. I hurriedly crawled under the door and started running towards the exit. My heart was pounding out of my chest. I could hear the other stall door open and footsteps behind me speeding up. As I looked back to see the scary man stumbling towards me, zipping his zipper up, my feet came from up under me as I slipped on the wet floor near the sinks. Quickly scrambling to my feet before the man could reach me, I dashed out the bathroom door, turning right, running through the hallway, speeding past the officer. I ran as fast as I could, jumping and squeezing past legs and bumping into people's arms and backs as I ran back between the tables. I saw Charlie and Mommy looking at me with a worried look on their face.

"Chena, stop running in here," Mommy snapped at me. But I ignored her, running right into her arms and burying my face into her chest. I started crying. "What's wrong, honey?" Mommy asked in a worried voice.

"There was a bad man in the girl's bathroom, looking at me pee! He's going hurt me, please don't let the bad man get me!" I screamed, holding on as tight as I could to Mommy's waist. She picked me up on her lap and cradled me.

"No one's going to get you, I'm here," Mommy said in a soothing voice.

"Chena baby, what did the man look like?" Charlie asked in a serious voice.

"He...he...he wa, wa, was white and scary," I gasped out between hyperventilating sobs. Trying to calm myself, I held my breath.

"What did his face look like? Was he wearing the same clothes as me?"

Looking up at Charlie I nodded my head up and down. "And he had a grey face hair and a painting on his neck of a skull," I mumbled.

"I know who that is," Charlie said, as he stood up and he walked away. He went over to a table two tables behind us and bent down and said something into a Mexican man's ear. This man was tall and big like Charlie, and he was wearing the same clothes as Charlie, except he'd rolled his sleeves up to his elbows to show the tattoos all over his arms. The Mexican man stood up and walked behind Charlie, both of them heading towards the bathrooms. Mommy and I sat in silence as they walked towards the policeman standing at the door. Charlie said something to the policeman, then all three men turned to look at me and Mommy. Then they all went into the hallway, disappearing from sight.

Mommy puts me down in front of my coloring book, and I started coloring again. "Chena, you want to go get something from the vending machines?" Mommy asked after sitting in silence for a while.

"Can I have a bean burrito?" I asked with excitement.

"Come on, let's go see if they have any left," Mommy replied and grabbed my hand. Before we could make it to the machine, though, Mommy abruptly stopped. "Where are all those guards going?" Mommy muttered under her breath as we watched five guards rush in from the brown steel door. They ran straight towards the bathrooms, pushing past people standing in their way, before disappearing into the hallway.

The room became silent as everyone stared at the commotion. Shortly after disappearing into the hallway, two guards came back out of the doorway holding up the scary man with the tattooed skull on his neck. His head dangling downward, his arms hung around the guards' necks with his legs are dragging on the floor as they struggled to hold his body up. A big circle of blood covered the front of his jeans, starting just below his zipper, and reaching all the way down to his knees.

"Oh my God," Mommy gasped, placing her hand over her mouth.

"Mommy, that's the bad man!" I mumbled, tugging on her warm arm. We both stood in silence as the guards walked past us, carrying the man's limp body through the brown steel doors. Mommy abandoned our vending machine mission and briskly walked us back to our table.

Looking towards the hallway in search of Charlie, we see the original guard who was standing at the wall near the restrooms return to his post, fiddling with his big straw hat as if nothing had happened. Then a few minutes later, Charlie and the Mexican man calmly came out of the doorway and turned to walk towards us. The Mexican man gave Charlie a dap, tapping his fist on top of Charlie's before Charlie taps his fist on top of the Mexican man's, and then he sat back down with his family. Charlie headed towards us with a slight smile on his face.

"That motherfucker won't ever touch another kid again," Charlie said and looked at me. I look up worried, feeling like I'm in trouble from the sound of Charlie's voice. "You're safe now, Chena. I'll smoke any motherfucker who fucks with you two," he said in a firm cold voice. Charlie then paused and cleared his throat. "Y'all my heart!" he said in a shaky emotional voice. Then he looked up at the celling, and back down at Mommy. Charlie's eyes were red and watery. Mommy reached out and grabbed Charlie's hand, squeezing it as she gave him a warm smile, and I returned to my My Little Pony coloring book.

CHAPTER 25
CHENA

Dear Diary,

Freedom or Revenge
Can't relax and let go
This is all I know

There is no safe place
To hide and go

Riding the line of morality
Indifference towards mortality

Can't trust another
With my deepest secret

Unable to laugh or cry
Until justice claims the damned

For me freedom is always
An eye for an eye

CHENA, THE MAKING OF AN ORPHAN

Dena didn't know what had happened between me and Becky, so sitting in traffic listening to her over-opinionated thoughts for the past hour and half as we headed to Timbuktu in the heart of San Frances had been pure torture. I didn't have the guts to tell her that the last words I said to Becky had been horrible, hateful, and probably one of the factors that had pushed her over the edge. God, I wish she'd just shut up and drive!

"Poor child had her whole life ahead of her...why would she do such a thing?" Dena exclaimed with cadence, attempting to strike up yet another conversation with me.

The more I continued to be nonresponsive to Dena, the more she continued on. "I just don't—"

"You can park right there!" I yelled, quickly pointing across Dena's body to the left, cutting her off in midsentence in a desperate attempt to halt her rambling. Dena put the black Ford Explorer into park and I quickly jumped out. "I'll meet you inside, okay?" I called, slamming the heavy SUV door shut.

I walked alone up what seemed to be never-ending beautiful white marble steps toward an entrance framed by gigantic wooden doors with small crosses carved into them, in a reverie. Numbness filled my body, and I acknowledged death. My eyes were drawn to the engraved words above the doors, "Saint Peter's Catholic Church."

"Wow! A Catholic church!" I mumbled in disgust under my breath, and drifted into deep thought. I couldn't help but think how fake this whole setting was. Becky's mother had decided to take over the planning of Becky's funeral, after Gwene had already made arrangements to have the service at

AX Baptist Church, Becky's favorite church, not to mention the place she had been baptized. Becky's mother had always tried to be something she's not, including a devoted Catholic. Two years ago she changed the pronunciation of her name April, to Ap'ril (but still spelled it the same), just because her married boyfriend at the time told her her name was too common. So every time I saw this phony fake witch, I went out my way to say, "Hi April," just to get the pure satisfaction seeing her roll her eyes and suck her teeth as she tries to correct me.

It's Ap'ril's fault that Becky was a loose cannon. Instead of just loving Becky for who she was, she always made Becky feel like she wasn't good enough. When Ap'ril's attempts to transform Becky into a miniature of her self failed, she gave up and just ignored Becky. When she did speak, it was only in the form of verbal abuse. Ap'ril's gestures were never original or sincere. She was only having the service at a Catholic cathedral because her boyfriend of the month was Catholic.

Bells rang out from the steeple of the church, startling me out of my daze. "Shit, it's noon already. The funeral's gonna start in thirty minutes," I mumbled as I started walking again, straight through the large wooden doors. Once inside the church, I started searching for Brandon. I walked down the dimly lit church aisle, slowly taking in the beauty of the church. I heard the voices of people trickling in behind me. Ignoring the sounds of people piling in to fill the empty wooden benches with their bottoms, I continued taking in the church's atmosphere. An altar to the right back side of the church, lit with white candles and featuring a large copper statue of Mary holding baby Jesus, grabbed my attention. Directly to the right of the altar was a large ivory font with a short line of people gathered near it. One by one, each of them dip their fingers quickly, then they use those same fingers to touch their forehead, chest, and each shoulder in the form of a crucifix before heading off to their seats.

I had to admit, I had never seen such jaw-dropping beauty in a church. There were magnificent red, blue, green, and yellow stained glass windows illustrating biblical stories spread all around the church, taking up enormous amounts of space on the massively high walls. As I looked upward, my breath was instantly taken away at the beautiful paintings of little blond and brown-haired white angels wearing white cloak-like garments. The angels were flying around between the painted-on clouds, and some were sitting on the clouds playing small harps. The painted sky spread all along the entire colossal celling. The dim lighting coordinated perfectly with the corner lights highlighting the ceiling, giving me the illusion that I was looking right up into heaven.

My eyes slowly climbed back down from the sky-high ceiling and focus straight ahead on the large poster-sized photograph of Becky standing on an easel. In the picture she wore a red cap and gown with a 1999 yellow tassel hanging to the side of her beautiful smiling face. In front of the photo were massive bouquets of white orchids, and to the left of it was Becky's open casket. "Wow," I whispered as I looked around and took in the size of the crowd, mostly people from our school, who quickly filled up the aisles quietly greeting each other.

"Chena!" Bee called, drawing my attention toward her well-put-together outfit. She wore a full-length form-fitting black Donna Karan dress, long black evening gloves, a pearl necklace, and a black hat with a fishnet veil that slightly covered her face. Smiling, I waved and began walking toward her and Tanisha.

"We saved you a seat." Tanisha pointed to the spot next to her on the bench, where she had placed her black cardigan and Bible.

"Hey," I said, reaching over the bench behind them to give them each a big warm hug.

"It looks real nice," Bee said, with a warm upbeat tone.

"Yes, it does, and you two look beautiful," I said. Embarrassed, I felt underdressed in Dena's oversized hand-me-down black button-down blouse, black ski pants, and black ballet flats. My hair wasn't flat ironed with neat pin curls like Bee's and Tanisha's, but just combed into a simple bun held at the the top of my head with black chopsticks.

"Where's Dena?" Bee asked, scooting her black Chanel clutch to the right to make sitting space on the bench.

"Uhmm, I don't know, but she's here," I said. When I looked up I caught Dena's tall form making her way through the crowd. "She's over by the altar talking to Becky's grand-mother." I began scanning the room for Brandon. "Hey, y'all seen Brandon? He was supposed to be here before me."

"Uhmm, I saw him with Ibrahima, walking by the stairs near the bathrooms, when we were walking in," Tanisha said, taking her seat and smoothing down her black and white polka-dot dress, which she had accented with a red bead necklace and matching red Mary Jane heels.

"Okay, I'ma go find them real quick. Save us a seat." I slipped back out through the crowded aisle, stepping over penny loafers, sneakers, six-inch heels, and flats, as I made my way toward the staircase.

Just as I turned right to head up the stairs, the sound of violins and flutes started echoing throughout the church, play-ing a beautiful melody. Rushing back to the open doorway to discover the source of this beautiful noise, I saw ten members from the school orchestra standing to the right of Becky's casket playing their instruments. The vague sound of male voices caught my attention, slowly pulling me away from the hypnotizing, tranquil music.

As I walked up the stairs, the voices became clearer. It's Brandon and Ibrahima, I thought in recognition as I quietly climbed the staircase, smiling.

"But the van's out back," Brandon said in a pleading tone.

"Yo dogg, this is some crazy shit we about to do," Ibrahima replied in a shaky voice, making me freeze in the stairwell. I had to listen; was the plan still a go? Just two steps away from the balcony entrance, I leaned against the wall and stand still.

"Man, I gotta do this. We gotta do this. We owe Becky," Brandon replied in a low voice.

"Pssh...Owe her. Yo, you act like you was fucking her or something."

"We were!...Uh...I mean, I did," Brandon said in anger, causing my heart to drop right out of my chest.

Tears of anger and betrayal instantly filled my eyes. This motherfucker lied to me, he's a phony fucking liar! I screamed inside of my head. I clenched my fist into a tight ball and held my breath to ensure that no sound escaped.

Ibrahima gasped at Brandon's words. "What?...For real?...Mr. Faithful! Mr. I-Would-Never!" he said in a taunting tone.

"Look dude, I'm not perfect, okay?...Shit, a man's got needs, and it was while Chena and I were broken up anyways," Brandon hissed in a loud whisper.

"So that's still fucked up, you know that was her girl."

"Yeah, I know it's fucked up. I was weak...and I can't take it back!...I love Chena, no doubt with all my heart, and if I could go back, I would. But I gotta live wit' it." Brandon paused, his voice getting caught in his throat.

Wow! Now this nigga is crying? I thought, standing still and quietly allowing my own tears to fall.

"How I dissed Becky was fucked up!...I called Becky that

night she killed herself when Chena went to sleep." Brandon paused again and cleared his throat. "I told her I loved Chena and to never call me again. Truthfully, I think that's the reason she killed herself...so I gotta handle her uncle...I owe it to her, and I need your help," he pleaded.

"Nigga, you know you my nigga, so on GP, I'm doing this for you!...I guess truth is, though, I owe her too." There's was brief silence between them before Ibrahima continued, "Man, not to mention, his perverted ass deserves this!"

"Hey guys," I called softly with a smile, trying to mask my hurt. Brandon and Ibrahima both jumped up off the bench where they sat and turned to face me with a shellshocked expression on their face.

"Hey Chena, when did you get here?" Ibrahima said nervously.

"Ooh, I was downstairs with the girls, and they told me they saw you guys come up here, so I just ran up here real quick to tell you we saved you some seats," I said in my calmest, warmest voice.

"Thanks, but we gonna stay up here, 'cause we got a perfect view of Leroy," Brandon replied as he reached for my hand to guide me to the edge of the balcony and point out Leroy, who was sitting three rows from the front, rubbing Becky's eight-year-old godsister's back as she cried into the palm of her tiny hands. Seeing Leroy's perverted hands on a child during Becky's funeral immediately redirected the anger festering inside me from Brandon's betrayal, and I threw it all onto him. I clenched my jaw down hard and rolled my eyes in disgust. Glancing up at Brandon and Ibrahima with a slightly raised eyebrow, I began to nod my head slightly without saying a word. Brandon and Ibrahima both returned my nod, agreeing that it needed to be done. Walking towards the stairwell without looking back, in a low voice I commanded, "Let's get this motherfucker!" Then I disappeared into the dark shadows of the stairwell, returning as quietly as I could to my seat next to Tanisha and Bee.

Sitting staring up at the priest, I listened to him as he read passages from the Bible in a mellow-toned voice, referring to saints I wasn't familiar with. I began to zone out, thinking about the plan. Right now, while we're all here at the funeral, Brandon's uncle should be breaking into Gwene's garage to get Leroy's chest. Then we have to wait for him to page Brandon. Brandon will wait twenty minutes and then go tell Leroy his car is being towed to get him outside. And then...

"Chena!..Chena!...Hello?" Bee whispered, poking me hard in the side with her elbow.

"Huh...what?" I asked, confused and caught off guard by her elbow.

"There goes Brandon!" Bee replied in a low whisper, pointing to where Brandon was bending down and whispering into Leroy's ear. I just sat there and watched as Leroy touched Ap'ril's shoulder, who sat in front of him silently crying. He whispered something into her ear, then both men stood up and started to walk towards the exit. Leroy walked out of the church, but Brandon lingered behind, looking at his watch. I have to be the first on the scene, but if I move now, it will look too obvious. I have to wait till Brandon leaves first. After the eulogy, I can go, I thought. I sat patiently waiting with folded arms while I planned the quietest route for an exit. Nervously shaking my foot as it dangled over my crossed leg, I waited for the perfect moment to move.

The thirty-minute eulogy finally ended, just in time, as my patience was wearing thin. "Hey excuse me, I'm going to the bathroom," I whispered to Dena, who moved her legs to the right as I rose. Before I could take a step, though, I heard my name being called from the altar.

"Chena, would you please come up and say a few words?" Gwene called out into the crowd, focusing her gaze onto me as she spotted me.

"Y'all come up with me," I snapped at Bee and Tanisha, who stood up and followed me down the aisle. When I reached the altar, Gwene reached out and gave me a tight hug, then went down the row hugging Bee and Tanisha before she broke down into a fit of sobs and had to be assisted to her seat by April. The rest of the A.T.C. mentees, Nina, Tamika, and Kelly, who had been sitting in the front row patting their eyes with tissues, quickly jumped up to assist April as her thirteen-year-old body struggled to hold up the weight of Gwene's collapsing legs. Bee glanced at me and then stepped forward to the microphone to speak first.

My body and mind were completely numb, my eyes are clear of tears, standing here feeling the trigger inside of me being pulled. It's the same feeling I had when I was four years old. Like a switch had been thrown, instantly all my emotions were turned off. I was no longer affected by Becky's death; I didn't hate Brandon, nor did I love him. He could have fallen off the face of the earth, and I wouldn't have given it a second thought. This is how it has to be. To survive, I can never trust anyone! All I have is me, and at the end of the day, I'm the only one that will ever love me and truly have my back...Oh shit! It's my turn to speak. Stepping out of my head and back into reality, I noticed Bee moving away back from the microphone. I quickly move forward. Looking to my left and to my right, I breathed in deeply as I studied the faces of the onlookers. Some loved and adored Becky, some didn't. The benches were filled with guys who were obsessed with her and hated her rejection, and with girls who disliked her because she stole their boyfriends' attention daily as she walked down the halls.

Everyone was looking at me as if I was going to give them the answers they wanted, as if I could explain why Becky killed herself. Tanisha cleared her throat, letting out two grunts, signaling to me that everyone was waiting for me to open my mouth and speak.

"Becky killed herself, and her body is gone, but each one of us will forever hold in our hearts the memories of her smiling, laughing, and brightening up the day. Becky was a—" I stopped in midsentence, taken aback by the sudden abrupt appearance of a hysterical middle-aged Mexican man in the doorway of the church.

"Eeeeii...vamanos, quick! Help!" the man yelled in his thick Spanish accent as he busted through the doors. He ran down the middle aisle, then fell to his knees and threw his hands in the air and looked to the sky, yelling at the top of his lungs in Spanish. His grey-and-green gardening coveralls were stained with blood from his chest to his knees. "Come, now!" he screamed, rising to his feet again and going back down the aisle, gesturing for us to follow.

Everyone stood up, murmuring in shock, and quickly followed the man outside down the marble steps. "Hay!... El hombre negro que cuelga," the old Mexican man yelled, pointing towards a baby weeping willow tree near the lagoon, just below the parking lot. Looking down at the tree, I could vaguely make out the side profile of a man's head and a leg. His body faced the Golden Gate Bridge, and all we could see was the rope wrapped around him that lashed him to the trunk of the tree. People started gasping as they reached the tree. There sat a nude man tied to the tree, with bruised eyes, a busted lip, and blood covering both of his legs. The part between his legs that made him a man was missing, and seemed to be the cause of the blood splatter. Next to the man, a big brown chest lay open.

Everyone screamed when they looked at the man, including Bee and Tanisha, who quickly covered their mouths and looked away from the horrifying sight. They backed away. But I remained still, standing right in front of Leroy, staring right into his swollen eyes. I looked down at his privates, watching the blood layered in air bubbles as it rushed out of the little bit of penis that was left, covering my mouth to mask the smile on my face.

"Get back, everybody! Someone call the police!" I screamed, trying to act normal and to keep Becky's secret out of the spectators' view. Looking to my right, I could see Gwene and Ap'ril making their way down the steps, and passing the parking lot while the distant sound of sirens became audible.

As she reached the scene, Ap'ril stood in shock. Screams tore out of her mouth, but she didn't move. Gwene briskly hobbled towards the man who she instantly recognized as her son. She begin pulling unsuccessfully at the ropes wrapped around Leroy's chest and arms, which tightly secured him to the tree. "Help him! Oooh Lord, somebody please help 'im," Gwen demanded as she put her hand to his face. "Baby, you gonna be just fine, hang in there," she said, just before she looked down and noticed something tied around his neck. She turned over the note that had attached with grey duct tape to a thin piece of string. Leroy started to speak, exposing the gap left by his two missing front teeth, but blood came out of his mouth instead.

Gwene continued to stare at the note as Leroy's head rolled to the right, slowly falling onto his shoulder as he passed out. Staring at the note with a confused look on her face, Gwene shook her head from side to side. She let the note fall out of her hands and looked at Leroy with a dawning look of discovery. "Ooooh my God!" she screamed and fell to the ground, looking up at her son. "No, no, no! Why?" She looked to the right, at the open brown chest lying next to Leroy's bloody left foot. She reached in and pulled out the black VHS tape that I had labeled "Becky's Lost Innocence." Dropping the tape, she moved her hand around in the chest, frantically picking up photographs, one after the other, screaming, "Get back! Get back! Get the hell back!" to anyone who stepped too close. She then closed the lid of the chest and slowly pulled herself up, using the chest and the tree for leverage. She hobbled in front of her son, wrapped her hand around the string, and snatched it right off his neck. Carefully folding the note in the palm of her hands, she reached up to the collar of her black blouse and placed the blood-stained note inside her bra. Then turned around to face the onlookers standing four feet away. "Somebody call the police!" she yelled in a authoritative tone.

CHAPTER 26
CHENA

Dear Diary,

Slipping away
into the abyss

Are the memories of
a wonderful,
kind, soft kiss

A kiss
given by one who
fulfills and completes the

Empty, fragile-sided me

Gone from thought
Shredded memory

The love once known,
and dear to me, was released
and set free
Now
I'm off to fulfill my destiny

CHENA, THE MAKING OF AN ORPHAN

"Hurry up and come on out so we can see you!" Bee screamed.

"Okay, but y'all better not laugh," Tanisha replied as she twisted the knob to her dressing room door.

"Wow, it's beautiful!" I exclaimed. Tanisha ran in front of the mirror and spun around, showing off the black satin and lace DKNY dress.

"That's the one! It's absolutely beautiful and it hugs your curves just right," Bee exclaimed, pointing to the low plunging neckline, which was very flattering to Tanisha's perky C-cup breasts.

"Aww, you think so?" Tanisha replied, tugging at the dress's lace bottom in an attempt to pull it past her knees. Every time she tugged at it, the dress instantly rode back up.

"Girl, you better rock what yo' momma gave you! But if you keep pulling that dress down, what yo' momma gave you gonna pop out the top o' that dress," Bee blurted out as she high-fived me and we broke out into a fit of laughter.

"Ha ha ha...y'all just jealous cause y'all's mommas didn't give y'all much to work with," Tanisha replied with a big grin, playfully hitting both of us on our shoulders. "Now get out, I'ma change. I'll meet y'all at the register." Tanisha turned and headed back into her dressing room.

"Okay, girl. We'll be right out here," I said. I scooped my brown leather Aldo purse from my lap, Bee swung her black leather Coach bag over her shoulder, and we jumped off the black velvet sofa and walked out of the dressing room. We started to browse nearby racks as we waited for Tanisha to come out.

"Girl, look!" Bee whispered as she poked my side with her elbow. Putting down an Eddie Bauer skully, I swiftly turned to look in the direction Bee was gazing.

"Ooh, great! Turn around! I don't want him to see us!" I demanded, speedily turning to walk in the opposite direction.

"Girl, it's too late. Here he comes," Bee said as she dropped to her knee, pretending to fasten the strap of her black four-inch-high Mary Janes.

"Hey! Chena!" Rolling my eyes and sucking my teeth at Bee, I slowly turned around.

"Hey Brandon," I replied nonchalantly.

"What y'all doing here?" Brandon asked, nervously waving to Bee. Trying not to make eye contact with Brandon, I picked up a red FUBU T-shirt and stared intently at the price tag.

"We're shopping for graduation dresses," I said.

"Oh, that's what's up. So what's up?" Brandon asked as he took a step closer, grabbing the T-shirt out of my hands and tossing it over his shoulder.

"Nothing's up." I opened my eyes wide and shrugged my shoulders.

"Why haven't you returned any of my calls then?" Brandon asked softly.

"Brandon, like I told you last month after Becky's funeral, we're over. I'm trying to move on and put the past behind me," I said, looking Brandon right in the eyes. I wanted to cry. The undeniable truth was I missed him so much it hurt, but the hurt from his betrayal had made me hard as a rock. I wanted to tell him that I knew about him and Becky, but what was the point, of bringing up the past, and acknowledging that our triangle of love caused her death. I also knew that my search for love would not end with Brandon, but my false dreams of happily ever after did the day of Becky's funeral. I would take Becky's true reasons for killing herself to the grave along with many other deep dark secrets. Trying with all my might to hold my angry yet sad tears in, I looked away.

Brandon reached out to grab my hand, but I instantly snatched it back. "Ma, why you gotta act like that? After all we been through you know you are my heart, and—"

Before Brandon could go any further, I cut him off. "Look I gotta go, the girls are waiting."

Brandon grabbed my arm and pulled me close to him. I could smell his Cool Water cologne, and the heat radiating from his chest was making me hot. "Yeah, okay. But look, I was calling to tell you to be careful...I ran into Becky's grandmother, and she said Leroy got out the hospital two weeks ago, and she and the police are looking for him...and I know he knows it was us," Brandon whispered anxiously. My heart started to thump out of my chest. I didn't expect for Leroy to every see freedom again. He was supposed to go to jail for the rest of his life. "Chena, you hear me?" Brandon shook me out of my daze.

"Yeah, thanks for telling me. I'll be all right. You look after yourself," I replied as I pulled myself away from Brandon's grip. I wanted to run right out of the doors of Lacy's department store, but instead I calmly walked out of the urban section, heading towards Bee.

Bee stood patiently preoccupying herself with watches at the jewelry counter. Bee, making eye contact with me as I walked toward her, immediately returned the diamond-studded watch she had been trying on back to the young man assisting her, and came over. "Girl, what was he talking to you about?" Bee asked as she put her arm around me, pulling me into a small corner between the handbag counter and the escalators, noticing the sadness in my eyes.

"Just same ole bullshit, why haven't I returned his calls, he loves me...blah blah blah..."

"He still don't know you know, huh?" Bee asked with a surprised look on her face.

"Naw, dumbass nigga, thinks he got away with it," I replied, shaking my head and rolling my eyes. Looking straight ahead I spotted Tanisha standing at a register in the young women's section with her hand on her hip, waiting for us. "Come on girl, there's Tanisha."

On graduation day, I jumped out of the shower with excitement, grabbed my towel, and headed down the hall toward my room. Stopping at Dena's bedroom door, I peeked my head in and knocked. Dena stuck her head out of her bathroom with her right hand holding a curling iron up to her head.

"Bee is going to pick me up, so you don't have to rush, I'll meet you there," I announced.

"Okay, perfect, 'cause this hair gonna take me all day," Dena replied with a smile.

Heading into my room, I closed my door and pressed play on my Prince CD. "Two thousand zero zero party's over, oops, out of time! So tonight I'm gonna party like it's 1999!" I started singing at the top of my lungs as I turned the volume up to match my vocals.

Dancing around the room stark naked, I already feel grown, and I'm loving it. Dena told me at the beginning of the week, "You don't have a curfew anymore and you can go and come as you please. You're gonna be out the house headed to college in two months anyway, so you might as well get used to it." So I had, staying out late at Bee's and Tanisha's house every night, and I'd been blasting my music, and Dena hadn't said a word. I kept dancing as I slid my white spaghetti strap linen dress over my head. I tighten my abs and pulled up the zipper on the right side, making the dress hug me like a corset.

Looking in the mirror, I was pleased with how the dress showed off my tiny waistline and pushed up my still-growing

B-cup breasts. Carefully untying my silk head scarf, I let my wrapped hair uncoil and fall past my shoulders. With precision I parted my hair down the middle and skillfully brushed the ends of both sides under, smoothing all of my hair into a perfect inward curve around my face. After applying my makeup, I stepped into my white canvas and cork platform sandals, then stepped back and looked into the mirror.

"Hey, Chena!" Dena yelled as she lightly tapped on my door.

"Come in!" I yell over the music. Dena opened the door and paused, placing her hand over her mouth, as she looked me up and down. Her light-skinned face turned pink and her eyes began to water.

"Aww, you look beautiful. Wow, you're all grown up! Look at you," Dena said and walked over to hug me.

"Aww thanks," I replied in the middle of Dena's tight embrace.

"Ooh...shoot...somebody's on the phone for you," Dena announces. "You so beautiful you made me forget!"

"Who is it?" I asked as I ran to Dena's room to grab the phone, a bright smile on my face. "Hello?...Hello?" I sang into the phone happily, but nothing but silence filled the other end. My smile faded. Focusing all my attention into the receiver, I could hear the faint sound of someone breathing. "Helllllllllllo!" I screamed into the phone. Irritated by the lack of a response, I quickly slammed the phone down. "Did they say who it was?" I yelled across the room to Dena, who was reaching into her closet toward the top shelf, trying to grab a shoebox.

"No, I didn't ask. It was a man's voice, though," Dena nonchalantly responded, focusing her attention on the box she was trying to reach.

That's weird. It was probably Brandon, playing on the phone, I told myself as I walked back into my room, but there was an eerie feeling running down my spine.

The fifteen-minute car ride was filled with silence as thoughts of Leroy and Brandon raced around my brain.

"Chena, what's wrong with you?" Bee yelled as she turned the volume down on her car stereo.

"Nothing!" I quickly replied, pasting on a smile.

"Girl, I know you thinking about Becky. I am too. She did some fucked up shit, but she was our friend and I wish she was walking this stage with us today," Becky said in a soft warm voice as she pulled into the full parking lot of Sal Valley High.

"Yeah, I wish she was here too. And I wish we didn't all have to split up," I said as I unbuckled my seat belt.

"Girl, you know me and Tanisha will just be a phone call away. We goin' to L.A., not the moon." Bee playfully hit my arm.

"I know, I just wish we could all go to college together," I whined as I hopped out of the car.

The loud sound of a whistle pierced my eardrums. The high-pitched ring went off three times directly behind me, and I jumped, startled.

"Hey! Where's your pass?" a woman's voice yelled. Turning around I saw Romonia, heading toward us with a Kodak smile on her face.

"Ha! A pass, we don't need a pass anymore!" Bee yelled back.

"Ha ha ha! That's right, soon-to-be graduates!" Ramonia smiled with a look of admiration.

"That's right in less than two hours we will officially be outtttta here!" I said excitedly, high-fiving Bee.

"I'll be watching. Congratulations! The halls won't be the same without you girls causing trouble." Romonia reached out to shake our hands. The black walkie talkie on her hip suddenly squawked, "What's your twenty?" She pulled it off of its clip and mumbled something into it as she walked away. Leaning against her Camaro, Bee and I stood observing for a quick moment as Ramonia transformed back into a nark. She skillfully wedged herself between some large bushes and the gym wall. Shaking our heads and laughing, Bee and I started to head towards the center quad to prepare for graduation. The cafeteria was packed with the entire graduating senior class dressed in their red and blue gowns, with big smiles on their faces.

"Hey...Johnson, Joons, Lexington...check, check, and check. Are you girls ready to say good bye to SVH?" Mr. Tobin asked as he checks our names off his list.

"I'll miss it, but I'm excited about starting a new chapter in my life," I declared.

"We'll miss you, Mr. Tobin. You were our favorite teacher!" Tanisha added as she snuck up from behind us, grabbing me and Bee by the waist and giving us a tight squeeze.

"All you girls go on now and get out of my face, before I start crying," Mr. Tobin replied, shooing us away with a wave of his hand. He continued taking roll with the group of Hispanic students entering the cafeteria behind us.

Walking through the crowded cafeteria scanning the signage on the floor to locate the J letter group, I spotted Brandon in the Ms, standing against the wall adjusting his collar. "Brandon McGee," I yelled. Caught off guard, he flinched, then searched the crowd until he spotted me. He quickly headed over in my direction, while Bee and Tanisha melted away into the crowd.

"Hey, Chena...big day, huh?" Brandon said with a big smile. Trying to avoid eye contact, I looked down, but my eyes were irresistibly drawn back up. I was overwhelmed by his sexy masculine aroma, his fresh shave and haircut, and his beautiful smile.

"Yeah, I can't believe it's really here....Umm, I heard you got into USC and I wanted to say congrats and—" Brandon leaned down, grabbing my face and kissing me in midsentence.

Rapidly melting in Brandon's arms, I fought hard within, reminding myself of his betrayal, and I pulled myself away. Looking up at Brandon in utter shock and disbelief, I fell speechless.

"The line will start moving in a few minutes, everyone get in position!" Mr. Tobin screamed across the room through his bullhorn, interrupting the silence between Brandon and I.

"I just wanted to say good-bye," I announced with a look of disgust. Briskly walking past Brandon and making my way through the crowd, I found my way to the J section. Lights were flashing everywhere as students posed, hugging, smiling, and making funny faces with their disposable Kodak cameras in hand.

A crowd of students surrounded P as he put on a show practicing his acceptance dance. "P, you are so silly." I commented as I reached over to hug him.

"Hey! You know it's not to late to join the team; I'll take all y'all as my wife," P announced as he went down the row hugging and kissing Bee and Tanisha's cheeks. Mr. Tobin yelled out one last announcement for us to get in line, this time banishing all niceness from his voice. All two hundred graduates immediately ran to our spots in line, forming a single file that wrapped around the entire cafeteria and zigzagged inward, forming four smaller loops within the outer ring.

The school band drums started to sound, signaling us that it was time to enter the stage. Walking out the doorway of B Hall, we were immediately greeted with a standing ovation. Proud parents, family, and friends jumped to their feet, clapping and whistling. Gratified, we took our places on the stage, contagiously smiling from ear to ear at one another. As the ceremony commenced, it seemed like an eternity before the speeches were over and the principal began reading out the names of the graduating class.

When he got to the Hs, I watched P dance across the stage, exactly as he had been demonstrating in the cafeteria. Then I stared into the crowd of parents, all dressed in their Sunday best, sitting patiently on the lawn in their fold-up chairs and clapping and cheering. Dena was crying her eyes out, taking tissue after tissue from Tanisha's mom. As I looked past Dena, though, my heart suddenly dropped. Ten feet behind her, standing under an oak tree just in front of the parking lot was a man who looked a lot like Leroy. Squinting my eyes, I focused on him, and though it was shaded by the tree's shadow, his face could still be clearly seen. "Fuck!" I said, quickly looking down the row at Brandon, who was so busy smiling and clapping for his fellow classmates that he didn't notice my state of panic. I looked back at the tree. The man spotted me looking at him, and he started to briskly hobble away, limping on his right side and cradling his left arm. I watched him intently as he slipped out of sight behind the building.

Bee poked me in the ribcage with her elbow, breaking my gaze. I looked at Bee. "They just called your name, stupid!" she whispered. Shaking my head to banish my fright, I thought, This is the biggest moment of my life, and I will not have it ruined by a pedophile! I will not live in fear! I quickly walked over to shake the superintendent's hand and claim my diploma. Standing at the front of the stage, posing with my principal and holding up my diploma for the official picture, I began to smile as excitement crept up out of my stomach and realization set in. I have my whole life ahead of me, and it starts right now.